THE END OF THE PLAYBOY

A NOVEL

HARLIN HAILEY

East of Lincoln

The Downsizing of Hudson Foster

The End of the Playboy

A NOVEL

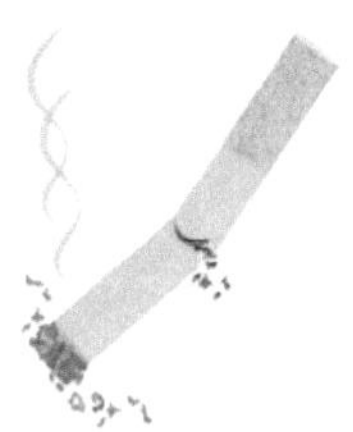

Harlin Hailey

Cover design by Edward Bettison

ISBN 979-8-218-39123-2 (Paperback)

First Edition

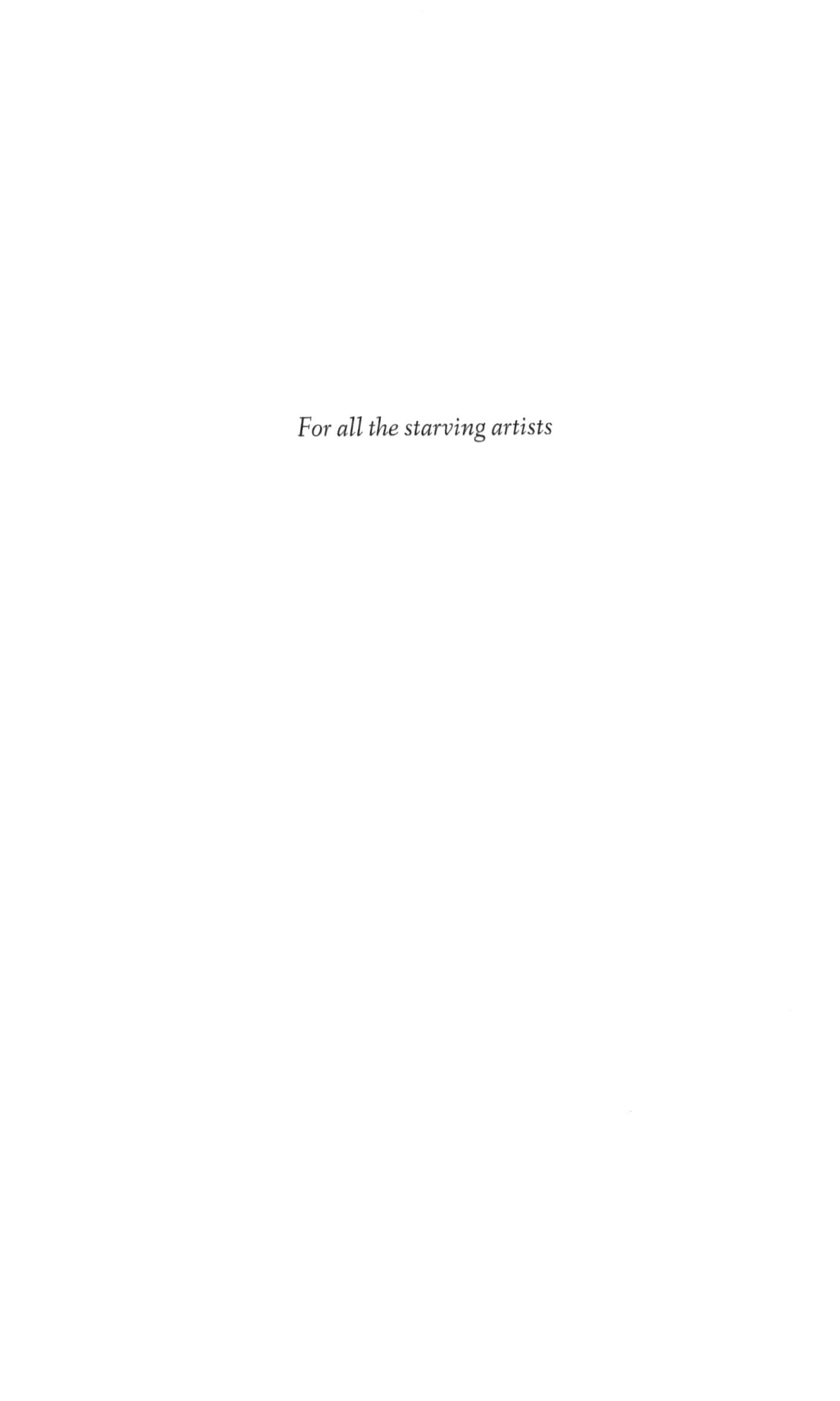

For all the starving artists

The only way to make sense out of change is to plunge
into it, move with it, and join the dance.

ALAN WATTS

TUESDAY

FUNK strolls the empty aisles of his favorite bookstore. It is late winter. The year rock died. The year we lost Bowie, Prince, and Glenn Frey.

Lemmy before that.

Tall and gangly, or what some would call skinny-fat, Funk cuts the swath of a man of leisure. He ambles past the writing and publishing section and thinks maybe he'll write his memoir one day. Although for the life of him, he's not sure who the reader of such a tome might be. If he had to guess, he'd pick the mentally deranged shooter or the aging strung-out groupie.

Both were ardent fans.

With a leisurely swing of his arm, he strides past the true crime section. No interest there. Just as long as he stays out of the morgue, it's all good. Ditto for the large-print books on the left.

Breezing down the aisle, he doesn't so much walk as glide. His elbow feels a little stiff, though. Not sure why. Maybe it was the ten knee push-ups he attempted yesterday.

Oh, look, it's the history section. He loves history, but he gets his fix from the History Channel now. The show *Vikings* being an overwhelming favorite. His mind drifts back to the eighth century, somewhere in Scandinavia. In a past life, he imagines the conversation between his fellow Norsemen going something like this: *"That Funk is one lazy Viking, man. He only raids twice a year now."*

"If that. I heard it was more like once every eighteen months. His last raid was pretty good, though. He practically sacked the entire village by himself. Cut off gobs of heads."

"That was over two years ago, bro. You know what he said last week when I asked him if he wanted to gut a few missionaries?"

"What's that?"

"He said his elbow was hurting. And that he wanted to give the old sword arm a rest. Yeah, and then three hours later I find him in the supply hut, fucking the water girl."

"That's bold."

"No kidding. And I'm no window peeper. But you see something, you say something. Am I right?"

"Does this chain mail shirt make me look fat?"

Walking down the aisle, the Nordic banter gradually fades from Funk's mind, his comfortable shoes shuffling across the well-worn indoor-outdoor carpeting. The bookstore is eerily quiet this morning, like a bomb dropped but didn't.

As he rounds the corner into the nursing section, he zeroes in on *The Drug Handbook*. It looks especially enticing this morning, its bold red and white Rx cover threatening to cure the ailments of our day.

Neck pain?

We've got you covered.

Opioid-induced constipation?

No worries, pop this pill, and in no time, you'll be singing "The Final Countdown" *in the shower. Clothes optional.*

Election fatigue?

Climate-change anxiety?

Comfort pony ate your homework?

Relax. Take two of these babies and call me in the morning.

Thanks, Doc.

Side Effects and Overdoses would be a better title for the handbook, Funk thinks. No need to sugarcoat it, just tell the people like it is. That guy he saw yesterday talking to a lamppost would probably agree.

At any rate, he remembers the sight of a pill bottle makes him queasy, and he moves on.

He cruises past section after section, seeking comfort in something that he has yet to know.

Philosophy.

Religion.

Astrology.

Fitness.

All books sit quiet, waiting patiently for a new owner. A new owner that will most likely be the dollar store bargain bin.

Like a lot of things these days, the venerable bookstore is dying. The comfy velvet chairs are gone, and the bathroom door is locked. In these politically charged times, books are out. And wearable technology is in.

Funk thinks of a new song he might like to write: "Where Have All the Customers Gone?" Possibly arranged to the tune of Simon and Garfunkel's "The Sound of Silence." But that thought is quickly erased as another man approaches. A nerdy-looking guy wearing a gray hoodie, a stingy brim fedora, and a Unabomber beard. He gets up in Funk's face and speaks in a hurried digital tone. "Weren't you in Davos?"

The smell of weed lingers on his breath.

Funk debates a moment. Was he in Davos? Or was that Cortina? "No, I'm sorry," he says. "You must have me confused with someone else."

"Huh," the guy says, scratching his bushy black beard and leaning against the bookshelf. "You look familiar."

Funk thinks the same about him, shaking his head at the man's Silicon Valley start-up look.

Dude, it's 2016. Do you even code anymore?

The digital man finally connects the dots and points enthusiastically. "I know where it was. It was at that TED talk with Larry Page." He laughs at the memory, his starry eyes lit up like two lightsabers. "You're the guy who challenged Bill Gates to an arm-wrestling contest. He would've kicked your ass, you know."

"I'm sure he would have," Funk says. "He's a man of great strength. But, no, that wasn't me. Now, if you'll excuse me, I have some porn to buy."

Which is true. For some strange reason, Funk has a hankering for some smut. Some open-gash, old-school smut. But not that bright digital Russian fare. That trash hurts his eyes. In addition, he likes a little foreplay first. Something the Russians have not yet mastered. But he realizes that he can't explore his aging lust here in the Barnes & Noble. The checkout lady would be all over his lazy ass before he got his hands on the nudie mag.

"Don't even think about it, buster. It's sealed in plastic."

Every dirty old man knows that before he can masturbate in the comfort of his own home, he must remove the plastic. It's just something you do. Or something you *used* to do.

So, with a polite over-the-shoulder wave, Funk exits the bookstore and heads for his favorite Los Angeles newsstand.

Another dying venue.

2

FUNK browses the racks at the local newsstand. More than any-thing, the magazines remind him of his advancing age. That he is even standing in a newsstand is a call to the wild. No longer does *Thrasher, Surfer,* or *Mad* court him, but rather *Smart Money* and *National Geographic.* As if helmeted hornbills and naked shorts were something we all grew into.

Funk knows that aging in L.A. is like a magic show—the older you get, the more you disappear. But that hasn't bothered him of late because like most people of a certain age, he is through chasing the shiny object. In these trying times of acri-mony and division, he is hunting for something more meaning-ful, purposeful. What that is, he doesn't have a clue. He just hopes that when he sees it, he'll grab it. Isn't that why he is here in this soon-to-be-extinct, dusty newsstand in Westwood Vill-age, sandwiched between two empty storefronts?

Filling in the holes of emptiness?

He is not sure that his life up to this point has etched anything important in the sands of time, save for the clipped toe-nail he deposited on Venice Beach last fall. Maybe the clipping will fossilize and be discovered one thousand years from now.

Future scientists might archive the findings, study them, and conclude that the extracted DNA came from a rudderless drifter.

An artist, perhaps.

He is certain that a much-improved version of him is waiting to break free from this self-imposed exile; he just doesn't have an inkling when that might occur. Maybe the Year of the Monkey.

The year he surpasses himself.

He lunges for a copy of *Fortune* magazine but stops mid-reach when a man says, "*I know you.*"

Geez. What is it with these people today? Bothering him in the middle of killing time.

Funk turns and stares at the middle-aged man. He looks like a lab technician in that white coat. Maybe a doctor. He's not particularly good looking, but he has a decent sense of timing and a full head of wild brown hair. Just handsome enough to play the lead in some hospital show.

Funk says, "I'm sorry, do I know—"

"Yeah, I'm Ryan fucking Gosling," the man says deadpan. He laughs at his own joke and taps his chest. "Dude, I'm just messing with you. I'm a fan. *A big fan.* You're Larry Funk. The lead singer and guitarist of Purple Onion."

Funk gives him a slack smile. "That was a long time ago."

"Yeah, close to thirty years."

Funk nods, squirming inside. Is this what his fans look like today? *Mad scientists in lab coats?*

"It would be an honor to shake your hand," the man says.

Funk shakes hands with Hospital Man, his sword arm getting pumped. He mumbles in a nonchalant tone, "I appreciate you for giving me this *Hot Tub Time Machine* moment. This blast from the past."

The man laughs. "Ha! No worries. But it's me who should thank you."

"Why's that?"

The man releases Funk's clammy hand and says, "For giving me the music. The memories. I still listen to all your old albums when I'm feeling down." He pauses. "And when I think of your famous jump-scissor kick, the one that looks like a cross between Eddie Van Halen and that Green Day dude, it makes me smile."

Time Life Music proudly presents...

"I'm glad you liked it," Funk says. "Life's always better when you don't know you're lost."

The man takes a step back, marveling at his good fortune. "Wow, I remember you playing the Whisky back in '88. That killer bill with Black Flag, the Butthole Surfers, and Social Distortion. Talk about ground zero for the counterculture."

"Yeah?" Funk says, trying to recall the show. "What song did we open with?"

The man's eyes are round in fascination. "*Dude*, I'll never forget it. You opened with 'Fool for the City.' You know, that song you covered by that other band?"

Funk's vision crystallizes. "Foghat."

"Whatever. Then you brought your babysitter up onstage. I think her name was Angie. And then you started talking about how you used to crush hard on her. First boner type shit. And then, bro, check it out. She really played a sick bass. I mean, my fucking head blew off that night."

A world-weary look from Funk. "Did it?"

"Yeah, man. Then you guys closed the show with 'Big Tits and a Bottle of Wine.' You remember that?"

Barely. It was so long ago. Every party, every gig, a mash of laughter and pain. But Angie, he remembers. How she used to babysit him when his parents went to the movies. How she let him stay up late and eat Lucky Charms and Frosted Flakes out of the box. Watch reruns of *Dallas* and *The Carol Burnett Show*. It was her that had turned him on to classic seventies rock. Everything from Rick Derringer to Boston. Heart to Jethro Tull. He still remembers playing a titillating game of Twister in the living room, both of them wrapped around each other while Foghat's "I Just Want to Make Love to You" blared from his JBL stereo speakers. The same orange-grille bookshelf speakers that had them singing duets late into the night. The year was 1978. He was twelve; she was fifteen.

"I somewhat remember that Whisky show," Funk says, scratching the stubble on his face.

Lately, Funk has taken to wallowing in vagueness.

"Dude!" the man says. "How could you forget? You took the stage like some prancing love god wearing a pair of humongous fake plastic tits and leopard-skin pants. And then you hoisted a magnum wine bottle over your head and started screaming at the crowd: '*Chug chug chug!*' That's when you started jamming on that string thing."

Funk smiles faintly. "The long zither."

"Whatever the fuck it was. It was awesome."

It had to happen. And so it does. The enthusiastic guy belts out the cult hit that Funk penned back in 1986.

"Big Tits and a Bottle of Wine."

The man uses his thumb as a microphone and starts wailing:

"*Big tits and a bottle of wine. A couple jugs and I'm feeling fine. She's coming over at half past nine. She's got big, big tits and a bottle of wine...*"

Real heady stuff, Funk thinks. But not half-bad.

It would be more palatable if his Spotify royalties amounted to something, but the truth of the matter is they are shrinking by the year. Pennies on the dollar. Fractions on the moon.

Funk doesn't have the heart to tell Hospital Man that he doesn't perform live anymore. That Artie the bass player now runs a Melrose thrift shop, and that the drummer, Coke Bottle, sells timeshares in Vegas. He's not even sure he could go on the road today. The touring schedules are grueling, and the revenues are dwindling. And when things are dying, it doesn't matter what hits you. A Bentley or a Ford Fusion. The pain is the same.

"Bravo," Funk says, fingering a *Rolling Stone* magazine. "You really nailed the chorus."

"Thanks," the guy says, raking back his thick wild mane. "Look, dude. I'm a raging fan. Let me know when the band is playing next. I'm all in." He hands Funk his business card and smiles. "Email me your newsletter. I couldn't find you online."

Funk shrugs. *Newsletter?*

"You guys were the real deal," the man says brightly. "The ultimate party band. None of that synth pop or new wave shit."

Funk secretly admires the man's nuanced palette. Purple Onion was the real deal—hardcore ska punk. They were definitely not the house band at the Hyatt. The groupies flinging their scented panties up onstage at the Roxy would attest to that. But now, on a hazy March morning in Los Angeles, there is a middle-aged man in a white lab coat drooling on his shoes. Not just any shoes, but his late dad's Rockports. It is not the first sartorial crime that he has committed, and it won't be the last.

Hospital Man continues, undeterred. He points and says, "I like your outfit. Post-whatever."

Funk is wearing a pair of baggy black Under Armour sweatpants and a Johnny Winter "Still Alive and Well" T-shirt. He calls it comfort couture. *What's not to like?*

"Look, fanboy," he says, searching for the proper designation, "enthusiastic *fan*—"

"The name's Ray. I may be glib, but my adoration for you is real. And believe me, I only worship gods who are worthy. I'm ready to serve."

"Dude, I'm not Vishnu."

"No, but you got that glow. Always have."

Funk has no ready answer to that. "I'm no god," he finally says. "I'm just lucky I made it out of that time period alive." He extends his arms out for inspection. "See? No needle marks, jailhouse tattoos, or piercings. I'm just a regular guy now. Some schmo on the street. Some *worthy* schmo who will turn fifty years old in five days."

"You look great," the man says. "I don't care how old you are. I'd just love to hear you play again. You could really torch the night. I'll be on the lookout for you. You and that ziller thing."

Funk gives him the highbrow. "Zither. The *long* zither."

"Yes, well," the man says, palms pressed together and bowing. "I'd better get going. I'm late for an appointment."

Funk nods, his silence deafening.

"I know, I know," the man says. "I'm hemorrhaging strange vibes. I can't help it. It's not every day you meet one of your idols. Anyway, it was really cool meeting you. And I hope to see you play again soon. I really do... I'll see you around."

"See ya around," Funk says.

Funk knows he will never be a bona fide cultural phenomenon in this age of time and convenience. But he will achieve cult status. And that's all one can ask for in the life of an aging rock star. That, and the occasional backstage blow job.

Funk watches the white lab coat exit the frosted glass door and hears a bell ring when it slams shut. Props to the guy for not asking for his autograph, though. But even if he had, Funk wouldn't have given it. Not unless he paid for it. *How else are musicians to earn a living today?*

Funk wanders into the smut section. It is time to get down to business. As he plods along the cracked linoleum floor of the newsstand, he sees vinyl koi fish stickers plastered to the dingy white walls. The fanciful aquatic decor calls to mind the time when his sister told him he was a Pisces. Evidently, being the twelfth astrological sign in the zodiac had explained his deviant behavior in the bathtub. He didn't mean to give her rubber duck a facial; it was just something that happened. At fifteen you forget about the rubber duck and let things fly. Something he thinks he should do more of now.

He stops and picks up a vintage edition of *Penthouse* magazine, staring at the hairy bits of a twenty-two-year-old centerfold. At this juncture, Funk feels he might not be the best candidate to write a romance novel. Dirty realism rarely sells. But oddly enough, the pristine vagina does not excite. It used to, of course. Over three hundred women notched would bear witness to that. (Although he'd two-stroked the last ten.)

Three hundred women are not legendary, he knows. It's not Wilt Chamberlain or Gene Simmons territory—not even close. But it's all water under the bridge now because these sexual encounters all took place in another era, in another life. It is a part of his history that he no longer trumpets, and he's neither disgusted by nor proud of it. It was just something that took place many years ago, at a very different time. The more important fact is that none of the three hundred women have been bedded in the last three years. Which is hella crazy because he's almost forgotten how to ride the old proverbial bike.

Funk raises his eyes from the *Penthouse* and sneaks a peek at the Mexican cashier. At the register, the cashier sits on a red swivel barstool munching on pork rinds, glued to a soccer match on a portable black-and-white TV. The loud, frantic voices of the Spanish-language soccer announcers provide the late-morning soundtrack. Satisfied that the Mexican can do no harm, Funk replaces the *Penthouse* and scans the rack of girlie mags. After a moment of scouring the flesh, he missile-locks on a copy of *Over 50* magazine.

Drum rolls fill his head. What can he say? Taste buds change.

He takes a nervous look around, chews his bottom lip, and slowly reaches for the copy of *Over 50*.

The second he grabs it—

cymbals crash from the TV.

He peels back the cover and grins like a Belfast schoolboy. "Reading" with an open mouth, he peruses the bounty of mature naked women. Suddenly, his face becomes panicked. Something is wrong. He doesn't have to see it; he can feel it. Horrified, he stares down at the stretched crotch of his dark sweatpants. He has an erection—an unwelcome middle-aged erection!

Rattled, Funk jams the X-rated magazine back in the rack and doubles over. The cashier speaks coolly, his eyes still locked on the soccer game. "I don't want a mess in there, chief. Either buy something or move on."

Funk doubled over: "It's all good."

Aware of his predicament, he scuttles away from the dirty books and grabs the first magazine he sees: *People*. Red-faced and flustered, Funk flashes a nervous smile and slaps the magazine down on the counter. He fumbles for his wallet. "Looks like Brangelina's out of Africa for good this time."

The Mexican cashier rolls his eyes. "*Transgender* or *Grannie's Garden*. It's all the same to me, chief. Six fifty."

After Funk pays, he walks gingerly for the exit like he's just taken a fastball between the legs.

TWO MILES away from Funk's position, in a sleek glass office tower, independent film producer Ronnie Slater sits at his desk thumbing through a stack of past-due bills. Business is dead, and he has not had work in over a year. He couldn't tell you the exact date when Los Angeles surrendered the title of entertainment capital of the world, but he thinks the nail in the coffin came when *The Tonight Show* left for New York.

Like most show biz people in L.A., he is just another cog in the machine, a board game piece of insignificant size and value. At fifty-five years of age, wrinkled and ball-bellied, he realizes now that his best days are behind him. Soon he will be played by the rich, fed to the young, and ground down by the late stages of capitalism.

The slide is inevitable.

He swears the fiery-red dye job on his long straight hair makes him look younger than his years (his natural color is slate gray), but in reality, people have called in to report a Bigfoot sighting.

Dialed 911.

An associate producer once described Slater's bloated pink

face and long ginger hair as "something that might have rolled off a Third World butcher's block." Rounding out his tired features are pale green eyes dipped in ice and a bulbous nose that has hoovered more yayo than the Sinaloa Cartel. He is a throwback to "the kid stays in the picture" days, the last emperor of eighties excess.

Slater's descent in Hollywood has been gradual, directly related to the runaway production of films to friendlier tax states and America's shifting tastes toward video games and mobile entertainment.

He reflects on the Academy Awards last month. The first time he realized there were no more film stars. Where once celebrities were as big as life, looked up to and admired, now they are just flimsy targets for the American dart-throwing public.

Nothing more than lost souls competing for likes and selfies.

Slater can almost feel the ghosts of Hollywood leaving the room. What used to be a destination, a state of mind, has become a dry spot on the map.

It's official, he thinks.

The movie star is dead.

Hollywood is dead.

Culturally, politically, and financially.

What used to be a town of glitz and glamour has now become a place just like any other. A sterile town of ones and zeros.

To make matters worse, Slater is a broken man of many depreciating assets, and like most of those desperate in Hollywood, he will do anything to survive. Including selling out friends and family—his specialty.

His big scarlet face is tight with worry today, somewhat scary, not unlike the creature-feature movie posters that line his wood-paneled walls.

"I'm cooked," he mumbles, raking the bills off his desk. "Hollywood is finished."

Rona, his business partner, whom he slept with but shouldn't have, enters the room. She is an aging blond starlet with an edge. The edge you get when Las Vegas calls, but *Saturday Night Live* doesn't. She thinks that fashion should be fun at any age, and so she has dug deep into her wardrobe this morning and covered her long blond hair with a red mesh trucker hat that reads: WHITE GIRL WASTED. And below that, in fine blue script, *Keeping it classy.*

It is not her first attempt at getting jiggy with it.

Slater takes note of her enhanced lips, her white T-shirt snug against her mature breasts, and yawns at her cutoff jean shorts that ride high on the thigh. All hallmarks of a lowborn, he thinks. Usually not one to prejudge, he notices that her lime-green snakeskin cowboy boots clash with the faded tattoo of two cherries on the stem that adorns her upper left calf. He laughs at the gaudy display, the ridiculousness of it all. How could any woman of a certain age expect to be taken seriously in a getup like that? She fires back and says the boots were a gift from an ex-lover, and they remind her of better times. Times of peace and love and all things, *not today.* He says, "Maybe you ought to dial it back a bit, ease off the Pinterest-style trends." He reminds her that fashion doesn't always have to be fun. There is a fine line between youth and looking like Ted Nugent's date at Cal Jam 2.

"Ha ha," she says, not amused. "You're one to talk. Wearing all black. Misery chic. You look like *The Matrix Reloaded.*" She cautions him that Mars is in Libra until the twenty-fifth of April. Which makes her slightly more aggressive. "So bear with me."

"Fair enough," Slater says. "What have you got?"

"It's the bank on line one...again."

Slater nods, braces himself, and reluctantly picks up the phone. "Ronnie Slater." A beat. "Yes, I'm aware my mortgage is delinquent." A pause. "Hey, if I had the money, I'd pay you. You know that. I've been a loyal customer for—what's that? Next week... Yes. Thank you. Thank you."

Slater hangs up the phone and rubs his seasoned temples. Rona stands by in truck-stop Boho, waiting for instructions.

After a long moment, Slater finally asks in a hushed tone, "Any word on the lizard project?"

"Carrot Top passed."

Slater looks at her in disbelief. "*Carrot Top passed?* The guy who never met a dollar he didn't like?" He pauses. "Or was that Jeff Bezos?"

"Your guess is as good as mine," she says, "but we still need a recognizable cast."

Slater nods. "What about Snooki? She in?"

"No. Her agent didn't think she'd eat a live horned toad on camera."

"*Oh, Marcia, Marcia, Marcia.* You're kidding me, right?"

"I'm afraid not."

Slater pounds his desk. "Fucking East Coast pansy. It's protein, dammit!"

The sound of his tumultuous voice startles him. Since when have the critics stopped singing his praises? It wasn't all that long ago that he won best feature film at the Independent Spirit Awards. He can almost hear the obsequious presenter now: "And the winner is...*Ronnie Slater!*"

He wonders how someone who soared so high once could crash to the ground with such a resounding thud.

The answer is Hollywood.

"Sorry for the sudden outburst," Slater says, "but I need a quick cash infusion." He chugs from a bottle of Evian water and swallows hard. "In case you haven't noticed, I'm broke."

Rona places a hand on her hip. "It doesn't take much noticing." She points at the sack lunch on his desk.

Slater shrugs, running several illegal schemes through his unvarnished mind. He speculates there's money to be made in stealing personal data, but he's not ready to go there yet.

"What about an equity loan?" Rona says.

"My credit's shot. I'm mortgaged to the prostate."

"There's always Call4Cash."

"Fuck those loan sharks. The vig's like twenty percent." Slater sighs and hangs his head. "I already called."

Bold Rona says what must be said, what Mars in Libra demands. "Long-form TV is where it's at now, Ronnie. Cable and streaming platforms. Unless you're a studio releasing a big superhero movie, there's not a lot out there for an auteur." She pauses. "And I know you don't want to hear it. But think about cutting your teeth on YouTube. Maybe build a new audience with shorts."

Slater with clenched teeth:

"I

am

NOT

filming

a

fucking

cat

TAKING A BATH!"

Slater's not big on cat videos. Nor does he want to see you hoisting your prized trophy fish off the bow of someone else's boat. But he agrees that there is gold in them thar hills, and once he opens himself up to the new medium, he will see the infinite possibilities. It is what the public wants to see. Will pay to see. And after a long career of making "Fire all you've got!" films, he has no choice.

It's adapt or die.

Slater lifts his soft chin and says with all sincerity, "Whatever happened to films about real people doing real things?"

"They bombed at the box office."

Slater snaps a pencil. "Christ! Where the fuck is John Wayne when you need him?"

"Off in the sunset," Rona says. "Sadly, they don't make movies about genuine people anymore. It's a shame too, because character dramas and westerns were my favorites." She pauses. "If it makes you feel any better, I actually paid to see *Kramer vs. Kramer.*"

Slater looks at her with incomprehension before frantically rifling through his desk. The urge to break something is strong. He, too, paid to see *Kramer vs. Kramer.* Thinking the better of the moment, he slams the pencil drawer shut and pleads with both hands. "Do we have anything at all? *Anything* to save us from ourselves?"

Rona hesitates, straightening her voluptuous posture. "There's that spring break project you passed on. That new game show pilot that MTV Classic is considering."

"Refresh me, please."

"You know, the one where old men try to pick up young women in a bar. Relive the glory days. But they don't want you to produce. They want you as a contestant."

Slater reflects a moment; he hasn't been in front of the camera in years. Not since he and his wife appeared on that house remodeling show. The same show where viewers called in saying that "icky old man" was touching himself. Slater admits he rearranged his penis, but he was by no means "playing with it." He was just adjusting his junk.

"What's the pay?" he asks irritably.

"Up to fifty thousand. But you gotta bring a wingman."

"Oh, yeah," Slater says, the light in his pale green eyes

sparkling with recollection. "The wingman who doesn't know he's playing a game. Who could I dupe into that?"

Slater nervously cracks his knuckles and ponders the possibilities. Wearing a black mock-neck shirt and black wool slacks, he now has the hysterical look of a coked-out undertaker high on his own supply.

"By the way," Rona says, tugging at the bill of her trucker cap, "your wife called."

Ah, yes. The wife.

Punctuating Slater's epic fall from Hollywood is an acrimonious divorce from a woman who enjoys rough sex and being choked out. *"Oh my God, the pool boy took me to the edge last night."*

It is not what he had in mind when he agreed to an open marriage. Not what he had in mind when a stranger showed up at his front door wearing camouflage tactical gear and polarized sunglasses, announcing he was here for the "home invasion robbery."

How do you answer that? *Sure, come on in. Mi casa es su casa. Can I get you something refreshing to drink, maybe a cold Fresca before the gasping begins?*

He shakes his head at the bloody thought of it and sweeps his bronzy hair off his face. He says softly but succinctly, "Did I tell you she's leaving me for the Boston Strangler?"

Rona crosses her arms and draws an uneasy breath. "I was not aware of that. No."

"Well, she is. We're in a spite marriage now. Motivated primarily by a desire to hurt. But she has one decent bone left in her bruised body. She's agreed to let me keep the house. That is, if I can make the monthly payment before the bank takes it back."

"You'll come up with something," Rona says.

"I hope so. Any other calls?"

She cocks her head and gives him the fisheye. "A girl named Sable. I mean, really, Ronnie. *Sable?* She sounded sixteen. And you know I don't care what you do with your C-list bimbos out of the office, but don't get me involved. You can chat with *Dateline* on your own time."

He waves a brusque hand. "Chill. She's twenty-three. Any other calls?"

"Just your friend Larry."

"Hmm."

Slater leans back in his Herman Miller Aeron chair and steeples his hands. Looking through the tempered glass doors of the cherrywood display case across the room, he stares longingly at the trophy he won for best picture in 1998. Now the only certainty is this: he is a nowhere man. A nearly man. A vile, undisciplined man lost in perpetual fidget. *But* he is an equal opportunity villain, and if he could grow a proper handlebar mustache, he would be twisting it now. That's because he has no intention of losing his house. Living in a yurt in Ojai holds zero appeal.

Which leaves him no choice.

Someone will have to be sacrificed at the foot of the game show altar. Someone whose last name rhymes with punk.

What can he say?

The entertainment gods need appeasing.

Slater looks pointedly at Rona and shapes his scheming face into a crazy batshit smile. "Funk called?"

FUNK STANDS ON THE SIDEWALK, a gentle offshore breeze blowing his thinning brown hair. With *People* magazine in hand, he stares blankly out at the Wilshire Boulevard traffic. The spacey gaze suggests something, but he's not sure what. It is high noon in Los Angeles, under an unclouded sky, and he's busy scaling the heights of apathy. The ennui pointing at him is not circuitous, he knows; it is a straight line.

The smell of marijuana is in the air. Which is no surprise. Every mom-and-pop business that closed during the Great Recession has now reopened as a vape shop, smoke shop, or cannabis dispensary. And as a result, all of Southern California smells like a Snoop Dogg concert.

After a moment of watching the cars whiz by, he tosses the gossip magazine into the trash can and marches north.

Under the glare of the scorching sun, he asks himself a question. *Where does a man go once he has seen the top of a mountain?* The answer is still uncertain, but he knows the question posed can only be asked by a lucky few. He should be thankful for this, for being born into a slice of history without fear of war, starvation, or judgment. And he is, but he is also mindful that the good life is a tiny capsule for some, a cruel dance for most.

He passes a man in a wife-beater T-shirt hosing down the sidewalk. He thinks about drought-shaming, but somebody beats him to it. "Hey, asshole," a man screams from a third-story building, "don't you know we're in a drought!"

To which the man with the hose says, "Fuck you, I took a three-hour shower last night."

The atmosphere, like the land and its people, is dry and ignitable. In these divided times, a tiny spark can lead to a huge explosion at any moment.

As he walks, Funk shrugs. *What's the point?* A recent report by scientists from Princeton and Stanford said the earth is entering a new period of extinction, including mankind. And after much mumbo jumbo, the study boiled down to we are all "essentially the walking dead."

Welcome to *Zombieland.*

The guy with the hose must have read the same report, Funk thinks. While he considers other, more quaint possibilities, his cell phone rings. He freezes on the sidewalk and looks up at the bright blue sky. He has no clue who it might be, but he senses distress. He steels himself, digs the phone out of his sweatpants, and glances down at the number. After shaking his head in exasperation, he slowly lifts the mobile to his ear. "Go, bitch," he says.

"Is this Old Man Funk?"

It's Slater. That so-called friend slash music video producer of "Big Tits and a Bottle of Wine." Until recently, they hadn't seen each other in over twenty years, but hard times and the love of music have brought them back together. Reconnected lost souls. Time seems to do that, he thinks. Bring older single men together.

"Go ahead, Slater," he says. "Humor me."

Funk listens patiently as Slater sings Neil Young's "Old Man" into the phone.

"I'm not fifty yet," Funk says.

"Not yet, my friend. But on Sunday, Father Time marches on. Got any big birthday plans?"

Funk sighs and looks into the window of a barbershop. A young man with a lustrous head of thick black hair is getting a trim. He looks robust, happy-eyed.

"You tell me," Funk says. "A middle-aged man living in a studio apartment with a hot plate and a beer fridge. Let me check my schedule."

"Don't forget the Presto Salad Shooter."

"It was a gift! Look, I'm steps away from your office. We'll talk there."

"Forget the office," Slater says. "Meet me at Ross."

"Since when does Mr. Neiman Marcus shop at Ross?"

Funk raises a good point. Slater has always fancied himself a Louis Vuitton–toting man. A man of both fashion and form. But times change, rainy day funds blow up, and lunch at Neiman's becomes less frequent.

This proposed Ross meeting is Funk's first red flag warning, and it goes unheeded.

"Just meet me there," Slater says. "Ross. Ten minutes. I've got a birthday surprise for you."

Funk frowns. "Not another hooker?"

"How did I know she had a peg leg? Just get over here."

Funk taps off the phone and reluctantly trudges up Wilshire Boulevard. For the first time in his relatively brief life, he has a sense of his own ending, a Julian Barnes moment. It is not something that unnerves him, it just is.

Warning: sea changes ahead, a new world order.

Funk arrives a few minutes later at the Ross Dress for Less. Outside the entrance, a homeless veteran sits cross-legged against the brick wall. He is barefoot and wearing desert fatigues, his sleeveless arms covered in POW-MIA tattoos. When he asks for money, Funk doesn't hesitate. He reaches into his pants pocket and hands the veteran his last five dollars. Then he thanks him for his service, and holds the door open for an elderly woman in a Los Angeles Clippers jersey and follows her into the store.

As he walks down the aisle, he feels the powerful presence of an old college girlfriend in tow. Her name was Paula, "Hey hey Paula," and she *loved* to shop. They would shop for hours together, trying on fancy clothes in every major department store in the city, and when they finally arrived home, usually late evening, she would lay out the "spoils of war" on the bed and admire her hard-earned "victories." After several marathon buying sprees, he quickly figured out that they were two different people. She always had stuff to buy. He always had stuff to sell.

Ever forward, he wanders into the men's section and sees a black blob with fiery-red hair fingering the shirt rack.

The Great Pumpkin?

No. He wishes. It's just Slater.

"Upping your game?" Funk says, wandering over.

Slater (still dressed in black) looks up and sees Funk standing in the aisle, and raises a cheap, trendy shirt. "No, yours," he says. "Come here. Check it out."

Funk approaches, and Slater pins the shirt against his chest. "Kenneth Cole. Twelve bucks. Clean lines. Minimalist gray. What do you think?"

Funk shakes his head. "What are you doing, Slater?"

"I told you, bro. Upping your game."

"Since when have you taken an interest in my couture?"

"Since you walked in wearing sweatpants and Rockports." Slater points. "Look at you. I don't know if you're ready for bocce ball or nurse duty."

Funk knows that being underdressed doesn't get you fired today; being overdressed does. "These shoes belonged to my father," he says. "You have a problem with that?"

Slater closes his eyes and nods sympathetically. "All I'm saying is please rethink your style choices. That's all I'm saying."

Funks turns and cruises down the aisle. Seconds later, he pulls a pair of cotton slacks from the rack and feels the fabric. Slater trails, then gently takes the pants from Funk's grasp. "No pleats."

"Why not?"

"Because pleats shout 'I'm from Utah and I own a pair of Tevas.'"

Funk takes the plunge. "I own a pair of Tevas."

"Oh," Slater says widemouthed. "Well, if anyone can make sport sandals cool, it's you." He coughs artificially. "I hear they have a great return policy."

Funk sees right through the two-faced mask. "Cut the crap," he says. "You said you had a birthday surprise for me."

"Only if you lighten up."

Funk nods, strolls the rack. Slater follows.

"All right," Slater says. "You want it? Here it is. I have been hired to produce a new reality game show this weekend—at the Skybar on Sunset. MTV is rumored to be interested."

"So?"

"So, I want you to come hang out. It's a spring break show, Larry. Spring fucking break. I'm talking horny coeds. Mattress squeaks and sex grunts. Yeah, that's right. The seasonal migration has begun."

Funk scoffs. "I'm turning fifty, Slater. I'm too old for spring break."

"That's your problem. You think old. Look at me. I'm fifty-five. I look thirty."

"Really, Slater? Your hair is the color of a rotten kumquat. If you're going to dye it, at least have it done professionally."

"What are you saying?"

"Your hair, man. *It's way too long* and way too vivid for a guy your age. And if you think it makes you look younger, it doesn't. To be honest, you look like Dog the Bounty Hunter after a hard day's night. Throw on a pair of Oakley wraparounds and you're good to go."

Slater sniffs at the air, seething.

"Don't believe me?" Funk says. "Google old men with long hair. You'll see the horror show."

Slater takes a freckled hand and sweeps back his thick tangerine mane. "Look at this hairline," he says proudly. "Look at it! A top surgeon couldn't have plugged it better."

Funk shrugs. "At least cut it. Let it go natural."

"And look like a corporate goon? No way. I'll let my mom read my browser history first—get a fucking flattop. There's no way in hell I'm gonna layer. Besides," he says, pointing, "you're one to talk. That windswept comb-over doesn't exactly scream 'do me.'"

Bull's-eye.

Slater has just struck the last shred of vanity that Funk still harbors: his hair. His thinning hair. For some unknown reason, it has declared jihad on his scalp, dead set on follicular destruction. Soon, he knows, there will be no more indulgent conditioners or fancy combs. Pat dries are the future. For a moment, he stands in injured silence, wishing he could turn back time and vigorously caress his fallen locks.

Lather, rinse, repeat.

"Say something," Slater says.

Funk finally snaps. "I will not wear a Bozo ring!"

"Shhhh, okay," Slater says, nervously looking around. "*De-escalate.* Do you wanna hear about the gig or not?"

"To be honest?" Funk says. "I'm not sure. I'm still reeling from your last *gig*...the time you made me super producer on the Hawaiian Tropic shoot."

"It's not my fault the parrot ate your Benadryl."

"Maybe, but with you I always know there's a catch."

In Hollywood, there's always a catch.

Funk ponders what that catch might be. He bows his head, resting his chin on his forefingers.

"No catch, dude," Slater says. "Everything's comped. Free food at the restaurant, entrance to the nightclub. And the best part—they gave me two VIP suites."

Funk looks off. "I don't know."

"Don't know?" Slater says. "Look, I'm aware the last few years have been hard. With your ex-girlfriend, the passing of your dad...and, you know...your creative center. But it's time you got back onstage, bro. Reclaimed the game. You used to be a *rock star*. Remember that guy? You can be him again. I mean, a hot plate is splendid company and all, but every once in a while, you need a weekend off. What do you say? You ready to slap on the Old Spice?"

Funk groans and looks at the ceiling.

Slater's hands move up and down like the scales of Libra, weighing each option as Funk thinks: *Young poon—hot plate. Young poon—hot plate.*

Funk jingles the change in his pocket before replying. He knows this goes against his better judgment, but his hot plate has provided little company this year. He finally agrees. "Okay, I'll go. But no Jell-O shots."

"That's my boy," Slater says. "And don't worry, nobody's forcing you to do anything you don't want to do. It's just fun in the sun. Maybe a little bottle service."

Funk takes that to be a good sign in general. He nods. "I like bottle service. But no political talk. I don't want to hear anything about the election. Nothing about Lyin' Ted Cruz, Trump, or Hillary. Or any of that 'Feel the Bern' stuff. I just want a quiet weekend away from it all. Is that too much to ask?"

Slater smiles. "No politics. But what do you say we make it interesting?"

"I don't like where this resides."

Slater puts his fat mitt on Funk's shoulder and says, "*Slap Shot.*"

Funk shakes his head and removes Slater's hand. "No way, definitely not."

"C'mon, man. Old-time hockey. The first guy to get laid wins."

"Wins what?"

"Three grand."

Funk reels back. "Three grand! I don't have that kind of money. Not to gamble with, anyway."

"I know you don't. That's the beauty of it."

"It's not beautiful to me."

"Yeah, but to the production company it is. They're footing the bill."

Here it comes.

"No, listen," Slater says. "You're background. All you've got to do is sign the release waiver and party. And then it's three grand, Funk. I know you're not destitute, but I also know you could use the cash."

Who couldn't?

"I told you," Funk says, "I don't mind hanging out for the weekend, but don't rope me into any commitments. Especially with MTV. I don't even watch it anymore. I mean, is it still on the air?"

Slater meets Funk's eyes. "Your hip meter has flatlined."

"Yeah? This coming from a guy who thought Napster was a backpack."

"Fine," Slater says with a look of displeasure. "Forget the money. Let's just hang. Be the guys we once were."

Be the guys we once were.

How many times has Funk heard that? How many times has he been grin-fucked by some nostalgic a-hole looking at him to make their impossible dreams come true?

Let me count the ways.

"I'm going to say this once," Funk says, "and only once. I don't want any faux producer duties. I don't want to be a PA, or a grip, or some dude who climbs cranes. No cranes! I am not lugging any cables or heavy equipment, and I most certainly do not want any cameras on me."

Slater nods in agreement. "No cameras. No cranes. Anything else?"

"Yeah," Funk says, folding his arms. "I'm not signing any release form. No release. No forms. Got it?"

Slater crosses his fingers behind his back and smiles at his lie. "I promise. But our gentleman's bet still stands. First guy to get laid wins."

Funk nods. "Old-time hockey?"

"Yeah," Slater says. "Old-time hockey."

Funk is not sure if he should be thrilled or terrified at the prospect. And why does he feel the sudden urge to belt out the theme song from the movie *Skyfall*?

Funk says, "We played that game over twenty years ago, Slater. Like, one time. And do you really think you've got a chance of hooking up before I do?"

"You used to be a player. Now it's more like the fifty-year-old virgin."

This fires up Funk's inner caveman.

"Oh, really? You got the blue pills ready, Gout Boy? Bring it on! Because it's a great time for empowerment."

Slater pauses. "You're hanging on way too tight, bro."

Funk runs a hand over his hair and points. "I'll see you on Friday. We'll see what kind of game you've got."

Funk walks off with purpose through the men's section, his dander still lit. Halfway up the aisle, he glances back over his shoulder and notices Slater trying on a black leather motorcycle jacket. "Hey, Members Only," he says. "I'd leave the leather on the rack. It doesn't flatter your plus-size figure."

"What?" Slater says. "It's DKNY."

Funk shakes his head and heads for the exit. Slater shouts across the store, "You're the one who better worry about his wardrobe!"

Slater turns and admires himself in the full-length floor mirror, mumbling under his breath. "Member's Only. Shit. What does he know about fashion? He looks like a *One Flew Over the Cuckoo's Nest* extra."

A stylish young black woman wearing a white lace dress and lemon-yellow ankle boots sidles up to Slater as he mugs with his reflection.

She says, "You look like that actor on *Dynasty*."

Startled that anyone would mistake him for a relic on a TV show that most want to forget, Slater stares her down in stony silence.

Then—

"Do I look like a fucking actor?!"

She does not flinch from the harsh sound of his gunshot voice.

She is from L.A.

Hardened by the years of jaded, demanding movie people, she stares at him like he's some slimy creature that has just climbed out of the sludge of the La Brea Tar Pits.

The stylish woman says calmly in a multi-state accent, "Have you ever felt that you were just muscling the material? That everything you do is met head-on by G-force winds?"

"What are you talking about?"

Her gaze drifts to Slater's corpulent body wrapped in a tight leather jacket. "It's not what you can wear," she says. "It's what you can pull off."

5

AFTER A LONG DAY OF DRIFTING, Funk arrives home.

It is night. The sky stippled with stars.

Home is a 452-square-foot studio apartment in West Los Angeles, affectionately named the "Bird Cage." He has, he thinks, through no effort of his own, joined the tiny house movement.

He saunters up to the brass-burnished mailboxes in the foyer of his stucco dingbat building and trips on a stack of phone books. "Goddangit," he mutters. How many times has he told the postman to stop dropping this dinosaur shit? Nobody reads phone books anymore. They just get stepped on and thrown away.

Just like old codgers.

He fishes the mailbox key from his sweatpants and grabs the mail. There is nothing special or important to act on, only pizza flyers and fan letters. More dinosaur dung. He tries hard to remember the last time a check arrived but draws a blank.

Exhausted, he keys the lock to his apartment and enters the room. The TV is on, flickering in the dark. The TV is always on, because TV is who he is. An old-school dude who doesn't swipe right. A brick-and-mortar man in an online world.

Trapped between the "groovy" boomers and the narcissistic millennials, he finds himself detached from his own generation. He is, by his own glum admission, a Gen X baby afraid of technology, a digital immigrant on the run.

Born the son of a groggy-eyed corrections officer and a classically trained pianist, he is at home with both high and low culture. A mutt who likes Bach and bagels.

He has never been a buyer of pitch-black sentiment, but for some arcane reason, he feels the world is in for a radical transformation. Sound footing giving way to slippery slopes. He does not believe the destruction of humankind is at hand, but it is close. And although he stands well on the other side of euphoria, he knows that somewhere in the void lies positive change; he can feel it. So can his little sister, who has tried to come to his rescue on more than one occasion. Last week she urged him to wade into the frigid waters of social media. Said she was utterly convinced that it would help revive his career and strengthen his brand. He said he liked it in theory, but not in execution. She said, "Fuck theory," and promptly uploaded a photograph of her brother to her Instagram account. An unfiltered photo of a forty-seven-year-old Funk posing on the Venice pier and squint-sighting with one eye shut. On this specific sunny afternoon, he wore beige Dockers (is there any other color?), a vintage '90s blue-and-yellow Nautica windbreaker, and an old pair of cordovan wing tips. Business casual is how he described it. Unfortunately, the camera had caught him at the most inopportune of moments, just as a gust of wind had lifted the thin patch of sandy hair off his blinding pate. So there he stood, frozen in time, eternally smiling like a man with an extra-large forehead. Or "fivehead," as his nephew had so eloquently put it.

There had been twelve likes on his sister's Instagram

account (mostly friends and family), and only one comment from some strange hipster dude with a muttonchops beard: *dad as fuck*.

If Funk were a different sort of cat, he would have lost it with that "dad as fuck" comment. Hunted the man down and squeezed his pimply balls until he cried uncle. But most of these keyboard commandos hiding behind their computers are angry cowards, he thinks, texting and tweeting their wicked ids across the dark corners of the internet. They comment or dislike with impunity, plotting their next character assassination. What they fail to realize is they're next.

Funk flips on the light and walks over to the dresser. The solid wood chest of drawers, finished in a dark walnut stain, is one of only three furniture pieces in the room, the others being an iron canopied queen bed and a black IKEA bookshelf.

He places his keys and billfold on top of the bureau, then peels off his sweaty T-shirt and tosses it into the hamper. He is unfazed by the potent smell of ammonia that suddenly seeps through the cracks inside the apartment. *Did the upstairs neighbor finally murder his brother?* It wouldn't surprise him. The frequent cry of "I will kill you, motherfucker!" is often heard floating above the courtyard.

Welcome to Los Angeles.

After opening a window to let in some fresh air, he plops down on the bed and glances at an infomercial on the TV. On-screen, a silver-haired doctor in a white smock combs the newly transplanted hairs of a middle-aged male patient. Peter, his least favorite son on *The Brady Bunch*, narrates the action. *"This patient was a Norwood 5A with excellent donor density. And as you can see, the results are natural and life-changing. The clinic was able to achieve a full look with only one mega session of twenty-seven hundred micro grafts. And the great thing is, we can do the same for you. It's time to reclaim your hair. Time to reclaim your life. So call or go online now. It's never too late..."*

A sound at the door rattles Funk. He thinks that what he hears is a knock. Barely audible, it has the faint click of paws on linoleum. Or, more untimely, the faint click of fingernails on wood. He prays that it's not another surprise visit from his Austrian neighbors. Their first sordid exchange had unfolded like a porn scene in the movie *Boogie Nights*.

In short, the unremarkable middle-aged couple had shown up at his doorstep unannounced last June. The wife, speaking in thick Austro-Bavarian English, and with a slight nasality, had asked him if he wanted to make love to her while the husband watched. At the same time, the antsy husband stood behind her in a belted khaki trench coat, death-clutching a videocassette tape of *Behind the Green Door*.

Shocked, Funk mumbled, "I'm flattered, but my back's a little tight right now. Maybe another time."

To which the husband grunted, "It's on with Dirk Diggler." Apparently, "Maybe another time" had been lost in translation.

But there was more to the fantasy Funk had yet to hear. More rolling drama. His role was to show up at their apartment, tired from a long day of battle, dressed in a US World War II combat uniform. A uniform, they said, provided by them, courtesy of the Western Costume Company. At a loss for words, Funk politely declined, citing combat fatigue and a shortage of clean underwear. Mercifully, he was relieved of his duty by another neighbor, Billy. The frat boy from Houston. Like a good American, Billy had answered the call of duty. With unending enthusiasm, he had bounded up the stairs humming "The Flag Still Flies High," whereas Funk had gone missing in action.

MIA.

Just as he had been for the last three years.

Shirtless, he sits up in bed, hoping it is anybody but the East

Alpine swingers. He turns his head toward the door and calls out, "Yeah? Just a sec!"

He hops up, puts on a flannel bathrobe, and cracks the front door. He sighs in relief. It's just his thirty-two-year-old neighbor, Judy. A pleasant-looking woman with a square face and a cute pageboy cut. As far as he remembers, she teaches school in Gardena. Third grade, he believes.

"Hey, neighbor," he says, tying off his robe. "What's up?"

"I'm so sorry to bother you at this hour," Judy says, "but I locked my key in the laundry room. Can I borrow yours?"

Funk smiles. "Sure. Let me see where I put it."

He walks over to the dresser and pulls the key from the top drawer and drops it gently into her open palm. "Here you go," he says.

"Thank you so much. I'll bring it right back."

"Don't worry about it. Tomorrow's cool."

"Are you sure?"

"Yeah, yeah. It's all good. I'm turning in early."

Judy nods and starts to leave.

"Hey, Judy," Funk says.

Judy freezes at the base of the stairs, her back hunched.

"Nutty question," Funk says.

"Nothing's nutty if it's on your mind."

"No, I guess not. I was just wondering. How old do I look to you?"

She laughs with the wisdom of a teacher. "Now that's the loaded L.A. question, isn't it? And one that a lady never answers."

"If you had to guess," Funk says, insisting.

"I really don't want—"

Funk presses, his head moving forward on his neck. "If you had to. Like, if you were on a game show or something."

"If I had to," Judy says earnestly, "I'd say you look as old as you feel."

Exhaling, he grins. "Way to wiggle out of that one, Houdini. Have a good night."

"Yeah, you too," she says, waving the key over her head. "And thanks."

As Funk watches her enter the laundry room, it dawns on him that there was zero sexual tension between them. *None.* Not even the remote possibility of a strong handshake. Since when has he become the safe neighbor? The guy who always says hello? In the past, she would've sensed he was hungry like a wolf and invited herself in and jumped his bones. Now he is the sensible neighbor, the harmless old guy in 4K who wears a full-length flannel bathrobe from Target.

Having lingered on that L.A. moment, he shuts the door and flicks off the light. He strips down to his plaid boxers and climbs into bed, thinking about his fiftieth birthday and his plans with Slater. Yawning, he picks up the TV remote and scrolls through the channel guide. He hates to admit it, but he hasn't been this deep in the lineup since the Kardashians stormed Thailand. A minute later, with his finger on the trigger, he lands on MTV's hit reality show *The Real World.* While watching the young cast whine and fight, he sinks into a deep sleep. It doesn't take him long to dream, and before he knows it, his subconscious has cast him as a new member of the beach house in the hit reality show.

EXT. Malibu Beach — Day

BIANCA, a twenty-two-year-old Dominican woman from the Bronx, lies out on the beach in a leopard-print string bikini. She tugs at her cornrow braids and speaks defensively into the camera.

BIANCA

Look, the world don't revolve around that old man. Straight up. You know what I'm sayin'? I mean, if I want to smoke two Janes, that's my business. No need to trip. I don't need some old, bald white dude tellin' me wuss up. Uh-uh. I don't roll like that. I strike it like I like it.

INT. MALIBU BEACH HOUSE — DAY

Inside the oceanfront mansion, JEREMY, a handsome young black man in a light blue polo shirt, sits in the confession booth and addresses the camera.

JEREMY

Yesterday, Funk led us all into the kitchen. He grabbed a frying pan and an egg from the fridge. Holding up the egg to Bianca's face, he said in an ominous tone, "*This is your brain.*" Then he cracked the egg and started frying it, scrambling it like some mad chef. He said, "*That sizzle you hear is your brain on drugs. Got it!*" We all looked at him like he was crazy. I guess that egg demonstration was from an old public service announcement. But it didn't seem to faze Bianca. She just laughed in his face and ate the egg.

EXT. MALIBU BEACH — SUNSET

On the beach, TINA, a pink-haired rocker girl, stands at the edge of the surf in cutoff jeans and a tie-dye T-shirt. She looks into the camera, hands on her hips.

TINA
(annoyed, appalled)

He's really pissing people off. Like, last night, he wanted to watch *his show*. And, like, I had forgotten to bring the remote down from upstairs. But when I tried to tell him, he went full-on rage balls. He's like, who's got the clicker! Who's got the *fucking* clicker!

EXT. MALIBU BEACH HOUSE — NIGHT

RANDY, a twentysomething white guy with a shaved head, sits on a sand dune under the moonlight. While drawing in the sand with a stick, he talks directly to camera.

RANDY

He's like our dad. He doesn't want to do anything with us. All he wants to do is watch TV. Like last night, Bianca suggested that we all just chill on the beach. But Funk said it was too cold. Said his knee was acting up. An old soccer injury or something. After he finished showing us the scar on his leg, he said in his fatherly voice, "But you kids go on and have fun." So we did. And when we came back from swimming, he was sprawled out on the couch, snoring away with one arm dangling. We tried to ignore him, talking about our plans and what we wanted to do with the rest of our lives. But when Bianca told us it was her dream to live near the coast someday, Funk rolled over and said, "That's nice, hotshot. But the more blue

you see, the more green you gotta cough up. That's the *real world.*"
Boy, was Bianca pissed. She told him he was a dream killer and that
his name, Funk, means a foul odor. But she didn't stop there. She
stormed into his bedroom and launched his can of Rogaine foam
over the balcony. That's when he went SEAL Team Six.
Screaming at us, accusing us all of stealing his Icy Hot patches. For
real, if this is what adulting is all about, I don't want any part of it.

CUT TO:
—Funk reading a newspaper on the toilet.

EXT. MALIBU BEACH HOUSE — NIGHT

Jeremy soaks in the hot tub. His voice is low and contemplative
when he speaks to the camera.

JEREMY

He cornered me the other day, and with this crazed, wild look
on his face asked me if I'd ever read *The Unbearable Lightness
of Being.* I didn't even know what that meant. Later, he asked
me if I'd seen his heating pad. Kinda implying that it was me
who "pinched it." *Wrong.* If you ask me, the brother's just too
old. Seriously, it took him an hour to drop a deuce last night.

Funk writhes in bed, semi-aware that he's been dreaming.
He mumbles, "Touch my Rogaine and I'll—"
A phone rings.
He lurches up, sweating in the sheets.
His eyeballs swing to a vintage Panasonic flip clock radio.
In big white digits, the time reads: 11:32 p.m.

Who would call at this hour? he thinks. It doesn't matter; he's not answering.

He turns off the TV and rolls over in bed. In the cool dark room, he hears Slater on the answering machine: "Hey, bro, it's me. Guess what I heard tonight on the news. The AMA, that's right, the American Medical Association, confirmed a study on two thousand men. Scientific proof said the more sex a man had, the younger he stayed. Shit. Like I didn't know that. I mean, you're only as young as the women you feel, right? Anyway, we're all set for Friday. Two suites at the Mondrian. The ultimate spring break staycation. And don't even think about backing out. Or talking to that quack shrink of yours. Every time you see that guy, he wants to claim you as his poster boy for a midlife crisis. I've got news for you, man. This is L.A. There's no such thing as a midlife crisis. *It's a whole-life crisis.*"

As Slater laughs predatorily, Funk smothers his head in a pillow.

FRIDAY

6

FUNK stomps around the stuffy waiting room of his therapist's office in bare feet. Nowadays, socks with flip-flops are about as formal as he gets. With head down, and hands folded firmly behind his back, he appears comfortable in a pair of tragically hip lowrider jeans and a gunmetal-gray Motörhead T-shirt. But looks are deceiving. The only thing remotely free and easy about him is his thoughts of Angie. All at once he yearns to become a part of her boy story, to share the limelight with her once again.

As he turns back and begins another lap of the room, he hears a door creak open. Looking up, he sees an expressionless woman with an outstretched arm. "You can go in now, Mr. Funk. He'll be with you in a moment."

Funk smiles and grabs his black rubber flip-flops from underneath the waiting room chair. "Thanks," he says, striding over the threshold in a casual manner.

Once inside, Funk appraises the room. It is sparse, or what he calls morgue chic. The walls are white and the floor is concrete. There are no baroque couches, Oriental rugs, or Freudian slips, just the stark reminder that you are not in a Lake Elsinore grow house. Two red plastic midcentury modern chairs dominate the middle of the space, along with a round gold mirror on the back of the door and an artificial pine tree in a braided sea grass basket that rests forlornly in the corner.

Wayfair clearance?

After tugging at his jeans, he takes a seat on one of the red plastic chairs. The March air is unusually humid for this early hour of the morning, thick and unmoving, but it's still his favorite part of the day. That quiet gray moment just before the sun breaks through the marine layer and the palm trees announce themselves. Soon, he knows, the angry uncivilized masses will hop in their overleveraged cars and declare war on one another.

A war he gave up on long ago.

On the sound system, a Muzak version of "Miss You" plays softly in the background. It is the original Rolling Stones tune. Not Purple Onion's speed metal cover that opened for Nirvana in 1990 at Raji's in Hollywood. That would be wishful thinking.

Peppered with regrets about what might have been, his thoughts return to Angie. He imagines what she might be doing now. Probably raising a family and playing guitar. Maybe a little goat yoga in her downtime.

Why hadn't he stayed in touch?

Why hasn't she?

As he bobs his head to the four-on-the-floor beat of the "disco" song, he pictures himself sitting atop a fine Arab charger. He is shirtless like Putin in the snowcapped Siberian mountains, his mighty white horse galloping under a crystal blue sky. In the distance, Angie waits patiently for him in a field of gold, but it is unclear who needs rescuing—him or her.

Stifling a yawn in the crook of his elbow, his thoughts drift back to the band. He wonders if, like a lot of the other groups at this stage, he'll sell his song catalog out. It used to be a re-sounding no, but his position has softened. Truth is, in this duck-and-cover society, nobody gives a shit about art anymore. They may say they do, but when you ask them when was the last time they bought a book or strolled through a museum, all you get is a guilty shrug. It might just be him, but as far as he can tell, most of the new artists working today lack artistic vision and integrity. All they seem to be interested in is the fast buck. Maybe they know something he doesn't, that anything and everything that can produce an income will eventually be sold out—all songs included. From hawking cars to ketchup, it's all about the gravy train now.

He knows Coke Bottle could use the dough. So could he.

So in his mind's eye, he runs through the band's catalog, searching for some buyout material. Side one of the *Screamers in the Night* album looks promising.

Side one
    No. Title
    1. "Screamers in the Night"
    2. "Guru Instrumental"
    3. "Sex on the Beach for All the Wrong Reasons"
    4. "Fool for the City"
    5. "Big Tits and a Bottle of Wine"

The potential is there, he thinks, although he can't imagine any corporation buying "Big Tits and a Bottle of Wine." He won't rule it out, though. Stranger things have happened. Ernest and Julio Gallo may decide to go in a different direction—get nutty with it. You never know. Humor may be a sinking ship, but it is not lost on those who still believe.

The therapist enters the room with a clipboard in hand, and his tinny voice clears all thoughts. "Good morning, Larry."

Funk gives him a two-finger salute.

The therapist sits in the red plastic chair next to Funk and crosses his legs. He is mid-fifties, short and frumpy, with round spectacles and thinning black hair. He is sporting the urban adventurer look today: an olive-green field jacket, khakis, and desert boots.

At least he isn't in a hoodie, Funk thinks. Last week's show-stopping garb.

Funk doesn't return the obligatory greeting; he just stares at the therapist's choice of clothes. "Just in from an archaeological dig, Doc?"

The therapist smiles, but it fades quickly. "Sig alert. The 405 freeway. It's a jungle out there."

Funk croaks, "End days."

The therapist nods curtly and says, "Yes, well, let's get started, shall we? How's your day so far?"

"All right," Funk says. "I had a great bowel movement this morning. An eight-inch, well-marbled masterpiece. And I didn't even need toilet paper."

"Congratulations. You ghosted a number two. I'm glad it went well for you." A pause. "Any other water closet thoughts you'd like to share before we get started?"

"No. Other than the fact that I was reading the newspaper in there. I still have a hard time looking at the carnage. I mean, that eye jump from the Macy's bra ad to the severed head is not an easy segue."

"The war on terror has been hard on us all," the therapist says. "It's natural to feel this way." He clears his throat. "I know we touched on it briefly last month, but how do you feel now about the passing of one of your heroes?"

"My father was my hero."

"I understand that, but I'm talking about your rock hero."

Funk feels like he has to say something. This clinical dude is making him hang on every word. But isn't that why he hired him? For his tough love, his Adlerian approach?

He tugs at his Motörhead T-shirt and says, "Lemmy was one of a kind. I'll miss him."

The therapist nods. "The art world has lost many icons this year. It gives us all time for reflection about how precious life really is."

Funk slumps in his chair. "Yeah, I guess...ever since my father died, I think more about my own mortality. I can see the end of things."

"They say a man doesn't become a man until his father passes."

"So that explains Jeb Bush."

The therapist fails to crack a smile. He takes off his spectacles and says, "I know it's been hard. A lot has happened in your life. Losing a loved one is never easy. But other than wearing your father's clothes, I think you've moved on the best one can. I'm proud of you. And so is your sister. But she tells me you've stopped writing and playing music. Why is that?"

"Because I'm still searching for my creative center."

"Ah, searching. You're not alone. Like a lot of Americans these days, you feel empty."

Funk closes his eyes and nods.

"Your sister seems to think it's taking too long. *This searching.* She thinks your rent-controlled apartment has thwarted your growth."

"Is she paying my rent?"

The therapist's eyebrows jump. "Is she?"

Funk hesitates, staring at a lump of bird poop on the window. "Not in this lifetime," he says, shamefaced. "Well, sometimes. In the past."

"Understood. How are you earning money right now?"

"I teach guitar and piano. Private lessons. Try to, anyway."

"Huh. Your sister tells me you were once a great studio musician. That you did session work for a lot of famous bands. The grapevine has it you play all instruments. Even the banjo."

Funk hasn't played the banjo in years. No wonder he feels a little banjo-deficient. He hopes the ghosts of Earl Scruggs and Pete Seeger will forgive him, cut him some slack from beyond the grave. "That was a long time ago," he says.

"Everything with you seems a long time ago," the therapist says. "What about the Pretenders? I heard they asked you to go on tour with them last year. What happened?"

"I went to Hawaii."

"Why?"

"To learn how to surf."

"Interesting."

"It's not interesting, Doc. Have you ever met a Pisces who didn't surf?"

"I'm not sure, but it sounds to me like you're running away from something, Larry." He pauses. "Possibly yourself?"

Funk has never run from himself—it was more like jogging.

"What I'm getting at is...," the therapist says, "you don't sound fulfilled."

"You're right. I'd rather be writing ringtones for Justin Bieber. Or thong twerking with Miley Cyrus." He sighs. "You don't get it, do you? It's chump change. For all my talents, I've never earned more than just enough to pay the bills."

"I can understand your frustration. You've come close to the brass ring many times. And now you find yourself getting older."

"How can you understand? You go home every night to your lapdog in your comfy Wilshire corridor condo and feed it quinoa treats from a remote-controlled trapdoor. Then it's go time with your wife on a firm Sealy Posturepedic."

The therapist looks dismayed. He taps his pencil on his notepad. "It's chicken."

"What?"

"The treats. The treats are chicken. Bacon and chicken, actually."

Funk lets loose. "I don't give a flying—"

"I didn't choose to be an artist, Larry. You did. And only true artists know that material success does not always follow the work. The reward is in the creation—the journey."

"I didn't choose to be an artist," Funk says. "It chose me."

The therapist leans back comfortably, an elbow planted on the back of the chair. "Then let it choose you. Don't fight the flow. The more you focus on past failures, the more the future will manifest itself. Just keep creating. The source will provide."

"Don't self-help my creativity. When I'm ready to write or play, I'll let you know."

"Okay. Let me ask you this. How do people find you?"

"What do you mean, how do people find me?"

"Technology has created an old guard and a new guard in the arts. It seems logical that you might try the new paradigm after the old guard—the gatekeeper model—has kept you out. You have no website. You're not on social media. You sneak peeks through your mother's Facebook page." He points at Funk. "So tell me, how can anybody find *you*?"

"That's just it. I don't want to be found. Real artists don't grovel."

"Ah. The age-old line between art and commerce."

"There's no mystery left, Doc. Nowhere to hide. Now they want to know what you had for lunch."

The therapist smiles. "Maybe they like your lunch. Maybe they find your lunch appetizing." He leans forward, his eyes resting calmly on Funk's face. "Maybe it's time you gave them a bite."

Funk shrugs.

"Very well," the therapist says. "Let's switch gears. Are you still seeing that woman from the salon?"

"You mean the one who specializes in thinning hair?"

"Yes, that's her. How's she doing?"

Funk looks down and stares pensively at his flip-flops on the polished concrete floor. "I don't see her anymore."

"Why not?"

"We broke up."

"Why?"

"Because every time I went in for a haircut she'd say, 'You know, Larry, you'd look a lot better if you stopped combing over.'"

"To which you replied?"

"'Like I have a choice, bitch!'"

"I see." The therapist reviews his notes, flips through a few pages. "So, Larry," he says. "Are you ready to tell me now?"

"Tell you what?"

"You know. This big secret of yours."

Funk crosses his arms. "No. Maybe at the end of the session."

"Okay," the therapist says, "we won't go there yet." He gazes out the window at the palm trees bending in the wind. After a quiet moment, he speaks in a bland tone. "You know, Larry, Christopher Lasch, the late social critic and author of *The Culture of Narcissism*, once wrote that adults 'cling to the illusion of youth until it can no longer be maintained,' at which point they must either accept their superfluous status or sink into dull despair." He turns his cold scrutiny back on Funk. "Does this remind you of anyone?"

7

SLATER STANDS AT THE WINDOW, peering through a bright midmorning sun, his burnt-orange hair bathed in fluorescent light. When he tilts his head to the left, he can almost see his expensive future off in the distance, beyond the grand mansions dotting the Hollywood Hills. *What happened to this town?* he thinks. *A town where a man was once judged on his actions and not his beliefs.*

He reflects on this question inside one of the Mondrian Hotel's posh, minimalist suites. The room is more palatial than he'd expected for such an old hotel, and it would be a shame if he didn't take advantage of its panty-dropping vibrations. Something to distract him from the decaying city below.

Funk is scheduled to arrive later this afternoon, and preproduction doesn't start until five. This gives him ample time to relax, collect his below-the-belt thoughts, and get his rocks off.

Why not? We can only deny nature for so long before it reasserts itself.

He hungers for "room service" but suspects that what he craves is not on the menu. He shuffles across the room and sits on the edge of his king-sized bed, wearing a white T-shirt and a pair of stars-and-stripes boxer shorts. He puts on his reading glasses and flips through the hotel's guest directory with a bitter look on his face—his suspicions confirmed. Turned off by the grammatically incorrect copy and no happy endings beyond the tourist drivel, he picks up his iPad and starts scrolling through massage parlors on Yelp. As is the custom, there are too many negative and phony reviews, too many whiny punks complaining about a twenty-dollar "foot massage." *My experience was bad the moment I arrived...Super pushy, rude and aggressive...Didn't soak my feet in hot water first, then offered a weak handy. Beware their free trials!*

Perhaps, he reasons, just like every other ordinary task these kids need to learn, they should turn to a video tutorial for tips. Tips on how to act, what to expect, and how to get the most "bang for your buck" at the local jerk shack. Usually, Slater will tell you, walking in with nine dollars in your pocket and asking to "see the whores" will not get you the desired results. Tact and diplomacy win the day. As well as a whole lot of dough.

Slater abandons the Yelp cesspool and heads for greener pastures—Yahoo. He types "sexual massage" into the search field, careful not to fall prey to all the clickbait titles that beckon. Titles like: "Why Young Slavic Women Don't Care about the Age Difference." Or, better yet, "Women Say This Is Their Favorite Trait for Men over Fifty."

It didn't take him long to figure out that their favorite trait was money, or lack thereof.

So why not spend it on a sure thing?

Tired of all the crabby reviews and pop-up ads, he tosses the iPad on the bed and grabs the phone book.

Dinosaur meets dinosaur yet again.

He eagerly flips through the yellow pages and a big advertisement catches his jaundiced eye: "Hollywood Nights Massage." His blood quickens at the prospect, yet it makes him feel vaguely guilty and weak inside. He thinks of his soon-to-be ex-wife, and his church where he has not attended Mass in over thirty years. And while he prefers Dr. Seuss over the Bible, he still believes in God. But since he has neglected Him for the last three decades, he has turned elsewhere for spiritual guidance.

The Magic Eight Ball on the internet.

He has asked it on more than one occasion, "Should I bang that bitch?" And the answer has always come back the same: *You may rely on it.*

With its wisdom gospel, he rips out the page, tosses the phone book across the room, and frantically dials the hotel phone.

A sultry voice answers. A little dark, somewhat husky. "Hollywood Nights. How may I help you?"

"Look, baby," Slater says. "I'm at the Mondrian on Sunset. How soon can you get a girl over? Preferably a nerdy blonde with big round glasses." A pause. "That's right, full service."

"We're close," the sultry voice says. "Twenty minutes, tops."

"Cool," Slater says. "But here is a list of my demands. And I want you to listen carefully because this is *very* important. Are you listening?"

"Yes."

"No, I mean, are you really listening?"

"All signs point to yes."

"Okay, good. Here's how it goes down."

Take note, incels. Class is in session.

Slater crosses his legs, aware that a testicle has just dropped from his boxer shorts. He speaks with an authoritative tone. "I don't want any women with piercings or tattoos of any kind. And if she shows up with a dragon on her back or any of that tongue shit—I will send her back. Repeat, I will send her back."

"You sound like a man who knows what he wants."

"I know what I don't want."

"What's that?"

"Blue waffle."

"Ooookay."

"I'm glad you agree. But no offense, I hope it's not you. There's a masculine quality to your voice that makes me uneasy."

"It's not me," the voice says, laughing. "But you don't know what you're missing."

Slater rises from the edge of the bed, draws the curtains. "I know what I'm missing. It's called cock, and I'm not interested. But we're getting sidetracked. Let's get back to the girl."

"Let's."

"No chicks over thirty. Repeat, *no chicks over thirty*. I'm not interested in mutton dressed as lamb. You hear me?"

"Yes."

"Good. And please, no caning victims, moles, facial hair, or chicks into urine therapy. I'm not into boner shock."

"Who is?"

"Right? And before I forget, no Russians. The last thing I need is to get roofied by Sergei on a Friday afternoon. You dig?"

"I'm not sure what 'you dig' means," the husky voice says, "but I think I can satisfy your demands."

I hope so, Slater thinks. Because the casting couch is dead. *What else is a predator to do?*

"Good," Slater says, clearing his throat in a series of thrusting grunts. "One more thing."

"Yes?"

"No penis haters."

"Excuse me?"

"You heard me. No angry women or woke freaks. Last chick I had played tetherball with my dick. The penis can take a lot of trauma, but this was warfare. A beatdown of the highest order."

"I can assure you there will be no haters." A lengthy pause. "You're not a cop, are you?"

"Hell no. Are you?"

"No. We are a legitimate massage agency."

"Yeah, sure you are," Slater says, "and the Easter Bunny is a superhero who fights crime on weekends."

"I'm serious."

"Explain that to the girl after my bull snake spits in her face."

Locker room talk is real, Slater tells himself, and any man that claims to have never heard it is lying.

You dig?

Slater hangs up the phone and reaches inside his stars-and-stripes boxer shorts, caressing his crusty balls. The anticipation is the best part of the process, he thinks. But what he doesn't know is that hidden cameras are already rolling inside his hotel room. At this very moment, a Hollywood camera crew has just captured his perverse booty call in front of a live studio audience.

First rule of Hollywood: *Always read the contract.*

———

Not far from Slater's hotel room, on the backlot of a Burbank television studio, a triggered Gen Z and millennial audience has just witnessed his crude "room service" call on a jumbotron TV.

In anger, the young crowd in Stage 1A pumps its fists at Slater's real-time image, shouting, *"Old man loser! Old man loser! Old man loser!"*

On the big screen, Slater throws off his T-shirt and liberates a set of large, hairy man breasts. Shocked by the meaty vision, the young audience is stunned into silence. They watch, horror-stricken, as a half-naked Slater approaches the vanity mirror, turns sideways, and begins sucking his prodigious gut in and out...in and out...like a stretched balloon losing its shape.

Fat-shame this, motherfuckers.

Slater pinches his love handles, and with his furry back to the camera, drops his boxer shorts and uncloaks a saggy white bottom. Hanging glutes with pitted acne scars.

Loud screams are heard from the live audience.

The disturbing image of Slater then freezes on the jumbotron, and in typewriter font, the words *Game or No Game?* zip across his historic ass cheeks.

Whew.

Onstage, the host of the show, a hip young black guy in a porkpie hat, stares at Slater's frozen image on the video monitor. He smiles and says into the camera, "Yo, yo, dawg, check it out. As gruesome as that is"—he points at Slater's naked body—"we have more to come from our new reality show, *Game or No Game?* Stay tuned for a special old-school edition, or as I like to say, boomers behaving badly."

He recoils at the sight of Slater's long apricot hair and crepey pale bum. "Whoa, dawg. Maybe you should read the release next time."

Canned laughter erupts.

8

"Look, Doc, I don't want to hear any more baloney about growing up. I'm doing the best I can. Los Angeles is no country for old men. Honestly, growing old in this city is like living in a fire zone. Dry and combustible." Funk crosses his legs and picks at the rubber of his left flip-flop. "Not only that, you try to find a decent wingman at my age. It's nearly impossible."

"Good point," the therapist says. "So, let's talk more about your age. How do you feel about turning fifty?"

"To quote William Hurt, 'I'm still evolving.'"

The therapist plays along, straight-faced. "And what have you eeee-volvvvved into now?"

"An old, balding hack with no direction."

"Why so hard on yourself? Look at me. I'm bald and quite content."

"Don't fool yourself. If I didn't pay your salary, you'd have zero game."

"Hmm. I think it's safe to assume that as a ladies' man, turning fifty is bothering you."

"Ya think?"

The therapist shifts his weight in the chair and stares back at Funk with a grave expression on his face. "I can't help you, Larry, if you continually puncture my professional insight with your sarcastic A-bombs."

Funk leans forward, his gaze sharp. "Let me steer you there, Doc. Are you familiar with the Jennifer Lopez song 'Love Don't Cost a Thing'?"

"I've heard it, yes. 'Even if you are broke, it doesn't matter. I will still love you.' Something to that effect."

"Your iPod list impresses me. But let me ask you something. First, substitute the word 'bald' for 'broke' in that song. Do you think she would have felt the same way? Even if you were *bald, my love don't cost a thing?*"

"I believe she's dating a younger man now with a bald head."

"Shaved heads don't count. Follicles do."

"Life doesn't boil down to a song, Larry. But reading between the lines here, one would surmise that your identity is tied to what you have or haven't achieved in life. In youth, the starving artist or rebellious rock star represents romance and adventure. But in middle age, to you, it just represents starving. Therefore, the reason you're still single, the very reason you still act the playboy, is because you haven't achieved a level of success worthy of the woman of your dreams. So, you have sabotaged any meaningful relationships that you may have perceived as intimate possibilities because of your feelings of self-worth, or lack thereof. And now you find yourself with your life half over and losing the only thing you think you have left to offer women. *Your looks. Your hair.*"

Funk slowly rises from the chair, stands expressionless, and raises both arms high into the air like a football referee.

Touchdown.

9

INSIDE THE CONFERENCE room of the Mondrian Hotel, Max Dungworth, the clean-cut twenty-six-year-old Machiavellian producer/director of *Game or No Game?* watches Slater's booty call on a NASA-like bank of TV monitors.

On the phone with the executive producers in New York, he sits with one leg over the other in a director's chair and speaks into a headset: "What do you guys think of that promo we just shot with the old fart? The audience ate it up."

A female executive responds. "The casting is perfect. Mr. Slater is a real character. Albeit a little scary. But we're excited about tomorrow's show."

"Me too," says Dungworth, his dry, stolid demeanor hiding the monster within. "It should be one great hour of television goodness."

Max Dungworth will tell you that he defies Hollywood stereotypes, but in actuality he is the embodiment of all that has gone wrong with today's youth: ruthless, robotic, and greedy.

Svelte and mean, with dark wavy hair and chunky black glasses, he stands well over six foot three in bare feet. He likes to think of himself as a driver of trends, an influencer of people, and that begins with his wardrobe—a crisp blue button-down Oxford shirt and a pair of socially conscious direct-to-consumer chino pants. Like Steve Jobs, he prefers to wear the same outfit every day. This reduces mental energy and allows for the brain to focus on the bigger tasks at hand. Tasks like how to exploit an old fart for TV ratings.

He goes off the rails with his shoes this morning, a pair of comfortable Birkenstocks with pearl-gray socks. Argyle when he wants to "lean into it."

Like most days, he wears a Fitbit. Counts his steps and tries to be the best he can be. He finds eating a nuisance and a time suck, and so a liquid diet of Soylent fuels his day. His conversations are interesting only to himself, and of that he is proud. Thinking of the rights and feelings of others is for fools, he thinks. Something he does not share with his millennial brethren. He does not care that he is not the most interesting man in the world. After all, he will tell you, what good is interesting without money?

That said, he has one serious chink in the armor. He takes drugs—*daily*.

Opioids, to be more precise.

Like his predecessors before him, the pressures of Hollywood are mounting. His crew believes he is just another sober, yogurt-eating asshole. But behind the detached mask lies the morning cocktail of fentanyl and ambition.

He doesn't have a dealer or "a guy" that gets him his dope. He buys his drugs straight from the gray web.

One keystroke at a time.

Hit the buy button, and the fentanyl arrives by mail in a small, tidy brown package. He often wonders when that package might arrive with the Amazon logo. It would certainly drive the price down. And what junkie wouldn't like that?

As he waits on hold, he thinks back to last Wednesday night. The night he was so out of it he couldn't see straight.

He was driving home stoned, boiled to the ears behind the wheel of his expensive SUV, when he hit something or someone in the crosswalk. He felt the car jerk and heave forward and thought he heard a dragging sound. But for all he knows, it could have been the song on the radio. It was dark, past eleven, and he should've stopped, but he didn't. Instead, he made last call at In-N-Out Burger and chomped down on a juicy Double-Double with a cheesy smirk on his face. When he got home and inspected the dented front bumper of the Land Rover, it looked like he'd hit a deer. But there are no deer in the urban streets of West Hollywood. Only people. But like everything else in Dungworth's life, he shrugged it off. Forgot about it. In a town like this, it would be hard to prove. L.A. is full of hit-and-run drivers. So go ahead, broflake, try picking him out of a lineup.

If it doesn't fit, you must acquit.

As with all drugs, there are side effects. And with opioids, constipation is one of them. Truth be told, Dungworth hasn't had a bowel movement in over a week, and as a result, he walks the line like the Tin Man in need of an oilcan, his legs stiff and measured.

Nonetheless, he has a job to do.

The show must go on.

The jarring voice of the female executive roars back to life in his headset. "It appears the lady of the night, or should I say, the lady of the day, has arrived."

Dungworth glances up at the wall of TV screens. Sees a nerdy blonde girl in high heels, big round spectacles, and a tight aqua-blue dress walking down the hotel corridor. On another monitor, a shirtless and bloated Slater is seen in his hotel suite, wrapping a white towel around his waist.

"Yeah," Dungworth says with a devilish grin. "The hooker's here. You guys want a private screening?"

The female executive answers in a sharp tone. "We'll pass on the private dancer, Max. We've seen enough ass cracks for one day."

"You sure? Because I've already got the working title. *Hookers, Bloopers and Blunders*. What do you guys think?"

An authoritative male voice crackles through his headset: "Take it to HBO, Max."

Dungworth nods and leans back in the director's chair. "Right. No worries," he says. "This is just for my eyes only."

"*Wait*," the female voice says hesitantly. "You're not actually going to watch the disgusting act...*are you?*"

"Not only am I going to watch," Dungworth says, "I'm going to participate."

An audible gasp from the female executive.

"Relax," Dungworth says. "It's not what you think. I'm just going to do a surprise pop-in on Gramps. Bum his Cialis high. After all, it's about access today—not ownership."

Dungworth cackles, not unlike an alpha hyena.

As a director and a producer of reality television, he is a master of the well-worn tropes. He has perfected the fine art of the awkward pause, the surprise pop-in, and the emotional family reunion. But it's the manufactured drama that puts the food on his table.

Bedlam and disorder rule the day.

Chaos, for lack of a better word, is good. Baby boomers, not so much. All they do is take and eat, he thinks. *Take and eat.* And looking at Slater's fleshy, hedonistic body on-screen has only confirmed his theory. Come to think of it, he has never met one cool boomer in his entire life. Not one. *Not ever.* There's something basically wrong with that.

Dungworth says, "I understand we can't air this on our

network, so I'll archive this little tryst for future endeavors. It's only a matter of time before I break down the barriers of good taste in America. Not that we ever had any."

The female voice sighs through the headset. "You're a sick man, Max."

Dungworth grimaces from the hard stool forming in his belly. "Thank you," he squeaks.

10

INSIDE SLATER'S luxurious hotel room, he lies in bed on his back with his eyes closed, his beefy hands clasped loosely behind his head. Underneath the covers, the naked call girl cups his shapeless heinie and vigorously deep throats his dry walnuts. In between gags, she tells him that she is an old-fashioned girl, one who doesn't want him to cum on her face or hair. She is not like her young peers, she says, those who enjoy a good facial splatter and a hint of danger with their small talk.

Uh-uh.

She doesn't roll like that.

"It's all good," Slater says.

And he means it. He pays, he fucks, he goes home. It's a lot safer that way.

Just as long as you steer clear of the Russians.

The music on the nightstand radio sets the mood: Stevie Wonder's "Part-Time Lover."

The nude nerd kisses his balls and says, "Do you like that?"

Slater winces. "It would feel a whole lot better if my pubic hair wasn't caught in your braces."

"No duh," she says. "It's the price you pay for straight teeth, mister. Which is why I gave you the short-timer's discount."

"Lucky me. Does it include the incisors?"

The young call girl's American English is blunt and salty, he thinks. *Breaking Bad* meets Appalachia. Maybe he should have listened to his Iranian grocer and chosen a foreign-born woman. Someone with a more "global" perspective. *"Forget American women,"* his grocer had said. *"Just take an English class at the local junior college and fuck all the immigrants. You'll thank me later."* In one discussion or another, he most likely agreed. It was crafty and wise advice in 1979, but worthy of Old Sparky today.

Slater guides the young woman's hand onto his joystick, but at first glance she seems reluctant to drive. "Jiggle the balls, baby," he says. "Jiggle the balls. Yeah, that feels good. Now go on ahead and run it up the flagpole."

She laughs and dives under the Egyptian cotton bedding—her white-sheeted head bobbing up and down.

Just as the two achieve perfect rhythm, a knock at the door jolts their harmonious arrangement.

The call girl, on instinct, abruptly emerges from underneath the duvet cover, doe eyes blinking.

Livid, Slater shouts, "Who is it!"

The answer comes through the door. "It's me, Max," Dungworth says.

Slater checks his watch. It is late morning, almost noon, the bright sunlight streaming through the crack in the oatmeal curtains. As much as he'd like to get his nut off, the producer is at the door. He evaluates the moment and lobs a softball; maybe he'll go away. "The meeting's not for another hour!"

"I know," Dungworth says. "But it couldn't wait. I've got some great ideas for the show. I'd like to share them with you."

Slater hears the keycard lock click, and rolls his eyes upward in disgust. The hooker squeals and dives under the covers as the door bangs open. The door opens with such force that it smashes and pins Slater's vintage tweed suitcase up against the luggage bench.

A stiff-legged Dungworth walks in like CSI entering a crime scene. He stops, stares at the two lovers in bed, and casually adjusts his thick black glasses. "Oops, my bad."

"Jesus Christ, Dungworth!" Slater says, sitting up. "What the hell?"

Dungworth closes the door. "It's just a suitcase." He points. "What's under the covers?"

Slater claws the reddish-orange clumps of hair away from his eyes. "A bedbug."

Dungworth smiles. "Hmm. Sounds dangerous. Does it bite?"

"In all the right places."

Dungworth gives him a smug nod. "Sounds like it's your year of taking action, Mr. Slater."

Slater feels the sudden urge to punch this sarcastic and patronizing a-hole. That's what he used to do. But these are different times. Times of mansplaining and manspreading and all things not manly. That's the problem with these young punks today. They're lost somewhere between manners and toxic masculinity. *I mean, whatever happened to float like a butterfly and sting like a bee?*

In "their" view, the days of Hemingway punching a guy in a bar are no longer heroic or cool, just pathetic and sad. And if you do play the man card, be prepared to go to jail—freedom revoked. But it doesn't mean that this arrogant kid standing before him doesn't deserve to get punched. God knows his long, pinched face is a big enough target. A steep slope, like El Capitan falling off itself. But restraint is the operative word of the times. And since Slater is a creature of comfort—loves his

Mediterranean house and his four-poster bed—he'll play the game until he doesn't.

Or can't.

"Look," Slater says, "can you give me twenty minutes? I've got company, in case you haven't noticed."

"Make it fifteen," Dungworth says. "It's time to get down to work. We've got to talk about your boy Funk."

Slater pulls the sheets up over his man breasts and nods.

"But make no mistake, Mr. Slater," Dungworth says. "Soon your day will be over. In the near future, you *will* be marginalized and pushed off into the shadows of late fall. I can see you now. Hunched and open-mouthed, aimlessly wandering the aisles of Home Depot. '*Valves? Valves? Where are the fucking valves?*'"

Slater holds his tongue, clenching his fists under the sheets.

"Retirement is a bitch, Mr. Slater."

Dungworth chuckles and heads for the exit. He turns and stares, standing dramatically with one hand on the doorknob. "Conference room. Fifteen minutes. I trust you will use them wisely."

Stiff-backed and brooding, Dungworth yanks the door open and slams it hard against Slater's suitcase. With one last glance over his shoulder, he leaves the room without another word.

Naked and irate, Slater bounds up from bed and hastily wraps a towel around his jiggly waist. He unwedges his vintage luggage from behind the door and inspects its tweedy body under the light. Satisfied that his classic suitcase will live to pack another day, he sticks his head out into the hallway and yells at Dungworth's fading back. "It's not just any suitcase, Dung-breath! It's a Hartmann!"

11

ACROSS TOWN, Funk's torture session drones on.

"How do you plan to celebrate your birthday?" the therapist asks.

"A friend of mine says he's got some spring break show he's producing on Sunset. He wants me to be an extra, hang out and party with a bunch of coeds. He says everything's free, but you never know with him."

The therapist points at Funk and gives him a paternal stare. "That explains your new look."

"Yeah, well," Funk says, "the jeans are new, but I had the shirt."

The embellished lowrider jeans with the crystal-studded back pocket flaps are a recent gift from Slater. He remembers the unboxing of the acid-washed denim left him breathless, though not in a good way. But in the spirit of friendship, he agreed to give them a try. Outfit inspo be damned.

"You don't sound too excited."

Funk sighs. "My star-spangled rodeo days are over, Doc. Swarovski crystals can only get you so far. But that's not what's bothering me."

"Okay, I'll bite. What's bothering you?"

"The bet."

The therapist looks alarmed, his pencil paused on the notepad. "What bet? You're gambling now?"

"What? No. It's something about, well..."

"Go on, Larry."

Funk shakes his head. "It's a dumb bet. Something about the first guy to get laid wins."

The therapist nods and unzips his field jacket. "I will not ask you what he wins. But citing the work of behavioral psychologist Daniel Kahneman, our first thought is 'often not the best answer we ultimately arrive at.'"

"You don't have to bring out the himpathy card," Funk says. "I can do that myself. But I know it sounds bad. So add that to a long list of things that aren't perfect about me."

They sit in silence for a moment, and Funk stares at his reflection in the round gold mirror on the door. He looks every inch of seventy with that wispy comb-over, he thinks. That's the thing about doctors' offices. They add twenty years to you. Not to mention those hospital mirrors. Try recognizing yourself on the gurney after an upper endoscopy. Shock treatment to follow.

The therapist speaks softly, careful not to scare his prey. "Care to elaborate on the bet, Larry?"

Funk crosses his arms and leans back in the chair. "It all goes back to the old days when we were clubbing. When people actually went out, you know? Slater and I shared a love for the movie *Slap Shot* with Paul Newman."

The therapist nods. "The Hanson brothers. Good flick."

"Yeah."

"And...how do they translate?"

"They used to have that saying between them. That they just wanted to play old-time hockey. So it became an inside joke. Slater would say, 'Let's go meet some girls. You know, play some old-time hockey. No women over thirty.' That was our war cry." Funk looks down, feels ashamed. "Or his. But that was over twenty-five years ago. I don't know how to tell him. I'm just not into it anymore. Haven't been for a long time."

The therapist crosses his legs. "Does this have something to do with your big secret?"

"You're good."

"That's why I make the big bucks." He pauses thoughtfully. "Perhaps it's time you tell me. I think you're ready."

"Lord knows I've watched enough sunsets."

"Go on."

"You know how I was telling you I never even noticed my switch from alternative rock to easy listening? And how one day it just happened? Here's the thing, the slide down the dial from Nine Inch Nails to the Glenn Miller Orchestra was surprisingly seamless. 'Moonlight Serenade' being one of my favorites. Well, it's kind of like that."

"You're dancing, Larry. Tell me."

Oh how I wish Newhart was still in practice.

"Larry?"

Funk points and blurts, "Plot point number one. I'm attracted to older girls."

The therapist lowers his chin and peeks over his spectacles. "Older girls. Or older—"

"*Women.* Older women, *okay.* I mean around my age. Maybe a little older. That good enough for you, shrink-wrap? Maybe I'll go all *Harold and Maude* on ya. Would you like that?"

The nod of approval from the therapist. "Breakthrough."

"I mean, don't get me wrong," Funk says. "If a Hooters girl wants me to go down on her, I'd have to think twice about it. Although nowadays, it's the HPV virus waiting to happen. You get or you give. You never know. So, it would probably just be the missionary position. Maybe a little slow stroke." He slides his fingers through his wispy hair. "It's just that even if a twentysomething woman finds me attractive, which is rare today, I just can't connect on any level. I don't care what color your iPhone is. I can't fake it anymore." He pauses, lips parted. "I guess that rules me out as next season's Bachelor, huh?"

The therapist smiles and claps. "Welcome to the club, Larry. You're an official grown-up now."

Funk wonders if there is a certain age where men start wearing their pants above their belly buttons. Has that day finally arrived for him? Or is this just another *waisted opportunity?*

Funk waves an enthusiastic hand like he wants to ask a question in grade school.

Ooh. Ooh. Pick me. Pick me.

"Yes, Larry?"

"Permission to hike my pants?"

The therapist chuckles. "Permission granted."

Funk stands. He steps away from the chair and, with great effort, wiggles his lowrider jeans high above the hips. In the process, a look of liberation comes into his face.

A smile beams from ear to ear.

He's officially part of the club now, he thinks, or has at least narrowed the divide.

12

AT THE HOTEL, Dungworth leads a disheveled and erected Slater into the conference room.

"Great shades of Satan, Dungworth. At least let a guy get off first. I didn't even get a chance to properly say goodbye to my girl."

"You can polish the banister on your own time, Mr. Slater. Right now you belong to me."

Slater understands that he is not being good-naturedly teased and nods agreeably. What else can he do? With his hands in his pockets and a manila envelope tucked under his arm, he trudges behind Dungworth, a bit self-conscious.

"This is our temporary control room, Mr. Slater. This is where the magic happens."

Slater stops and gawks at the vast bank of NASA-like flat-panel TV screens on the wall. It almost resembles the Apollo Mission Control Center, he thinks.

Help me, Houston, I've got big fucking problems.

Nodding in admiration, Slater looks up at the primary LED display screen in the center of the operation. It must be at least eighty inches, he figures. *At least.*

Slater estimates it will take a crew of thirty to operate all the fancy equipment. Maybe more. Taking a step forward, he counts three rows of white plastic-top tables and ergonomic chairs on casters that divide the room into interim workstations. Anchored on the tabletops are computers and monitors, vision mixers with dials and levers, switchers, cameras and servers, and editing and audio consoles with colorful lights.

In the heart of it all sits Dungworth's director's chair—his throne—a thirty-inch bamboo number with a white canvas back and seat.

Slater rearranges his flagging unit and mumbles, "Pretty elaborate stuff."

"Yes, it is," Dungworth says. "This is where we herd the cats. Countdown to 'on-air.' The hotel has been kind enough to lend us their executive conference room for our little on-location setup, so if you need anything during production, this is base camp. HQ. The Samsung big-screen you see is where our crew will watch and monitor most of the game's action. So you'll report back here during filming."

Slater says, "Looks like you've got all angles covered."

"We do." Dungworth points at a bar cart on wheels against the wall. "Can I get you some coffee or tea? Little Debbie snack cakes?"

"No, thanks," Slater says.

"You sure? Because if you're hungry I can make a run for some Swanson pot pies."

Slater waves him off. He's more of a Banquet type guy. Salisbury steak and mashed potatoes.

"Okay," Dungworth says. "Feel free to help yourself anytime. And if you have any digestive problems during the shoot—like you people are prone to get—we have a bowl of Tums antacids at the ready. Berry Fusion or Extra Strength. Your choice."

You people?

Dungworth gestures toward the conference table. "Now please, Mr. Slater, have a seat."

Slater sits meekly, a manila envelope in hand. As he squirms to get comfortable in his chair, a fat drop of sweat falls from the tip of his cauliflower nose and lands on the brown envelope. Looking down, he sees that the sweat droplet has left a dark stain on the envelope in the shape of an avocado.

A ripe avocado?

Slater brushes the stain with his left thumb and says softly, "Ronnie. I prefer you call me Ronnie."

Dungworth looks at him strangely. "With all due respect, Mr. Slater, you're on a collision course with the Smucker's jar."

"Which is another way of saying I'm old and expendable."

Dungworth nods. "Precisely."

Slater knows well that once you pass the age of fifty in Hollywood, you no longer set the trends. All you can hope to do is be part of them.

"C'mon," Dungworth says. "It's all about the numbers—the demo. You know that. Sure, you've been involved with some decent projects in the past, but you're three months shy of fifty-six."

"What does that have to do with anything?"

"I'm guessing you need this job. Am I right?"

Slater lowers his eyes. "Badly."

Dungworth shakes his head. "Pitiful. Look at you, coming in here with the scent of a professional woman on your clothes. Stinky and unkempt. Frankly, you should be ashamed. You look like the Golden State Killer out on the prowl. Remind me to have your DNA checked after the show."

Slater runs a quivery finger around his collar. *Is it just me, or is it hot in here?* He hates to admit it, but Dungworth is right. He is a little gamey. His long-sleeved black shirt is soiled with bodily fluids, wrinkled, and unbuttoned to the belly. In the full light, his ungodly man breasts roam free, and his hair is a rat's nest of orange spikes and dollar store gel. Exasperated, he throws up his hands and asks for the sale. "I didn't have time to wash up. Can we just talk money, *please?*"

Dungworth's cruel mouth forms a half-smile. "Only old people ask that question, Mr. Slater. Hint, hint. The mortgage due?"

Slater pounds the table. "Rates are fucking rising!"

Dungworth fixes him with a gruff expression. "Don't pop a rod on me, old man."

After collecting himself, Slater rakes back his freakish hair and says, "I'm sorry. I'm good."

"You sure?"

Slater nods. "Yeah, I'm sure."

Glasshole.

Dungworth leans back in his chair and pushes up his glasses with an index finger. "Okay," he says. "You want to talk money? Here it is. The winning team gets fifty thousand dollars. The losers—ten grand. That's provided Mr. Funk signs the release form. No signature, *no dough.*" Dungworth narrows his eyes. "Are these terms acceptable?"

"Yes. And please don't worry about the release. I'll have it signed by Sunday."

"Super," Dungworth says. "Let's run down logistics."

Dungworth rises and walks pigeon-toed over to a workstation desk. He pushes several lighted buttons on the video switcher, and the bank of monitors on the wall flicker to life. The images on the TV screens now display various locales within the hotel:

The lobby.

Funk's empty suite.

The restaurant, pool, and Skybar nightclub.

"Briefly," Dungworth says, "the show is called *Game or No Game?* It's basically a hidden-camera reality show in the same vein as *Punk'd* or *Candid Camera.*"

"Cool. What's the concept?"

"The concept," Dungworth says, "is quite simple. Two alpha male contestants will compete against each other to pick up women in a bar. I believe in your day the term was called...*score.*"

Slater smiles idiotically.

"It's our first old-school episode," Dungworth says. "Sort of like history in the making. And unlike today, where the young guys employ PUA coaches or manuals on how to get the girl, this is all about pure back-in-the-day game." He pauses. "Or just another excuse for our audience to laugh at old people."

"I get it," Slater says. "What's the hook?"

"The catch," Dungworth says, "is that one player doesn't know he's playing a game. He's out there all alone, loose fodder for the cannon." He snickers at the prospects.

"Right," Slater says. "And that player would be Funk."

"You are correct, sir. It gives the show an air of suspense. High stakes. Even danger, when you factor in strokes or heart attacks."

Slater stares at him quizzically. "Strokes?"

Dungworth pushes another button, and the naked image of a red-faced Slater "making love" to the nerdy call girl fills the big screen. He is frozen in the missionary position, caught mid-pump, with his grizzly scrotum peeking out of his gleaming white caboose. "Overexertion is a killer," Dungworth says. "And the beauty of that is, I don't know CPR." He pauses. "Smile, Mr. Slater. You're on *Game or No Game?*"

Slater looks up, fighting the urge to vomit on the table. "That's a little dark. *Hey*, you didn't tell me you were filming me!"

"You didn't read the contract or the release you signed, did you?"

Slater rubs his weak chin. "It wouldn't be the first time, Hoss. So go ahead...*exploit me.*"

"That's exactly what I intend to do."

He is certainly singular in his performance, Slater thinks.

At that same moment two brawny workmen in dark blue coveralls dolly in a large solid oak armoire, momentarily interrupting them. One of the workmen grunts, "Wardrobe said you wanted this, Mr. Dungworth."

Dungworth wheels. "Do you idiots ever knock?"

The taller of the two workmen says, "It's kind of hard, sir, when we're holding this beast."

"Oh, all right," Dungworth says, motioning with an irritated hand. "Just set it by the bathroom and get out. I have no time for low-level morons."

"Yes, sir," the taller one says, sharing a concerned look with his work buddy.

Slater and Dungworth watch the two workmen do as they are instructed. And after a moment of considerable exertion by the movers, the armoire is finally set in place by the bathroom door.

The smaller of the two workmen with blond curls says, "Anything else you need, sir?"

"Yeah," Dungworth says. "Get the fuck out."

The movers nod their heads in unison, grab the dolly, and quietly shuffle out of the control room. Slater takes a moment and stares fondly at the stately oak armoire—a country French Normandie with a carved clover cartouche. It is a beautiful piece, he thinks, with paneled wood doors and floral scrolls. He used to own one like that. One where he meticulously stored his designer suits, his XXXL Robert Graham shirts, and the fresh white Italian sneakers he purchased in Milan. He misses those glamorous days, but he does not miss moving the heavy piece around.

That armoire must weigh a ton. One man alone could never budge it. Those young workmen were butt-strong, and yet watching them bulge and grunt, positioning the armoire into place, only reaffirmed his limits. He couldn't imagine doing that for a living today. Much less help a friend move.

But wait, did he ever help a friend move?

Dungworth sighs and takes a seat. "Not the most mentally robust, those two. Now, where was I?"

Slater says, "Before naked me, or after?"

"Before."

"You said Funk doesn't know he's playing a game. So what I want to know is, how do you determine the winner? That is to say, are you filming the actual hookup?"

"This is not *Debbie Does Dallas*, Mr. Slater. Implied game wins the day. You can danger-wank off camera."

Slater shrugs. "So a kiss will win it?"

"Maybe," Dungworth says. "The focus groups will decide that. In keeping with old-school traditions, we'll have two very diverse groups. One male. One female. They have all answered an ad in *Casting Call* for a new reality show pilot and range in age from eighteen to twenty-four. Both groups will watch the action via a television monitor in separate hotel rooms, then vote on which contestant has more game. Or who gets the girl. Make sense?"

Slater nods.

"Good. Moving on." Dungworth points to a curved computer monitor on the console with two jockeying vertical bar graphs. One red, one green. "The votes are tracked here on a virtual scoreboard," he says. "Your boy Funk is green."

Slater perks up, rubbing his hands together greedily. "The color of money."

"I like your enthusiasm, old boy. At the stroke of midnight on Saturday, the winner will be crowned. You, Mr. Slater, want to see that rectangular green bar high above the red. Any questions?"

"What about the people in the nightclub? Are they in on it?"

"No. To them it's just another spring break night. Another chance to get lucky. This keeps it authentic. But we do have plants, or actors, if we need them. And a few mobile production trucks on Sunset if he decides to catch a breath of fresh air."

"Where do I come in?" Slater asks.

Dungworth smiles. "You're the wingman, Mr. Slater. The man who sets the honey traps. Your job is to keep Funk moving toward the hookup. Keep him engaged and inside the venue. Also, keep in mind that the victor's woman must be younger than fifty years old and met here at the hotel. That's it. There are no other restrictions. We have several hidden-camera events planned for the contestants. I'll keep you posted."

Slater gives him a thumbs-up.

"Great," Dungworth says. "You ready to see the competition? Who your boy's playing against?"

"As ready as I'll ever be," Slater says.

Dungworth flips a switch and cuts the lights. The room goes dark. In the black, Dungworth says, "They call him the Latin Satin. His name's Lopez. Phil Lopez. He's a forty-eight-year-old personal trainer from Encino, California. He's rumored to have a forked tongue."

"Like a lizard?"

"Apparently so. Not only that, he's reportedly hung like a Malaysian tapir."

"*Jesus.*"

"He can't help you now, Mr. Slater. Only Funk can do that. Let's look at the video."

A shaky homemade movie of Phil Lopez at the gym thunders to life on the big screen. He is shirtless on the bench press, lying on his back, jacking serious iron to the music of Bruce Springsteen's "Born in the U.S.A." Lopez is strong and charismatic, a chiseled mass with boulder shoulders and a perfect head of jet-black hair. In between reps, his smooth brown skin glistens with sweat.

"As you can see, Mr. Slater, less is never more."

Slater sits slack-jawed. "Look at the frickin' arms on that guy."

Dungworth laughs. "Yeah. Looks like a python swallowed El Chapo."

Slater says under his breath, "This is gonna be a slaughter."

"Did you say something, Mr. Slater?"

"I said it's going to be a holler. A real hoot."

Dungworth flips on the lights. Slater looks deflated, white as a ghoul.

"So that's the competition," Dungworth says, looking at Slater's sallow face. "You look a little spooked. You all right?"

"No, no," Slater says. "Just a little hot."

Dungworth slides a box of Kleenex across the table. "I understand. A minor case of the sphincter trembles. No worries. It's natural."

Slater nods, grabs a tissue, and wipes his brow.

"Now, let's see Mr. Funk." Dungworth puckers his lips like he has a sour taste in his mouth. "By the way, what kind of name is that? *Funk.*"

"It's of German origin," Slater says softly. "It means a spark or something. But I think they named him after a big band leader."

Dungworth cuts him a frosty side-eye. "Really? Sounds like a fungal infection. Personally, if I were voting? Guy's got no game right off the bat. So who is he? What's his North Star?"

"He's a pretty chill dude. He used to play in a band of some renown."

"Fantastic. Let's see him. What do you got? Snapchat? YouTube footage?"

Slater smashes a silverfish crawling across the conference table. "I don't have a..." He clears his throat. "Any elaborate footage. Just a few old Polaroids."

"Polaroids?" Dungworth says grimly. "Like, taken back in the day with Eastman?"

Slater grits his teeth and slides the manila envelope across the table. Dungworth opens it and studies a faded sepia-toned photograph of a young Funk playing a Fender guitar onstage at the Roxy. He is slender and shirtless, with long brown hair and faded Levis.

"Looks like a worthy contender," Dungworth says. "Let's see him now. Or was that it for the Instamatic?"

"Well, actually..."

The conference table phone buzzes. A flustered Slater freezes, looking at the wireless apparatus like his fate hangs in the balance with one call.

Dungworth punches the speaker button and answers, "Yeah, Marty?"

"Contestant Lopez is out by the pool," the voice of Marty says. "He's asking for you."

"Tell him I'll be down in a minute."

"You got it."

Dungworth stabs the speaker button and hangs up. He looks at Slater with loaded eyes and says, "We'll talk about your boy later. Phil Lopez is here. I want you to meet him."

13

SLATER FOLLOWS Dungworth out to the hotel pool, where contestant Phil Lopez and his wingman lounge in a cabana in plush white robes and flip-flops—umbrella drinks in hand.

"Phil, Phil," Dungworth says, approaching the cabana with open arms. "You're looking good, my man."

Slater shields his vampire eyes from the early-afternoon sunlight and watches a chameleon-like Dungworth change his tune. The producer's voice and face have now turned smarmy and fawning—a dorky white boy trying to act street.

Lopez raises his blade shades and shakes hands with Dungworth. He says, "Wuss up, Max?"

"What's good, what's good," Dungworth says. "You wanted to see me?"

"Yeah," Lopez says. "I want you to meet my wingman, Backstreet. He's my homie. My primo. He just touched down from Puerto Rico."

Slater aims his hooded eyes at Backstreet—the short and plump wingman. The reclining sidekick appears to be in his late thirties, with a sculpted beard and a Chicago Bulls flat-brimmed hat framing his chubby face. His faraway look gives Slater the impression of one that has been recently concussed.

Backstreet, chomping down on a bag of Lay's potato chips, wipes his greasy hand on his terrycloth robe, and extends it to Dungworth. "Tsup," he says.

Nonplussed, Dungworth offers a tepid fist bump. "Nice to meet you...Backstreet. Of boy band fame?"

Backstreet shudders. "Fuck that. I owned this name long before those pole-smokers."

A lukewarm smile from Dungworth. "Sure you did." He turns abruptly, arm outstretched. "Oh, and this here's Ronnie Slater. Your competition's wingman."

Slater chin-nods.

An excited Lopez sits up and swings his toned legs over the chaise lounge. "Oh yeah? Nice to meet you. But no offense, Red. You know you're going down, right?"

"Yeah," Backstreet says. "My homie here has grazed on so much pussy, he gets a nose bleed every twenty-eight days."

Team Lopez laughs and high-fives.

"I wouldn't count your chickens," Slater says. "We're in it to win it."

"No shit, Fabio," Backstreet says.

Lopez stands and removes his robe, revealing a V-shaped body in neon-green swim briefs. All watch as he grabs a bottle of suntan lotion—SPF 2—and squirts it freely on his bare, ripped torso.

Slater counts an eight-pack. A far cry from his fat pack.

"So, Max," Lopez says, gently rubbing the lotion into his smooth chest with the tips of his fingers. "I wanted to ask you, do you want me to trash-talk this guy or what? What's his name?"

Slater blurts out, "Funk. Larry 'Uptown' Funk."

Slater does not know why he has just labeled Funk

"Uptown." It was just something that jumped from his big mouth. Even worse, he isn't familiar with the hit song of the same name. Still thinks Bruno Mars is a vacuum cleaner.

Backstreet chokes on his fruity drink. "Funk! Sounds like a circus clown, bro. And it rhymes with punk." He laughs at his own joke. "Might as well cut us a check now."

Lopez joins in. "Flunk, junk, gunk..."

"Hunk," adds Slater, throwing out a Hail Mary.

If Funk were here now to defend his surname, he would happily trot out all of its inglorious permutations—from high school to present day. There was Grand Funk Railroad. Space Funk. Funky Brewster. Grandmaster Funk. Funk the Punk. Drunk Funk. Classic Funk. Vintage Funk. Bunk Funk. Funk the Lunk. Skunky Funk (earned after a bad batch of home-grown). The Funkmeister. Funk Can Dunk (more to come). Funkytown. And finally, Play That Funky Music White Boy (which he can, and did).

Dungworth raises a hand and halts the playful banter. "To answer your question, Phil, trash-talking is fine, even encouraged. Anything short of violence is fair game. But I wouldn't jump the gun just yet. Mr. Slater brings us a California rock star with long brown locks and natural highlights." He pauses, picks a grape from the fruit bowl and pops it into his mouth. "Supposedly, he's quite a legend in the L.A. club scene. Had many a panty hurled his way. Well, let's just say he has sown his wild oats extensively. Even rumored to have given Warren Beatty a few tips. You're going to have to earn it, Phil." Dungworth looks at Slater. "Isn't that right, sir?"

Slater nods, trying hard to convince himself. "It's going to be a really big show. A real dogfight."

"You hear that, Phil?" Dungworth says. "A real dogfight. That means you gotta give me one hundred percent out there. Don't short me, bro. Don't give me the homie hiccup."

Backstreet answers, points a stiff finger at Dungworth. "We don't short nobody. You can bank on that."

Slater's cell phone rings, momentarily rescuing him from these barbarians at the gate. He quickly checks the screen and sees it's Funk—the fifty-thousand-dollar man. "Excuse me," he says. "I've got to take this call."

Slater treads lightly across the wooden deck and finds a secluded teak lounger under a towering queen palm tree. He sits, runs a nervous hand over his burgundy hair, and glances out at the stunning panoramic view of L.A. The urban sprawl below spreads across the land for as far as the eye can see, baking under a clear blue sky as vivid as an LSD trip.

Sinking into the soft white cushion, he takes a deep breath and answers calmly but firmly. "Where are you, man? I'm counting on you."

———

"Why the edge?" Funk says. "I'll be there in a few hours. I'm running a little late."

Typical.

Funk sits on his canopied queen bed, clutching the phone and watching reruns of *American Idol*. He has a soft spot for the latest contestant. A twentysomething woman from Iowa with big pipes and an infectious smile. Harry Connick Jr. says no. But Keith Urban wants More. That was her name, More. And then it's welcome to Hollywood.

Funk used to smile like that.

"It's all good," Slater says. "And sorry for the edge. The producer's an egotistical prick."

"Takes one to know one."

"Ha. Ha. Do you know what that punk kid said to me?"

"What?"

"He said I should be on the Smucker's jar. You know, referring to that whole centenarian birthday bit on *The Today Show.* I almost smacked him."

Funk laughs. "Save your energy for the weekend, Champ. I'm on my way."

"You'd better be. The sun's out. The beautiful people are lounging by the pool. And I got you the best VIP suite at the hotel."

"Cool," Funk says, sounding as upbeat as possible. "I'll be there soon."

Funk hangs up and leans his head back on the pillow, pinching the bridge of his nose. He glances at the vintage 1989 Jane's Addiction concert poster on his bathroom door and remembers what fun he had that May night in San Francisco at the Fillmore. The venue was packed, the vibe was electric, and nobody was shitting in the streets.

Outside, it is a cold world we live in, he thinks, and despite the cramped quarters of the Bird Cage, he takes comfort in the roof over his head, thankful for the shelter.

Systematically, his eyes drift to the dusty musical instruments that sit stacked in the corner on the brown floor carpet. They're all there, everything from bongos, guitars, banjos, and yes, even the long zither. None of which he has touched in ages.

Where has all the time gone?

He charged into thirty, loped into forty, and now drifts into fifty. What will sixty bring? he thinks. A crawl? A hesitant baby crawl?

He picks up the remote and zaps off the TV. Reluctantly, he drags himself out of bed and wiggles out of his tragically hip lowrider jeans. He wads them into a tight ball and tosses them into the hamper with all the other clothes to be donated to the Goodwill.

Slipping on a pair of tan chino pants over his new breathable underwear, he wonders how he is going to break the news to Slater. That he's just not into chasing tail anymore.

Whereas Slater is controversial and antagonistic, Funk likes to keep his mouth shut. Dialogue turns into diatribe, he knows, and he prefers to tiptoe in the shadows, watching the show from afar.

A bag of Cheetos in hand. Doritos on deck.

They are two completely different men now. Slater the "benevolent" arms dealer who will sell to anyone, and he the aloof artist, marinated in rectitude.

He hasn't seen a divergence like this since his ninth-grade school dance.

Maybe he won't tell Slater anything and just let the weekend dissolve into itself. Blurred by so many alternative facts.

He had originally placed the call to Slater to back out of the spring break soiree. But since he has backed out of everything for the last three years, he figured a rare appearance would be the first step back into the limelight.

Give the fans something to root for.

There could be worse things than celebrating your fiftieth birthday with a charmless snake, but he's not sure what they are.

Celebrated and famous, but still reachable.

That's him.

14

FUNK'S ARRIVAL IS IMMINENT.

It is 5:29 p.m.

Inside the control room, Dungworth and Slater stand hunched over a video display monitor, watching the Mondrian Hotel's valet attendants scramble at the vehicle drop-off zone. The statuesque people have arrived, and expensive cars and SUVs roll in.

A Mercedes-Maybach.

A black stretch limo.

A Land Rover Discovery.

The new Tesla Model X.

And so the evening dance of enchantment begins, a ballet of winks and smiles, air-kisses and bro hugs. Keys jangle, and there are several park-it-up-front requests from uppity media influencers and wannabe stars. The scene is hip, horribly pretentious, and one hundred percent Hollywood.

But there is no sign of Funk.

"Where's your boy?" Dungworth asks, nervously clicking his nails on the console. "I need to start preproduction."

"He'll be here any minute," Slater says. "Trust me, I'll know his car when I see it."

Moments later a mint 1979 silver 911 Porsche coupe glides slowly into the car park. Under the harsh white lights, the silver metallic paint job shines like a showroom mirror.

Earl Scheib would have been proud.

Slater points at the screen, excited. "That's him. *The Sexy Beast.*"

"Sexy beast?" Dungworth says.

"It's the car," Slater says. "The name of his car."

Dungworth shakes his head. "It is a classic. I'll give him that. But it's a tough look to pull off over fifty. I mean, at that age you look like the old guy going out for a joyride in his boyhood jalopy. Dick Van Dyke in *Chitty Chitty Bang Bang.*"

Slater shrugs and says, "Dick got the girl. Remember that?"

"I'll reserve judgment until I see him."

Dungworth and Slater huddle over the monitor in anticipation of Funk's exit. The classic Porsche rolls to a complete stop, and the valet attendant, a polished Hispanic man in a dark pinstripe suit, opens the door. Funk steps out of the vehicle like an appreciative costar, all eyes upon him. Wearing a white polo shirt, baggy tan chinos, and aviator sunglasses, his thin brown hair whips in the breeze.

Dungworth is furious, his neck red with rage. He points at the screen and says, "That's him? You gotta be shittin' me! He looks like a campus groper."

"He grows on you," Slater says. "Trust me. He's what the women call sneaky good looking. Like Nick Cage or Chevy Chase."

"Sneaky? I ask for a California rock star, and you give me Half Dome!"

"Listen," Slater says.

"No, you listen. This isn't a morning show. We don't have

time for ambush makeovers." Dungworth slaps his forehead. "This is a disaster. The show's off. I'm finished."

Slater makes an emotional appeal. "I know there's a lot to unpack here, but I'm telling you, he's a baller—a master fornicator. He'll make great TV."

Dungworth rests his head on the console. "Ten million years of evolution, and all the unbroken strand of DNA can produce is this?"

"Hard to believe, I know," Slater says. "But the women love him. *I swear.* Double major at UC Santa Barbara. Music composition. Writing and literature. He's a multi-instrumentalist and leader of the band Purple Onion."

An angry Dungworth gets up in Slater's face. "When? In 1962? When he opened for the fucking Beatles!"

With adrenaline running high, Slater cups Dungworth's shoulder and sells him hard. "You don't understand. He's loaded with intangibles. You'll see. He has this knack, this uncanny knack of producing extraordinary acts in ordinary moments. Just give him a chance."

Dungworth puffs his cheeks out and blows a breath. "And the next thing you'll tell me is he's a kind man, a good man."

15

FUNK carries an overnight bag through the hotel lobby with the easy gait of an ex-athlete. Which he is, or was. His favorite sport is basketball, but he doesn't get out to the park as much as he used to. Yet he still changes the hoop nets on the public courts faithfully once a month.

He smiles and greets the disinterested staff with a half-wave and a chin nod and heads toward the Mondrian's mushroom-shaped front desk. The purple-hued lobby is sparse this after-noon, hot and sticky, and smells of floral sprays mixed with amber. The flowery scent is so overpowering that he holds his nose for a moment. That's the problem with America today, he thinks. They cover everything in a heavy sauce.

He prefers a light glaze.

Funk has been to this hotel twice before, but he can't recall the exact dates. He believes one of those times was the same day that he recorded his first—and only—hole in one at the Penmar Municipal Golf Course in Venice, California. He was in his mid-thirties at that point and ended up shagging the ball girl in the concession stand. She said the hamburgers were good, and he'd said, "I'll bet." Then he put his hand up there and fell in.

Started swimming breaststroke.

Or the time this wild, spiky-haired chick "kidnapped" him after the show at the Troubadour and brought him here to an after-hours party at the Skybar. She wore a black tank top with a crystal skull on it, he a faded denim jacket over a navy T-shirt. She introduced herself as Tomorrow Knight and said that she was a mystic with clairvoyant powers, and that if he ever wanted to know anything about his future, she would be happy to do a reading. *For a fee, of course.* Her story unraveled when she told him she used to play drums for the Runaways. He didn't believe her, so with a gentle squeeze of her hand and a polite smile, he passed on the "psychic session." He didn't bother to tell her that the Runaways had disbanded in 1979, and that they only had one drummer, the late, great Sandy West. Arguably one of the greatest rock drummers of all time—male or female. As the night wore on, Ms. Knight's drinking became a problem. Way too much vodka. So he did the gentlemanly thing and booked a room at the hotel. Lying in bed after a bout of rowdy lovemaking, she'd asked him, "Is it so bad that sex and death occur simultaneously?" Then she started chewing rather hard on his left shoulder. Drew blood, in fact. After another minute of vigorous gnawing, she followed with, "Is that such a bad thing, this offering of blood and strangers?" He, being only slightly inebriated, said, "No, of course not." But inside, he was quietly terrified, plotting a fast and furious getaway. He had no intention of being anyone's chew toy.

"Dammit!" he hears someone shout in the lobby.

Funk's amble down memory lane is cut short. He glances over his shoulder and spots a young pudgy guy with curly black hair and cargo shorts, wrestling with a large video production case. On closer examination, Funk sees the blocky red font on the guy's white T-shirt reads: "I'm Fat. Let's Party!"

At least the kid has a sense of humor, Funk thinks. Something that many lack today.

Funk walks over to the portly dude and says, "Here, bro. Let me help you with that."

Funk grabs the silver hard-shell case and, with a tiny grunt, hoists it up onto a dolly. It is heavy and unwieldy, but he doesn't dare tell the young man that.

"Thanks, man," the guy says, his unblemished face pink and fleshy. "You never know what's inside these things."

Funk smiles. "As long as it's not a bomb, it's all good."

16

DUNGWORTH AND SLATER have just witnessed Funk's kind act on the control room monitor.

"Now I ask you," Slater says, arms out, palms up. "Is chivalry dead?"

Dungworth stares up at the wall of TV screens and sighs. "He helped out one of my crew members with an equipment case in the lobby. So what?"

"Women love compassionate men," Slater says. "I read that in a Chinese study. It's called the halo effect."

Dungworth looks as if he'd rather be chained to the front row of a Bon Jovi concert. "I'll try to salvage the show," he says glumly. "I don't know what else to do. I've got no choice. I'm stuck with Funk. The balding man with a halo."

"He's no beauty queen," Slater says, "but *do not* underestimate him. Do so at your own peril."

They exchange a tense glance.

Dungworth says, "You better be ready for tomorrow's show. Cameras roll in the early a.m." He waves a dismissive hand. "Until then, Mr. Slater, just go. Go have dinner with this...this...*Uptown Funk* of yours."

Slater smiles and crosses his fingers behind his back. "Tomorrow we make magic, Dungworth. You'll see."

Dungworth takes a seat in the director's chair, his hard green eyes scoping Slater. Disgust overtakes him. "Just get me Funk's signed release, old man."

17

IN THE SLANTING light of late afternoon, Funk unlocks the door to his hotel room and strolls in. He stops in the center of the spacious suite, lifts his sunglasses, and surveys the scene. The ethereal decor is white and modern, he sees, with oversized furniture and looking-glass mirrors. The air is slightly stuffy and holds a faint scent of fresh laundry and bong water. On the nightstand, a clock radio softly plays the Eagles' "One of These Nights."

Randy Meisner singing high harmony on the refrain.

Up close, the glossy furniture looks dinged and tired, like an old set of *Password*. But the hardwood floors are new. Definitely an upgrade over the beige pile the spiky-haired chick had puked on back in the day.

This hotel has been trashed over the years, he thinks, punished by inebriated rock stars, flighty jet-setters, and bratty Hollywood royalty. He guesses one could place him in that category, albeit with an asterisk. Unlike the beautiful furniture-throwing glitterati, cult heroes like him are rarely seen as glamorous—or rich.

But you do not come to this hotel for the rooms, he knows.

You come for the after-party at the Skybar and the stunning, up-in-the-cloud views of the city. It is here in the magic of nightfall, staring down into the bright and shimmering lights of L.A., where you can lose yourself and dream. Here, for a few hours anyway, where the stars are all yours, and you can be anyone you want to be.

It brings him back to a simpler time when the world was invincible. A time when people actually liked each other, talked to each other, and anything was possible.

He doesn't miss the old days; he just dislikes the new ones.

Haunted by his rightness, he tosses his overnight bag onto the curvy white sofa and places his sunglasses on the night-stand. He positions himself at the foot of the king-sized bed, spreads his long arms out like wings, and flops back-first onto the fluffy mattress. A short catnap would be nice—a minute to rest his eyes. But the clattering of a service cart and the shrill voice of a young woman shouting "*Selfie!*" in the hallway shatters the peaceful moment. Next, through the thin hotel walls, come the excited cries of sorority girls shrieking and squatting and bumping up against his door. He knows that sound. It is the familiar sound of spring break. The sound of rebellious youth, unending vitality, and primates in heat. Anybody that has ever experienced it will tell you that spring break selfies only lead one way—to fornication. So Funk has already decided that if he has to hear the pounding rhythm of a banging headboard, it might as well be his own.

Twenty years ago, he would have swaggered out there in his red boxer's silk robe that had FREE SEX INQUIRE WITHIN embroidered across the chest and invited them all in for tequila shots and fresh limes. He was as horny as a male sage grouse during mating season back then—his stiff dick like a sawed-off bat. But now things have crawled up inside themselves, and all he wants to do is sleep. The drive over has left him moderately fatigued.

He closes his eyes and folds his arms across his chest, willing the noise away.

Moments later he imagines...

The picture of an old, bald man wearing aviator shades on the Smucker's jar.

Funk then hears the famous voice of Willard Scott of *The Today Show* inside his head, as if that large, jovial reporter was at his bedside.

"God bless him. Larry Funk from Los Angeles is one hundred years old today. A handsome fellow. He dislikes poseurs, reality shows, and snivelers of all kinds. He recently won a fiddle contest and writes in his journal twice a day. A lifelong bachelor, he says the secret to longevity is following your heart and the ability to say no. Sounds like a feisty old cuss just like me."

The hotel phone on the nightstand rings.

Funk's eyes pop open, staring at the ceiling. Three ringy dingys later, he rolls over and answers in a muddled voice. "Yeah?...Food...Good. I'll be down in a few."

18

7:25 p.m.

Dinnertime.

Funk and Slater sit with open menus under the stars in the outdoor section of the hotel's hip new restaurant, Ivory on Sunset. The food is seasonal, the vibe Old Hollywood. There is no need for outdoor heaters this evening. The March night is warm. The moon almost full.

Slater says, "What did I tell you about wearing grandpa clothes?"

Funk, still in a white polo shirt and a pair of baggy chinos, shrugs. "The sparkly jeans didn't fit."

"Christ, man. What happened to you? You used to be cool."

Funk rebukes him with a cold look. "You're one to talk with that man blouse. Last I heard, the Peacock Revolution was over."

Slater is wearing an orange satin camp shirt with a spread collar, his initials, RJS, silk-screened in white across the front pocket. It is short-sleeved, tight against his paunchy body, and unbuttoned to an unruly thatch of silver chest hair. "This is retro Americana, bro," he says defensively. "Made in Japan. It's very expensive."

"It's full-on Gary Glitter is what it is," Funk says. "But at least it matches your hair." He pauses, staring at Slater's enlarged breast tissue. "Though I'd probably tuck the girls in for the evening."

"What are you saying?"

"I'm saying nobody wants to see your sweater meat. Wearing your shirt flamboyantly unbuttoned is no longer cool, Ronnie. Just creepy."

Slater sets his menu down. "Yeah? This coming from a guy wearing stain-resistant slacks."

Funk smiles disarmingly.

Slater sighs and leans back in his chair. "Don't you ever feel like you're missing out on something?"

Funk has never suffered from FOMO. Fear of missing out. He learned long ago that when the time was right, the world would present itself. And it had—in spades—just not for a very long time.

"I've never missed out on anything in my life," Funk says. "In fact, I've gorged."

"Maybe in the past. But you're parched now, dude. It's time you drank from the river."

"What river is that?"

Slater leans forward and whispers, "The River Narcissus. It flows right through the center of Los Angeles. And the sooner you take a drink from it, my fine-haired friend, the sooner you'll enjoy her fruitful bounty."

"I'm not getting my hair done, if that's what you're hinting at."

"You're the one who said you were headed for horseshoe country. I just want you to feel good about yourself."

Funk closes his menu and sets it down on the table. "I know I'm losing my hair. You don't have to tell me. It's called growing old. Besides, I'm not asking you to get your tits lipo'ed. So stop bothering people."

The sudden noise of a barking dog causes Slater to flinch. He looks over at the commotion, unnerved. A fresh-faced twentysomething couple a few tables away, blissfully unaware of their surroundings, eat avocado toast with a shaggy white dog at their feet. The dog, equally unaware, laps at a stainless-steel bowl and wears a red bandanna around its neck.

"What is that dog doing here?" Slater says.

Funk shrugs. "Looks like it's eating."

"It's unsanitary is what it is. These kids today think they can bring their pets anywhere. Fucking mangy mutt. Look at it, looks just like its skinny punk owner. I mean, look at that dude. His sunken chest is so hollowed out I could use him as a salad bowl." Slater rises, both hands on the table. "I'm going to say something."

"Let it go," Funk says.

Slater twists his body and cranes his neck for a better view. "You gotta be kidding me. You see that? They're feeding the dog avocado toast. And it's eating it! *Unbelievable.*"

"The dog likes avocado," Funk says. "Who doesn't?"

Slater, seething: "I bet it's a rescue dog. Seriously, when was the last time you found a teacup poodle at the shelter? Almost never. It's filled with mutts and pit bulls. Did you ever stop and ask yourself why that is?"

Funk sits quiet, staring into his water glass.

"Because nobody wants them!" Slater throws his napkin down in disgust. "I've had it with these millennials and their pets. Along with their thrift-store clothes and stupid Mason jars. This is not a pop-up food court. I'm going over."

A young waitress approaches the table. She steps with caution. "Umm...are you guys ready to order?"

Slater turns, quickly harnesses his anger, and takes a seat at the table. He looks up at the waitress and gives her a lewd smile, a real lopsided beauty. "I'm always ready, baby."

Ick.

Slater has just committed the first of many old-man boomer faux pas. *Baby. Hun. Honey. Sweetie.* All capital offenses today.

The patient waitress plays through, a benign customer-service smile on her face.

"You'll have to excuse him," Funk says. "His parents locked him in a hot car in Key Largo as a boy. He actually inspired the hit song 'Hot Child in the City.'"

Funk's deadpan coaxes a hearty laugh from the waitress. She puts a hand to her mouth and composes herself. "I can see it's going to be one of those full moon nights," she says. "What can I get you?"

Slater flashes Funk a black-ops stare. "Well, go ahead, smart guy. Order."

Funk looks up at the moon. It appears bright but bruised, just like the ego before him. "You go," he says. "I'm still debating."

Slater doesn't hesitate. He grabs his menu and spits out his order in rapid-fire jabber. "I'll start with the crab croquettes in mango sauce," he says. "Two orders. But don't bother with the sauce. I won't eat it. Feed it to the dog over there if you want. And no vegetables. If I see too much color, I'll send it back. Go big or go home, am I right?" He pauses, running a crooked finger down the menu. "I like animal products," he goes on. "I'm a carnivore by nature. *Stalk, hunt, kill.* So I'll take a double order of the strip steak with Cuban black beans, and a petite filet on the side—medium well. But go easy on the beans. I don't want to be meat-gassing all night between the sheets. Get my drift? Also, a vat of drawn butter would be nice, along with an order of mashed potatoes and one lobster mac and cheese. And keep the booze flowing. In fact, bring the whole bottle of Grey Goose and several mixers. I like choice." Slater hands the menu to the waitress. "Oh," he says, "and one order of avocado toast. I'm feeling extra frisky tonight." Another unholy smile. "That'll do it...for now."

"You sure?" Funk says. "How about a side of stroke-out stew?"

Slater's face tightens. "What? It's on the production. Which means tonight I'm going big. Meat-and-potatoes big. None of that astronaut food. I plan on sticking it to the producer. Showing him my middle finger. I strongly urge you do the same."

Funk hands the menu to the waitress and says, "I'll just have one order of the Scottish salmon and a side of the farmer's market vegetables."

Buying in bulk is not Funk's style.

"And to drink?"

"A Heineken, please."

"Got it. Thanks, guys," the waitress says. "Your food will be out shortly."

The waitress leaves and Slater says, "What the fuck was that?"

"What?"

"I give you carte blanche to order anything you want and you order *farmer's market vegetables* and a beer. *Christ,* pull yourself together, man. Is it your GERD?"

Funk looks away. "Yeah."

"Did you bring your blue wedge pillow?"

Funk scowls and emphatically checks the air with a fore-finger.

"Good," Slater says. "Gonna have housekeeping elevate the bed?"

Another Funk finger check. Only more aggressive this time.

"Attaboy," Slater says, changing the subject. "Guess why I'm so hungry. Go ahead, guess."

"I don't know. Because you haven't eaten in a while?"

Slater stands up and lunges his face across the table. "Do you see that?"

Funk, uncomfortable: "What? Jesus."

"On my face."

"I see nothing but pasty."

Slater jerks his face to different angles in the ambient light.

"How about now?"

"*No.* Sit down. You're embarrassing me."

Slater sits, excited. "Pimples. It's beautiful, man. I'm breaking out like a teenager."

"And you're proud of that...*why?*"

"I'm on HGH. Human growth hormone. Doctor says in six months, my organs will be sixteen again. I'm ravenous."

"That's insane. You don't even know what that does to your body."

"I don't give a shit. It works." Slater crosses his arms and smiles. A smile that is meant to convey wonder. "Do you know that I've had morning wood all week?"

Funk opens his mouth but doesn't speak.

"Yeah, it's like that," Slater says. "I'm talking full-on diamond cutter."

"More than I need to know."

"When was the last time you had a hard-on?"

Funk pretends to think. "This morning."

Slater picks at a pimple on his neck. "A urine boner doesn't count."

Music pipes from the outdoor speakers, saving Funk from

further explanation. He does not need to elaborate on what kind of boner he sprouted this morning. Especially to the soundtrack of Ambrosia's "How Much I Feel."

Beyond that, he knows, old boners are a lot like old electronics. You never know what you're going to get. It might just be a blown fuse, or the whole damned motherboard.

19

INSIDE THE SHADOWY CONTROL ROOM, Dungworth and a skeleton crew of six observe Funk and Slater dining at the restaurant on the flat-panel displays. With all eyes locked on the screens, they watch the arrival of the appetizers.

It's chow time.

Dungworth points at Slater on the monitor and says, "Twenty bucks Honey Boo Boo yarks on the table."

Another man says, "You're on."

The crew sits at their workstations, watching the dinner scene happen in real time.

A female assistant with a dark beehive hairdo and big wandering eyes says, "Hey, Max, you want me to get some B-roll on this?"

Dungworth looks spacey, preoccupied. "How many times have I told you, Amanda? Your B-roll is your A-roll."

She nods. "Got it."

Dungworth shakes the chemicals from his cloudy mind and says into a headset, "Give me a soundtrack on this. Something eighties. But check your levels first. Audio is everything."

On the monitor, the scenes of Funk and Slater eating dinner unfold like a movie montage.

The music starts.

Phil Collins warbling "In the Air Tonight."

Oh Lord.

The crew watches in disbelief as Slater grabs a handful of crab croquettes off the plate, eats them whole, and stuffs them down his throat with a twisting motion. He smiles with his mouth full and gives the Hispanic busboy a big thumbs-up.

Oh Lord.

When the salads arrive, Slater pours a half bottle of Grey Goose vodka into a hammered copper mug. He adds a dash of ginger beer and daintily stirs it with his pinkie finger. After downing the entire cocktail in one dramatic chug, he signals the waitress for more of everything, giving her a round-trip gesture with a flip of the hand.

Oh Lord.

Slater grins like a heathen in a Turkish bathhouse with the arrival of the strip steak and salmon.

New cutlery is provided.

And finally—

The crew watches Slater attack a steak like a homeless animal, drawn butter glistening on his jowls. Funk sits disgusted, watching him shovel it all in.

Amanda, the girl with the beehive hairdo, says, "That big guy can really put it away. Hungry Horace for sure."

"I'm impressed," Dungworth says. "The old dude hasn't lost his appetite."

"Apparently not," another female crew member adds, watching a server precariously stacking up all the empty plates at the table. "But that dinner's going to be a thousand-dollar tab. *Easy.*"

Dungworth nods his head in appreciation. "Nobody makes

a living in Hollywood being gracious in defeat. Good on Mr. Slater for fisting the production budget like that. That's old-school."

Satisfied with the supplemental footage, Dungworth removes his headset and says to the crew, "That's it for tonight, people. Get some rest and be ready for tomorrow's show. We've got an early call time."

In a wired, troubled voice, Amanda points at Slater's image on the monitor and says, "Is he teasing that dog?"

Dungworth looks up at the screen and sees Slater waving a piece of avocado toast toward the scruffy mutt. "He is," Dungworth says. "He's a heartless serpent. That's why I hired him."

On the monitor, the mongrel growls at Slater from a few tables away, straining at its leash. "That is so uncool," Amanda says. "You can see by the dark light in Mr. Slater's eyes he's enjoying it."

"Karma will take care of him, Amanda. The cycle of cause and effect."

"Which means?"

"Whores always get their due."

20

IN THE RESTAURANT, Slater tilts uncomfortably in his chair, clutching his pregnant belly. He moans and groans, his face pained and twisted.

Funk says, "Are you gonna burp or fart?"

"Don't know yet. Maybe a shart. These jeans are like a noose around my gut."

Funk shakes his head. "Serves you right for shopping in the young men's department."

Slater lifts his blue-jeaned butt, angles it slightly toward the millennial couple and their dog, and emits a strained squeak. Unhappy with the outcome, he leans back in his chair and unloads a loud, yodeling belch.

"All good?" Funk asks, waving his hand in front of his face to dispel the wicked stench of digested meat products.

"Better," Slater says. He tosses his napkin onto the table like he's throwing in the towel. "Much better."

"So that'll do it?" Funk asks.

"No, no," Slater says. "I'm thinking about dessert. Maybe some Key lime pie." Slater's face suddenly drops. He looks alarmed. "Uh-oh."

"What?" Funk asks.

Slater trains his eyes over Funk's left shoulder. "Two goons on the set," he says. "Just let me do the talking."

It is Lopez and Backstreet, strutting into the restaurant like Crockett and Tubbs.

Don Johnson on the hammer.

Philip Michael Thomas trailing.

The dynamic duo wear white linen suits and pastel-colored T-shirts, along with pink and turquoise espadrilles, respectively.

The heat is on.

Slater lowers his eyes, hoping to avoid contact, but the fiery shade of Just For Men that colors his hair has already given him away. The two men spot Slater and immediately make a beeline for his flaming nob.

Lopez stops at the table and puts his hands in his pockets. Concern darkens his face as he speaks with a serious tone. "We heard rumors of a brush fire that had broken out in the restaurant." He points at Slater's head. "Turns out it was a false alarm. *Thank, God.*" He laughs and throws a playful uppercut. "What's up, Slater? You keepin' it real?"

Slater nods and sucks on his spoon. "Just fine dining under the stars. Is there anything better, gentlemen?"

It's an eighties flashback, Funk thinks, and he can almost hear the synthesized instrumental music of Jan Hammer accompanying the duo's unwelcome presence.

While Slater engages in small talk, Funk takes a moment to study Lopez. The charismatic man has dark eyes like Brazilian coffee, a square jaw, and the look of infidelity on his face. There is absolutely *nothing* androgynous about him. He is one hundred percent pure testosterone. If he has a taste for the ladies, Funk supposes, he will do well here on spring break. Put simply: they made the holiday for men like him. Not so for the short one.

Funk's cultural critique quickly fades as Slater introduces him.

"This is my buddy, Larry," Slater says, squeezing Funk's shoulder with a grubby hand.

Everybody nods. No handshakes. Just the inconvenient murmurs of "Tsup" between strange men who will never become friends.

Lopez and Backstreet stare at Funk for a moment before exchanging glances and giggling. Funk is unsuspecting, but Slater quickly takes charge.

"Well, it was good seeing you both. But if you don't mind, we're going to finish dinner." Slater smiles aloofly and waves his fork. "A quiet dinner." He nods to Lopez. "Miami." And to Backstreet. "Vice."

"It's all good," Lopez says. "We get it." He turns to his wing-man. "Let's roll, Backstreet."

"Yo, yo," Backstreet says to Slater. "We'll see you and Uptown tomorrow."

Uptown?

"Yeah," Lopez says in his best vice cop voice. "It's nothing personal...it's just business."

They laugh and low-five. As they leave, Lopez spins his head around and flicks his long, fleshy tongue out at Funk.

Flabbergasted, Funk says to Slater, "I'm not sure if that righteous act was meant for me or some other lucky patron, but I do hope your friend's housebroken."

"He's not my friend," Slater says. "He knows the producer. Just ignore him. Unfortunately, he's part of the ecosystem."

Funk nods, forgets about it. He has more pressing matters on his mind. He leans forward in his chair and stares into his dinner plate. "About tomorrow," he says. "I'm not feeling the old-time hockey vibe. This stupid bet on who gets the girl."

"Why not? It was fun in the past."

"The past is over, Slater. I'm not that guy anymore." Funk pauses, spears a fork into the salmon. "Never was."

Funk chews his food slowly and looks down at the bright lights below. It strikes him as funny that he has been able to remain vertical for so long in a city of horizontals. He thinks about Rebecca, his last girlfriend. She was a dancer with long legs who liked to practice in his tiny studio apartment and do the splits and touch the walls with both feet. It was she who had suggested that he take smaller bites when eating. Said his mandible was working overtime. On the face of it, she thought his aggressive chewing had aged him. Last he heard, she was doing soft video porn in the Valley, her new boyfriend's Ferrari Testarossa double-parked outside.

"Okay," Slater says. "I'll admit the bet's a bit Harvey-esque, a bit obscene. But it might be fun to chase a few ladies. It is spring break."

Funk winces.

"Then forget it, bro. I just thought it might help jump-start the weekend. Gird your loins. So we'll just hang. If something happens, it happens. Fair enough?"

Funk absorbs this, nodding to himself. "Right on."

"Good," Slater says. "So are you glad you came?"

Funk shrugs. "It was either this or the National Cornhole Championships."

Slater laughs. "Dude, do yourself a favor and change your name to Alejandro. Just for the weekend."

"What? *No.*"

"Why not? Birds love that name. You can be the mysterious Spaniard from Seville. Or better yet, the reclusive billionaire bad boy from Madrid. There's a lot of ways to game it."

Funk cuts his eyes and sets his fork down on the plate. "I have never had to lie to get any woman in my life. You, on the other hand..."

Slater stuffs a half-slice of Key lime pie into his mouth and mumbles, "I'm going to make a prediction here. Mark my words, you will meet a hottie this weekend, and she's going to *blow... your...mind.*" He punctuates his statement with a celebratory "blow it up" gesture with both hands, his fingers fully splayed.

21

AT THE SAME moment Funk and Slater dine, fifty-three-year-old singer Angie Gunn croons a romantic ballad to a slow-dancing wedding party in the hotel's main ballroom. The guests clutch each other tightly, with heads on shoulders and eyes half-shut. The faces of an energetic, older couple, possibly the groom's parents, are full of pride as they spin gracefully and confidently around the dance floor. All bodies sway in harmony with the soothing music as Angie's classically trained voice fills the room. Her sound is both raspy and angelic, and when she reaches the upper register of her voice, she holds the last note.

The money note.

The audience is spellbound. Some wipe away tears. Others whistle for more and applaud wildly.

Angie, earthy and elegant, wears a delicate white lace dress and platform leather sandals. She flips back her feathered brown hair and says, "Thank you so much. It was a pleasure entertaining you tonight. The name of our band is Sound Lady. And I speak for all of us in saying good luck to the bride and groom...Mr. and Mrs. Arnold P. Gerkin. Goodnight."

More applause from drunken simpletons.

22

AT THE DINNER TABLE, Funk and Slater hear the roar of applause rising up from the wedding reception.

Funk scratches his thinly haired head and says, "Don't tell me we gotta rave all night."

"Dude, it's just a wedding. Some poor sap taking the ball and chain. Tomorrow we rave all night."

Slater is drinking martinis now. Three? Six? It's no fun to count. Stalling for time, he musters his courage and gulps his drink. The hallmark of his entire operation rests with Funk signing the release.

There are no contingency plans.

Slater's mind races with what-ifs. *What if he bails on me? What if someone tips him off? Worse yet, what if he can't perform?* He is sure that Funk can see him blushing. Or is it the booze? He scrunches up a napkin, eats the olive from his glass, and glances over at the millennial couple. They are holding hands across the table, talking softly under a clear night sky, the mangy white mutt asleep at their feet. He's not sure what bothers him the most about millennials. Their propensity to start every sentence with *So*, or their blatant disrespect for their elders.

Look at them over there eating that Michelin-starred avocado toast, he thinks. Like they've discovered something new. Hey, asshole! I've got the skinny for you. I've been eating avocados for fifty fucking years. *And not just on toast!*

"You got something to say?" Funk says, breaking the silence.

"What?"

"I know that quiet, smirky look. Squirming like Marta on the bed in *Scarface*. Machine gun under the covers. C'mon, man. What gives?"

Slater sighs, his eyes resting on the martini glass. After a moment of anguished contemplation, he grabs the cool stem and necks the last of the drink. He shakes his head from the throat burn and says, "Okay. So this is how it is. I know you said you didn't want to be on camera. And that's cool—*totally cool*. We'll be able to shoot around that. But if you can just help me out and sign this release, they'll pay you three grand. No questions asked."

Funk sits mute.

Slater looks down, unable to look his friend in the eye. The table is filthy, he sees, the white linen cloth cluttered with left-over giblets from his food orgy. There are pieces of meat gristle, empty potato skins, and chunks of avocado scattered about. It is a real pig trough.

Summoning up what little gumption he has left, Slater rakes an arm across the table and sweeps away the leftover food. He then pulls the document from his back pocket and unfolds it like a map, carefully smoothing out the wrinkled paper on the linen tablecloth.

Funk looks at it like it's roadkill. The document is unsigned, a chunk of avocado smashed on the top right corner. After a moment of shaking his head, Funk finally says in a measured tone, "I told you no. And if I can't hang out without it, I'll leave tonight."

Slater throws his hands up in surrender. "No, no. It's cool. I just thought you might reconsider because of the money." He smiles sheepishly. "I mean, we can all use more money, right?"

Funk stands, tosses his napkin on the table. He is distant but not mad. In a subtle nod to John Cameron Swayze, he cocks his wrist and checks his vintage Timex watch. It is a quarter past nine.

Close to bedtime.

"I'm gonna chill in the room awhile," he says. "Maybe turn in early."

Slater rises, a frantic light in his eyes. "Larry, they just want you to sign the release in case you accidentally stroll in front of the camera. It's boilerplate stuff."

Funk, over the shoulder: "There's no such thing as boiler-plate in Hollywood."

FUNK meanders into the hotel lobby.

It is crowded and loud, and the air smells of dried fruit and tasty chemicals.

Almost sweet, like Raid.

The wedding guests have flooded the reception area now and are aggressively heading for the exits. Most are young, inebriated, and self-consciously white.

Funk shoulders past an ill-mannered dude in a rented tuxedo who shouts above the crowd, "It's the last day to register your drone, bro!" He laughs drunkenly.

At this, another degenerate with a clip-on tie blows vape smoke from his nose and says, "Who gives a shit. I bet you still have an AOL account."

Funk still has an AOL account. Has for twenty years. But he dare not speak it. He stands rigid, like an outcropping in a sea of beauty. The young bridesmaids dart obliviously by him, parting at his rocky presence and swimming back into formation once passed. People used to applaud him, he thinks. Now they just get out of his way. By hard adventure, he has the foresight to recognize that turning fifty is close to eighty-five in culture-war years.

Maybe it's time I left the battlefield.

For a moment he looks out the window into the car park and watches a limousine carry away the young newlyweds. He is happy for them. A future waits.

Feeling a bit bedraggled, he soldiers on through the lobby, looking for the elevator. All he wants to do now is get ready for bed, slip on his "Old Guys Rule" T-shirt, and fall asleep to the news.

He strolls around the corner and spots the ballroom door. It is open and inviting and he peers in. The garnished room is now empty and quiet, and all that remains of the wedding reception is a beautiful mess—and a grand piano. As he stares wistfully at the piano, a burning longing stirs inside him.

He slowly spins his head and checks for lurkers, then side-steps into the room like a cat burglar on the prowl. Once inside, he walks lightly toward the piano, almost tiptoeing, but the golden silence is soon broken when he steps on a red plastic party cup.

Crunch!

The grating sound startles him and almost forces his mouth open. Must have been a real grind-fest in here, he thinks. Maybe he should leave, but the baby grand is calling his name, drawing him in like a melodious magnet.

He resumes his march forward with a look of calm determination on his face, his Converse sneakers kicking cups and clearing the way. When he finally reaches the piano, he just stands there staring at it, like it is a long-lost friend or an estranged family member. His mind begins to drift, thinking of false hopes and missed opportunities. He ultimately comes to the realization that maybe his dating practice of catch-and-release wasn't the best of mating calls.

After a long pause he sits on the cushioned piano bench and straightens his spine. But he does not play. While contemplating it, a young couple from the wedding reception surprises him.

"Hey, play us a tune, Mr. Piano Dude."

Funk turns his head and examines the couple standing beside him.

They are glowing and sloppy, maybe early twenties, he thinks. The young blond man wears a dark suit and no tie, his white shirt open to the navel. There is a large hickey on his neck, the color and shape of a mashed strawberry. She wears a black sleeveless gown, her crimson face the same color as the rose tattoo on her left forearm.

"So what do you say, sir?" the young guy asks. "You got a couple more songs in you?" He clutches his girlish date and she giggles under his arm.

Funk processes the moment. "I'm afraid I'm not the—"

"*Please*," the young woman says. "Just one more."

Funk shrugs. Who is he to deny punch-drunk love?

"Okay," Funk says. "But just one. Any requests?"

The childlike woman twists her long black hair around her finger and says, "A love song. Something sappy."

Funk nods. Sappy he can do. He extends his long, nimble fingers across the keyboard and plays the perfect tune: the plaintive and emotional theme song from *Love Story*. The mournful melody moves the couple, and this moves Funk. When he finally finishes, the young woman wipes tears from her eyes. "Oh my God," she says. "That was so beautiful, and *so sad*. What was it?"

In the doorway, Angie, the wedding singer, watches the performance. "It's from the movie *Love Story*," she says. "One of piano dude's favorites."

They all turn toward the raspy, sweet-sounding voice at the door.

"Huh?" the young man grunts.

Funk squints, can't believe his good fortune. "Angie?"

"Hi, Larry," she says, smiling. "I see you're still wowing the crowd."

Funk, excited: "Talk about *wow*. What are you doing here?"

"My band played a wedding tonight. And you?"

"A buddy of mine's shooting some spring break show here tomorrow." He shrugs. "I'm basically hanging out on his dime."

Angie approaches. With each graceful step, her long, feathered brown hair bounces like a seventies rock star.

Funk slowly rises from the piano, his eyes trained on her billowy white dress. They meet in the middle of the room and stop at the wedding cake table. Only crumbs remain, pink icing smeared on the white tablecloth. They stand silent for a moment, soaking each other in like old lovers. She is taller than he remembers, not yet eye level, but close enough to see into him. It might just be the chunky platform shoes she is wearing, he thinks, or maybe his six-foot frame is shrinking. Both are genuine possibilities. Until recently, Funk would have squeezed her in a bear hug, swept her off her feet, and danced around the room. But this is not the end of the Second World War. Like Slater, and all modern men today, he knows the times call for more reserve. Maybe that's why he feels a sudden urge to give her the aw-shucks buddy tap on the shoulder. Luckily for him, in this moment of great indecision, as has always been the case, she hugs him first.

"It's so good to see you," she says, kissing his cheek and pulling back. "You look great."

The young couple thank Funk and drunk-walk for the exit. But he doesn't hear or see anything but Angie. His being, every ounce of his fiber, is wholeheartedly locked on her.

With his heart beating like a big bass drum, he finally says, "So, how are you? Everything good?"

"I'm really good," Angie says, nodding. "For the first time in my life, I'm actually comfortable in my own skin. What about you?"

Funk glances at her ring finger and sees nothing. Then back up at her prominent ears that catch the edge of the light. He has always loved the way they stuck out, like some cute little mouse in a children's fairy tale. Imperfect, yet sensual, they are adorned tonight with exotic silver teardrop earrings.

"I'm still shedding mine," he says. "I mean, my skin, that is. But yeah, other than that, I'm good." He clears his throat and smiles like a nervous groom. "Anyway, last I heard, you were married and living in domestic bliss in Riverside with what's-his-name?"

"Bob."

"Oh yes, Bob."

She smiles. "I'm in West Hollywood now. Divorced, with one beautiful daughter named Megan. You'd love her. She plays a mean bass."

"Sweet. I like the name Megan. It's grounded, you know? Not like Palm Shadow or Planet."

"And you? Married? Kids?"

Funk looks down and stuffs his hands into his pants pockets. "Still in West L.A.," he says. "Not married, no kids. I guess I just haven't found the right gir—" He stops himself and his eyes travel up to meet hers. "Woman yet."

He pretends he has it all together, but it is clear that he's been floating these last few years. Same for the women he's been with. He runs through roll call in his head and thinks about Maggie. A Scorpio woman he almost married. It's impossible to believe that their relationship lasted over six years. They met at Gazzarri's nightclub on Sunset, she a groupie for another band, and he a one-man wrecking crew of one-night stands. At first, being a Pisces, he enjoyed swimming in her deep and intense waters, but ultimately, he said he wasn't ready for a long-term commitment, and she drifted away. He had chalked up his dissatisfaction to the almost-seven-year itch, but she said that he was just a pussy, someone afraid of intimacy and true love.

Maybe she was right.

Not long ago, she sent him a picture of her baby and said that she wished it were his. Said that her unsettled heart had finally healed. He didn't respond, but he was happy for her and flattered in a middle-aged and unheroic sort of way. He thinks a baby might have passed him by, but he won't rule one out. And to those who say he's too old, he will quietly remind them that it takes a village to raise a baby. Travel to any Third World country and you'll see that. People go. People die. Other people step up. That's just the way life is.

Angie nods, looking at him with a newfound sense of compassion. "I understand," she says. "Finding the right one is hard. But I bet you're slaying it on all those online dating apps. Scrolling left. Or whatever it is people do on there."

"Me? No. I don't do a lot of scrolling, and I don't look good on paper. I guess you could say I'm old-fashioned. Just a simple guy looking for someone to go the distance with. Like Eli Wallach and Anne Jackson."

Angie arches her eyebrows. "Paul Newman and Joanne Woodward?"

"Yeah," Funk says. "Somebody that gets it." He waves a hand over his face. "Gets whoever this is."

She beams. "It's really good to see you, Larry. I miss our babysitting duets."

"Yeah, me too."

He also misses her baby-lotion smell, the warmth of her whiskey-brown eyes, and her staccato laugh that he once declared the eighth wonder of the world. His knees tremble when he says, "Hey, can I buy you a drink? Some coffee? Maybe catch up?"

Angie spies the time on her cell phone and grins. "Sure, I'd like that. Let me check in with the sitter. I'll meet you by the pool in a few minutes."

Funk, with rubbery legs: "No bathroom stalling."

24

9:54 p.m.

Wound tight, a barefoot Slater paces the bamboo floor in his air-conditioned hotel suite, anxiously talking on his cell phone to a call center in some faraway land.

"Wait," he says, "I know I'm in default…no, please, talk with the manager, Margie, in the loss mitigation department. She assured me I could make the mortgage payment next week."

"Hold, please," the voice from afar says.

Slater stands in silence, his face flushed by the stress of the call. As he listens to the hold music from another country, he walks slowly over to the high window and faces the L.A. night. The moon sits big and heavy over the twinkling city, the heat-blurred skyline barely recognizable. He knows spring will come soon, and his seasonal tree allergies will return. Along with that, he feels the faint pangs of guilt over deceiving a good friend in need. The grim reality is, by this time tomorrow, Funk will be lunch meat for a nest of entertainment vipers eager to exploit a decent man down on his luck. He hopes that one day, for the sake of art, Funk will forgive him. But he expects no sympathy.

Only the fifty grand.

The brassy voice on the line startles him. "Mr. Slater?"

"Yes, yes," he says tensely, taking a seat on the edge of the bed. "I'm here."

"It's confirmed. You have until next Friday to make the payment. You can expect a confirmation email."

Slater closes his eyes and blows a sigh of relief. "Thank you, thank you," he says. "I'll have it in by then. I promise."

He clenches his jaw and hangs up, refusing to believe the universe has caught on to him. Let alone figured out his reindeer games.

He rises off the bed and pads across the cold hardwood floor, resuming his place at the window. Out there, beyond the lavish hotel grounds and the upscale confines of the walled-off mansions, the naked and the walking dead inject lethal drugs on dirt floors, staring blankly at their own comatose reflections in the blazing moonlight.

In his mind, the homeless encampments below seem far away, but to many Angelenos, they are oh so close.

In exactly twenty-six hours, at the stroke of midnight, the winner of *Game or No Game?* will be crowned. In a perfect world, Slater will walk with the fifty grand, and Funk will, once again, fall into the loving embrace of an adoring public.

I am Icarus now, he thinks.

Flying way too close to the sun.

25

UNDER THE SILVERY light of the big moon, Funk and Angie lie on comfy lounge chairs at the hotel pool. She holds a glass of red wine, he a blue margarita glass. Angie is barefoot now, her chunky leather sandals resting on the teak deck. Her painted red toes wiggle when she says, "So the last I heard, you were touring with the Pretenders."

Funk stares at the pool. It is still and flat, a glassy turquoise rectangle. "I guess we've been out of touch awhile."

"Over twenty years."

"I knew I should've updated my Facebook page."

"I didn't know you had a Facebook page."

"*I don't.*"

She smiles warmly and sips from her wineglass. "Maybe that's why I couldn't find you."

Funk swallows hard. "Maybe so. As for the Pretenders, I was supposed to audition for lead guitar, but I opted to go party with a buddy in Hawaii. Got on a plane and did the whole luau thing. And when I came back...they'd found another guy. Strike one. I guess I just wasn't into it after Purple Onion broke up. The band wasn't making any money, and all we were doing was getting older. It felt like the whole L.A. music scene had died. So I stopped playing music and started writing. Looking for anything to fire the creative spark."

"Novels?"

"Screenplays."

They share a look.

"Yeah, I know. Stupid idea."

"No," Angie says, her hand touching his arm. "What were they about?"

"My first was a wacky thriller. A lot of plot twists and pop music dialogue."

"What happened with it?"

"Quentin Tarantino beat me to the punch. Came out with *Pulp Fiction.*"

"Like, with all the musical references and stuff?"

Funk looks at the pool again, glowing like an emerald in the dark. He feels the urge to jump in, swim to the bottom and touch the drain. "Yeah," he says. "Strike two. After that, I wrote this espionage thriller about a terrorist plot to blow up the Empire State Building."

"Don't tell me."

He nods. "Yeah. Strike three. Can you believe it? I finished the script in August 2001. There was a bidding war amongst the studios, and I was this close to buying a house. Well, we all know what happened on September 11. It was a no-go after that."

"How did that make you feel?"

"I was mad at first, broke some things. All I could think about was the money, or my lack of it. But then, just like everyone else, I felt this terrible sadness set in. I felt really guilty for thinking that way. So sad about losing all those people. And for the families." He draws in a hard breath. "I guess I felt responsible for releasing that whole negative vibe out into the universe."

Funk sips his drink, a cone of moonlight splitting his oblong face.

"That's not your fault," Angie says. "You were just using the energy already in the universe. All artists do that."

"Maybe. But after that, I turned to ringtones. Some session work. Music for corporate films. Stuff like that. Just to be sure it wasn't my fault." He pauses. "Then my dad died. *Strike four.*"

"I'm so sorry. I didn't hear."

"It was a couple of years ago. Cancer. Anyway, I've been searching ever since. Had to rethink my whole career path as a starving artist. I've played thousands of gigs, written countless songs, screenplays, and articles, with nothing to show for it except 'Big Tits and a Bottle of Wine'—which nets me about four bucks a month in royalties." He shrugs. "That's my definitive moment. That's all I've got to show for my efforts."

"I don't believe in definitive moments," Angie says. "Sure, they happen, but I think life is all about the day-to-day. You know, the smaller moments, the grind-it-out moments. And when those bigger moments appear, you've got to grab them with gusto."

Funk nods, her wise words hitting home. "You're right," he says. "I just hope I'm ready when it comes."

"Oh, you'll be ready," she says. "You'll be able to see it coming from a mile away."

Funk crosses his arms over his chest and looks up at the stars. Her voice is gentle and caring, and the more she speaks, the more confident he feels about grabbing those moments. He inhales purposefully and steers the conversation away from himself. "So," he says, "how's your brother? He finally finish his MBA?"

"No. But he succeeded in getting his MFU."

"MFU?"

"Master's of Fuck Up. Pardon my French."

"Ah," Funk says. "I hold the same degree. Which is why I'm thinking about getting a real estate license."

She laughs. "You? On bus benches? I can't see it. You're way too talented for that."

"Your lips to the creative god's ears. Anyway, enough of my Ken Burns saga. What about you? What do you want?"

Angie leans back, her legs bent at the knees on the chaise lounge. "I don't need much. I used to think I did, but now I'm kind of into this whole voluntary simplicity thing."

"Me too," says Funk. "Except that mine's involuntary."

She smiles. "You're richer than you think, Larry. Millions of artists would kill for your life. As for me, I've got a wonderful daughter, and I've just started a new band. I'm looking forward. But practical, you know?"

"What about *Bob*...still see him?"

"Not much. He moved out of state. He's a left-brain. That was our problem."

Funk winces. "Ouch. I mean, all you can really do with a left-brain is pack it up and move to suburbia. Am I right?"

They share a smile. Two minds think alike.

"The crazy thing is," Angie says, "he started writing and self-publishing novels to impress me. His first one was a wacky thriller, too. If you can believe that."

Funk's eyes widen. "Really?"

"Yeah. It was horrible. I'll never forget the title: *Fatal Defection.* But there was a mishap at the printers, and the hardcover came back with a different title. *Fatal Defecation.* The blurb read: 'When defecation becomes survival.'"

Funk laughs. "I can see how fecal harassment might deter a man. So he stopped writing?"

"I wish. He just switched genres."

"Let me guess. Space opera? The flight attendant raised by wolves?"

"Mountain man romance. For women who love beards and Colorado. You know the protagonist. Guy opens a microbrewery and complains about the traffic in Boulder."

Funk nods. "A lot of chicks dig the Columbia fleece."

She points. "That's what he wears!"

They laugh.

"That's the problem with self-publishing," Funk says. "Any idiot can write a book and stick it up on Amazon. Seriously, what's left to write as satire anymore? I mean, my dentist is writing mysteries now. He titled his latest *Between a Molar and a Hard Place*. I kid you not. He took out a full-page ad in the *L.A. Times* last Sunday. Wanted a jacket quote from me."

"Did you give him one?"

"No. What was I going to say? Good campy fun?"

Funk has never been a write-to-market kind of guy.

The music of Nicki Minaj suddenly flares up from the Skybar, the hotel's storied nightspot. Funk suspects the hip-hop beat signals the end of tranquility, the end of quiet time.

Angie swirls what's left of the Syrah in her wineglass and says, "Sounds like they're getting ready for the after-hours crowd. It must be getting late. I'd probably better get going."

"What?" Funk says. "And miss the glow sticks and foam cannons on the dance floor? Binge drinking to follow."

"Been there, done that," she says. "But if body paint is involved, you might convince me to stay."

He laughs. "Whoever thought spring break was a good idea?"

"Not me," she says quietly, looking down at her bare feet.

After the long pause that follows, Angie finally says, "Hey, what are you doing tomorrow night?"

"I'll be here. Having dinner with my buddy. Why?"

"My band's playing up the street."

Funk sits up in the recliner. "At the Whisky?"

"Yeah. We open for the Motels. I can get you on the guest list. Your friend too."

"Really? The Motels? That'd be great. What time?"

"We're scheduled for eight. But if you have other plans, we can do it another day. My band's touring all summer. Going on the road. I'll be firing up my new RV, *The Lazy Faze*."

Funk likes the sound of *The Lazy Faze*, especially how easy it rolls off her tongue. He looks directly at her and says, "I definitely want to go. I'm just not sure what my buddy's got planned. He may be—"

"Planning a birthday party?"

Funk smiles like that twelve-year-old kid getting tucked into bed. "You remember?"

"I never forget a birthday, Larry. Sunday, right?"

"That's right. Clock strikes midnight on Saturday."

Funk nibbles on his lower lip, his shelf life half over.

"What a wonderful occasion," Angie says. "But don't worry. I'm not going to ask you how old you are."

"Good, 'cause I'm not going to tell you."

She laughs at his mischievous grin.

"I'm fifty," Funk says. "The big *five-oooo*."

She raises her wineglass. "And still holding on. I'm fifty-three. Just getting it out there now. In case you want to hightail it."

"Not a chance," he says. "I'd never run from you."

A beat.

"Look," Angie says, "I understand if you have plans for tomorrow. But call me on Sunday. I'm available for celebrations."

Sunday! Sunday! Sunday!

And just like that, the Funkmeister is back.

Mildly nervous, he says, "Does that celebration include *The Lazy Faze?*"

She smiles. "Maybe, and if you're lucky, I might even let you drive."

Funk tips his glass toward hers. "Then it's a date."

They clink glasses and savor the moment in the warm winter night. Angie says, "I'd love to stay, but I gotta get home."

She slides into her sandals and stands, slinging her suede fringe handbag over her shoulder. "It was really great seeing you, Larry."

Caught off balance, he looks at her and blurts, "Likewise."

Likewise? What the hell was that? Get up and hug her, you fool. The air is charged! It's a firestarter night!

Funk stands, his white Converse sneakers planted firmly on the wooden deck. He is ready for action now, ready to make the first move. He closes his eyes and cranes his neck, the undulating blue light from the pool rippling across his body.

Then—

"Oh, I almost forgot," Angie says, her arm outstretched. "Gimme your phone."

Timing. It's his timing. It's been off the last few years.

Funk fumbles for his phone and hands it over.

She's punching in numbers; he's thinking about stairwell sex.

What ordinary man could throttle such thoughts?

Funk's eyes drift in his sockets, his vision slightly aware of his surroundings. Is that a full moon? Or is the universe just happy to see him? He knows that L.A. will give you reinvention. But awakening? Not so much.

Angie grabs Funk's hand and slaps the phone into his palm, closing his fingers tightly around it. Funk senses that she senses that this artist of leisure—*him*—needs a swift kick in the pants.

"No excuses this time, Larry," she says. "My number's in your phone. *Call me.*"

————

At this exact moment, Slater looks down onto the pool from a high window like a cagey villain in a *Hawaii Five-O* episode. His face displays a look of grave concern as he watches Funk and Angie hug.

A stark realization hits hard:

This isn't a game. This is war.

SATURDAY

26

8:45 a.m.

Funk sits naked on the toilet in the Thinker's pose, softly humming The Motels' "Only the Lonely."

What he doesn't know is that a hidden bathroom cam is capturing this very private moment inside his hotel suite.

It's game time.

Inside the hectic control room, Funk's vulnerable image fills several flat-panel monitors. Dungworth and a pitted-faced male production assistant stand near the big screen, staring at Funk on the throne—still humming.

Dungworth shifts his feet uneasily and says with a modicum of concern, "How long's he been in there?"

"At least an hour."

Dungworth nods glumly. He can relate. The pain in his lower abdomen feels like a border collie is chewing on his large intestine.

"I know the feeling," he mutters.

The ruddy production assistant looks thoughtful. "You know, Max," he says, "the Italians use olive oil when a baby gets stopped up. They place a little oil on their first finger and slide it up the baby's bum. They say it works miracles. Manual evacuation. Maybe you ought to try it."

Dungworth stands a little crooked, as if his back is bothering him. He places a bracing hand on his hip and says with a half-dose of venom, "Do I look Italian, Pizza Face? Furthermore, I have no intention of discussing natural irrigation methods with you. I am numb from the waist down—*impacted*. And passing hard rocks is in my future. So just do me a favor and do your job."

Pizza Face lowers his head. "Yes, sir."

"Good, now where the fuck is Marty?"

The assistant stares up at the ceiling tiles and shrugs. "Beats me."

Opioids, Dungworth thinks. *More opioids.*

Dungworth turns his head and shouts to a crew of twenty. "Where the hell is my TD! Marty! Marty!"

The bathroom door bangs open and a short, chubby kid with curly black hair enters the room, fumbling with his fly. He scrambles to his workstation on the long curved desk, sits, and puts on his headset. This is Marty, the technical director of *Game or No Game?* The same affable twenty-two-year-old geek that Funk helped yesterday in the lobby.

Marty now wears a fresh pair of navy cargo shorts, flip-flops, and a new slogan T-shirt that reads: "What Can I Say? My Mom Likes Slayer."

Dungworth stares at Marty's fat calves and dirty uncut toenails. He shakes his head in revulsion and wonders when did America go from *No shirt, no shoes, no service* to *No shirt, no shoes, no problem?*

Dungworth says, "It's about time, Marty. You were this close to spinning signs on Sunset."

Marty, in true slacker fashion, ignores the comment and kicks off his Reef flip-flops. He looks up at the big screen and sees Funk on the throne. He points. "I know that dude. He helped me out yesterday. He's a nice guy."

"I'm glad you like him," Dungworth says. "Because it's time to get intimate. Say hello to the star of the show. Mr. Larry Funk."

"Rad," Marty says. "But I hope you're not filming a guy on the can. Toilet humor is so passé." He stares back at Funk's image. "Is he humming the Motels?"

"Does it matter, Boy Genius? Just get me some light on the subject." Dungworth walks down the row of workstations, his legs bowed inward. "All right, people, it's game time. Let's do this. Camera three. Bring up Lopez."

In an instant, half the TV screens on the wall switch to the image of a bare-chested Phil Lopez doing one-armed push-ups in his hotel room. The other half show Funk on the toilet.

Dungworth shouts, "Mac! Get New York on the line. Do it now! And get that dotard Slater in here. It's showtime."

Mac, a bald, muscular PA, scrambles for the door. "Right away, Mr. Dungworth."

As he turns, Dungworth says out of the corner of his mouth, "Marty, get the focus groups up."

"Roger copy clear," Marty says, gripping a computer mouse.

Two 30-inch monitors flicker to life on the center desk. One screen reveals a room of thirteen restless young women seated on a black L-shaped sofa centered around a wall-mounted flat-screen TV. Their mobile devices have been temporarily confis-cated, and all wear the terrified look normally associated with phone-separation anxiety. The other screen shows a group of fourteen exuberant young men in their late teens and early twenties, fidgeting in metal folding chairs, staring at a TV monitor on top of a mobile production cart. They are all here for two reasons: money and fame. Most will end up settling for a few bucks and two catered meals. Domino's if they're lucky.

Dungworth slips on his headset and says to a woman assistant, "Can they hear me?"

She nods emphatically, two thumbs up. "Yes. You're good to go."

Dungworth leans forward with his elbows on the desk and addresses the two groups on-screen. "Good morning, people. If you can hear me, please wave."

Both groups wave back on the monitor. All except one tight-faced, high-haired young man in the men's group, who flips the bird with a flourish.

Fucking Jimmy Neutron, Dungworth thinks.

No lunch for you!

"Great," Dungworth continues in his lordly tone. "Again, thank you all for being a part of our new reality show, *Game or No Game?* I know that we have briefed all of you on the rules, but I want to make sure you're clear on how to vote for your favorite contestant. Under your chairs, or sofa, you'll find a handheld game console. Please grab that now."

The focus groups grope under their seats and fetch their consoles.

Dungworth continues. "Super. As you can see, there is one green button and one red button. The green button represents Mr. Larry Funk. The red button for Mr. Phil Lopez. When it comes time to vote, the TV screen in your room will flash the question in big red letters: *GAME OR NO GAME?* VOTE NOW. You will then push the button for the player you like, or the player you think has the most game. This should not be hard if you are familiar with Nintendo or Game Boy. Are we clear?"

Both groups shake their heads yes.

"Perfect," Dungworth says. "It's time for the first vote." He whips his head. "Marty, give the women's focus group the split screen. Funk on the toilet, Lopez doing push-ups."

Marty slides a T-bar lever down on the video switcher and

mutes the sound. He looks over at Dungworth, uncertain. "A little unfair, don't you think? A guy on the can and—"

Dungworth silences him with a raised hand. "It's called the money shot, lard bag. And if you question me again in front of the troops, I guarantee your next job will be holding the crotch light on the set of a dystopian gang bang. Bring in the cuck fluffer!"

Marty stares at him, astonished. "Wowzers, who gave you a hanging wedgie?"

———

Inside the hotel room of the women's focus group, they all sit slumped on the sofa, staring oddly at the images of Funk and Lopez on their TV set. While they are diverse in age and background, they all share the same everlasting look of dissatisfaction customary of young, privileged L.A. women. Some giggle at the sight of a strong, half-naked Lopez skipping rope and doing push-ups, but all "*EEEWWWW*" in unison when they see Funk on the toilet, nonchalantly flipping through a copy of *The Economist* magazine.

On-screen, the words *GAME OR NO GAME?* VOTE NOW blink in red.

The women grip their consoles and begin voting.

Fingers punching buttons.

———

Back in the control room, Dungworth tracks the votes on the vertical bar graph monitor. The red bar—Phil Lopez—rockets up past a tiny slice of green.

"We've got a ball game," Dungworth says.

Marty shoots him a scalding look just as Slater enters the room.

"Okay," Slater says, clapping his hands together with energy and enthusiasm. "What did I miss? Funk on a roll?"

Dungworth chuckles. "A Lopez landslide."

Slater looks up at the wall of screens and spots Funk on the toilet. "Oh, come on, man! You're not showing that to a bunch of random nobodies. That's hideous."

"The first vote already revealed that, sir. It's game on."

"Game on?" Slater says. "This is not a peep show!"

Dungworth stretches his animatronic frame and adjusts his clunky black glasses. "The world is fast, old boy. It's all you can do to keep up. How many times do I have to remind you... always assume you are being watched."

"I'm just trying to keep it fair."

Dungworth looks at Slater without expression. "Was it fair when your wife threw away your *Playboy* collection? Then tossed Miss November 1976 into the beach bonfire?"

"Hell no, it wasn't," Slater says. "She was my favorite."

"Or was it fair that your brother scratched your Black Sabbath *Paranoid* album and replaced it with the Nitty Gritty Dirt Band?"

How does he know that?

"It's going to be a glorious new world, Mr. Slater. No longer will you hold my generation hostage with your selfish desires. Soon, we will all live in a new paradise free of boomers, one where we will never have to listen to 'Cat Scratch Fever' ever again. So you still want to talk fair, or just stand there looking guilty?"

Slater grits his teeth and says, "Hardball, huh?"

"No. Basketball."

"The what?" Slater wheezes.

Dungworth sips from a bottle of Soylent and circles the

desk. "Roundball, pops. You might recall nailing a peach basket to a post."

Slater looks bewildered, like a moose staring into a campfire.

"Scientists have been telling us for years that memory for autobiographical events, also known as episodic memory, is pliable and unreliable, Mr. Slater. Do you really need me to spell it out for you? Or did you forget where you are?"

"But, but...I don't even know if he plays basketball."

Dungworth shoves a stick of gum into his mouth and lobs the wrapper into the wastebasket. "That's the beauty of live TV. We're going to find out."

Live TV? Slater thinks.

Funk will have my head for this.

But what Slater and Dungworth don't know about Funk is that he was a star basketball player in high school, and a holy terror on the intramural courts in college. He is what basketball fans call a rare bird, a guard who can crash the boards—a guard who can dunk.

Funk the Dunk. That's him.

Other talents include a golf swing as smooth and buttery as a California chardonnay, a wicked drop shot, and a decent game of foosball. All of which he would rather be doing now than entertaining you.

This is quite an impressive resume, you might say, but then you'd have to ask yourself: how can a man of fifty pull off a slam dunk? Kobe and Shaq both cashed it in before the age of forty.

Three words: eight-foot basket.

Funk is not particularly quick, but he covers a lot of ground for an aging rock star. Just ask the poor sod who tried to chase down one of his nasty drop shots and ended up limping off the pickleball court with a blown Achilles. Shit happens, and just like life, live TV doesn't always follow the script.

Dungworth will soon find out the hard way that he has

committed one of the world's great moral sins and judged a book by its gangly, long-armed cover.

"We've got a basketball goal set up on deck by the pool," Dungworth says. "We have hidden cameras planted in the land-scaping and trees. Wireless mics on the perimeter. Get Funk out there any way you can. The next vote's on the hoop court. Mano a mano with Phil Lopez." Dungworth's mouth opens in a consti-pated half-smile. "Like *Highlander*, Mr. Slater, there can only be one."

An anxious Slater scratches his gray beard stubble. "But what if it gets rough? Are you calling fouls?"

Dungworth leans back against the oak armoire and cracks his knuckles. "The only foul that needs calling is on you, Agent Orange. Now get me Funk's signed release, and get your asses on the court."

27

LATE MORNING.

Bright sunshine dapples the ritzy hotel grounds on yet another bluebird California day.

Funk and Slater head for the pool wearing gold mesh tank tops, faded white gym shorts, and well-worn sneakers.

Funk spins a basketball on his right index finger, and casually transfers it to the middle finger of his left hand—still spinning.

The man's got skills.

Funk has been told that a simple game of Horse awaits. Something to get the blood flowing.

"These vintage jerseys are a little tight," Funk says, looking at Slater's protruding belly. "Where did you get these rancid throwbacks? Etsy?"

"It's all wardrobe had," Slater says. "Don't sweat it. It's a short workout." He stares ruefully at Funk's balding pate. "But you're gonna have to start wearing a hat, dude. I don't want your head to get burned by the sun. Next thing you know, brown spots on the pate. Not good. I don't want you to look like a speckled trout."

Funk, with unexpected clarity: "Okey dokey."

Without warning, Slater's right ear twitches when a spinning Frisbee hums by at high speed. Shell-shocked, he ducks just in time as the flying disc curves out of sight. "Grilled cheezus! That was close."

Slater rises from his crouch and sees the shaggy white-haired dog that annoyed him at dinner last night chasing down the Frisbee into the shrubbery. Slater yells at the furry blur, "I'm fresh out of avocado, you mangy—"

"Easy," Funk says. "It's just a dog."

"I know, but it's not cool. That soy boy letting his dog roam free like that. I'm going to say something to management."

"Management doesn't care," Funk says. "Do you think the dog checked in by itself? He's part of the ecosystem, as you like to say. Get over it."

Slater watches the dog root in the bushes. "Keep digging, you pie-eyed mongrel. No avocados there." He looks back at Funk, puts his game face on.

"Guess what," he says.

"What?"

"The producer called an audible."

Funk looks over with an expression of fear and anxiety, the basketball still spinning on his finger. "Yeah? Is that good or bad?"

"It's all good," Slater says. "The production company wants to film in South Beach instead. Which means we're not shooting in the nightclub tonight."

"So no cameras?"

"That's right, buddy. No cameras. I knew you'd be happy." He grabs the spinning basketball off Funk's finger and smiles. "It's party time. Just two wild and crazy guys letting it all hang out. I've still got a lot of fun stuff planned, but all you gotta do is relax and concentrate on this..."

They round the corner to the pool, and Slater points at all the beautiful, bikinied girls being filmed playing water volleyball.

"This is it," Slater says. "We wrap after this pool scene."

Funk dodges a cameraman like he would a leper—or a man with whooping cough. L.A.'s latest outbreak. What's next? he thinks. A global pandemic? *Murder hornets?*

"These women are gorgeous," Funk says. "But what are they, *eighteen?*"

"Twenty-one, twenty-two," Slater says. "They're coeds. It's spring break, remember? But the beauty of all this is, every one of these hard-bodied fillies will be at the Skybar tonight."

Funk shakes his head. "I'm too old for them."

"Stop it. Was Bob Barker too old to date the help on *The Price Is Right?*"

"There were lawsuits, Slater."

Slater pauses, scratches his neck. "My bad. Hugh Hefner, then. Was the Hef too old for the twins?"

"He's ninety, Slater. God bless him, but he's not exactly a bon vivant about town anymore."

"True. But *Playboy* magazine is bringing back nudity. Which means some things just go together. Like mature men and foxy young women."

An amazed Funk says, "You'll never tire of coaching your own blow jobs, will you?"

Slater smiles and tosses the basketball back to Funk. "Never."

"You're unbelievable."

Slater pulls his long greasy hair up in a ponytail. "By the way," he says, "who was that old chick you were with last night?"

"What old chick?"

"The MILF by the pool."

Funk stops on the teak deck. "So that's it? You're stalking me now?"

"My room has a pool view, Larry. I just happened to look down."

Funk scowls. "First off, she's not old. Her name's Angie. We went to high school together. Her band played the wedding gig last night, and we just ran into each other."

"How romantic," Slater says flatly.

"*I know.* She used to babysit me. I was a sophomore; she was a senior. We played in the band together. Can you believe that?"

Slater nods. "Uh-huh. Did you stuff her?"

"No."

"Nothing? Not even a jean rub? A little outercourse."

Funk with a death stare. "What are you, five years old? I want you to repeat after me. I am not a regressive creep. I am not a regressive creep. I am not a regress—"

"Okay, okay," Slater says. "I'll drop it. Cripes."

The conversation falls quiet. Slater looks as if he's just endured a TSA reach-around at the airport. He exhales and looks off, watching a young woman with braids and a plunging black one-piece swimsuit pushing up out of the pool. "This is bad, man," he says under his breath. "Historically bad."

The sudden sound of a bouncing basketball grabs their attention. Funk glances up and sees Lopez and Backstreet strutting into view on the concrete footpath.

All geared up.

Logos flashing.

Unlike Funk and Slater, whose faded and ratty playing attire looks like the ball boy just copped it from the junior varsity practice squad, Team Lopez looks shiny and new in all-black uniforms and custom Air Jordans.

Are those anti-pilling jerseys? Funk thinks.

Backstreet dribbles the ball between his legs with flair and confidence, smiling like a street jockey high on quaaludes.

"Oh gosh," Funk mumbles. "The lizard man cometh."

The two men approach.

"Well, well," Lopez says, taking off his mirrored sunglasses. "It's the old patrol. What's up, homies?"

Slater ignores the dig and grins. "It's always a pleasure, Phil. Your timing is impeccable. We were just about to play a little game of roundball. Care to get schooled?"

Backstreet laughs. "Shit, Phil could lock you both up."

"Perhaps," Slater says. "But I've got odds on my boy posterizing his ass."

Funk looks at Slater with apprehension. "What are you talking about? I haven't played in three years."

"Don't worry," Slater says. "The rim's only eight feet. It's a baby's game." He gives Funk a gentle elbow nudge. "Now get out there on the court and make your wingman proud."

Funk palms the ball, glares at Slater. "I gotta warm up first."

Three wooden steps down from the pool deck is a small garden courtyard. The outdoor furniture has been removed, and the producers have laid a bright green outdoor tile court over the plank decking. A Spalding NBA angled pole backboard system now anchors the area. Advertised as the perfect system "for a laid-back pickup game between friends," the angled pole allows for more action under the basket.

Just like the pros.

Funk steps onto the makeshift court, dribbles twice, and promptly shoots an air ball. Backstreet snickers behind a balled fist and glances at Lopez. They both carry the look of "*we got this*" on their faces.

Funk's next shot rims out, but the third hits nothing but net. *Swish.*

He's finding his range now, his rhythm.

Unimpressed, Lopez steps onto the makeshift court. "Let's do this."

————

Inside the control room, Marty and the production crew watch the basketball game unfold on the Samsung big-screen. Apparently, Dungworth is on "break" and set to return "as soon as humanly possible."

Keep calm and carry on.

So far the hoop game has been a lopsided affair, with Funk dominating Lopez on both ends of the court.

The crew marvels at the moves of the soon-to-be fifty-year-old and cheers when Funk swats a Lopez jump shot into the pool.

Marty, the technical director, sits motionless at his desk, gnawing on the cap of a ballpoint pen. He's not much of a basketball fan, but watching Funk dribble behind his back, stutter-step, and score easily with a finger-roll layup gives him the itch to suit up and get off the bench. There is an elegant quality to the man's game, Marty thinks, a musical rhythm of pivots and leaps.

Aside from this, there is a very distinctive jump kick that happens every time Funk leaves the ground and shoots the basketball. It's as if he were onstage, performing for a sold-out crowd.

Marty suddenly has the feeling that he has met this man before. He's not sure if it was just the chance meeting yesterday in the lobby that has triggered the notion, or if he's somehow been enriched by his presence in another time—another place.

He is convinced it is the latter.

On-screen, with a Lopez hand in his face, Funk steps back and sinks a three-point shot from long range.

Bang!

Nothing but net.

Marty smiles as a frustrated Lopez slams the ball down in defeat. On another monitor, he observes the focus groups watching the game. The men are devoted to the competition, gnashing their teeth as they sit on the edge of their seats, but the women seem bored. Three of the women share a *Vogue* magazine, while another files her nails like the cops are dragging the lake for her dead husband. Across from her, a reserved woman dressed in a blue blazer and gold buttons stares blankly out the window.

Marty knows what she is thinking. That her agent deceived her. Which is true. He did, along with the rest of his untalented clients.

The bathroom door flings open and Dungworth exits stiffly. The eyes of the entire crew follow him as he melts tremulously into the director's chair, his starched blue Oxford shirt as rigid as his movements. He appears pensive, brooding.

After a moment, Marty peers over the top of his computer monitor and asks, "Success?"

Dungworth shakes his head. "No. So what's happening with the game between these two geriatric gigolos? Is it ugly?"

Marty shrugs. "It depends on who you want to win."

Alarmed, Dungworth's head jerks like a news anchor talking into the wrong camera. "*What?* Somebody get my challenge producer in here. Do it now!"

———

Inside the hotel room of the men's focus group, they are jittery and intense, highly invested in the outcome of the basketball game.

A floppy-eared kid in a bomber jacket points at the TV and

says to the group, "Funk's gonna break him down right here. Curry style. You watch."

On-screen, Lopez talks smack as Funk dribbles. "You want some of this, bitch? You think you can score on me? Go ahead, Pale Rider, try to take it to the hole."

Funk dribbles with his tongue out, sticks his bony butt into the body of Lopez, and slowly backs him down toward the goal. He is methodical, workmanlike. Comfortable in the paint.

"Here it comes," says the kid.

The muscular Lopez tries to rake the ball away with his short alligator arms, but Funk keeps his distance. Keeps powering forward. He stops under the basketball rim and looks around. There is nowhere to go.

He is trapped.

Lopez laughs and says with one hand on Funk's back, "What are you gonna do now, *ese*?"

Funk, calmly: "Go to the house."

In one lightning-quick motion, Funk jumps straight up and tomahawk-jams the basketball.

The net rips and the backboard shakes.

The men jump from their seats and "OOOOOOHHH" in unison, cheering and high-fiving Funk's victory.

The floppy-eared kid in the bomber jacket points enthusiastically at Lopez and yells, "It's Funkalicious!"

28

TWENTY MINUTES LATER, after a thrilling game of basketball, Funk and Slater limp toward the lobby elevator. Funk drips sweat, a white towel wrapped around his neck.

"A friendly game of Horse, you said. Next thing you know, I've got a lizard on my back."

"Hey," Slater says, "you're the one who said he wanted a little sun on his face. Besides, you won, didn't you?"

Funk wipes his forehead with the towel. "At the expense of both ankles. At least the hospital is close by."

Cedars-Sinai Medical Center. One of the best in the nation. It is something he thinks about now as both ankles swell.

Welcome to the world of fifty.

They arrive at the elevator door and Funk stabs the UP button.

"Shake it off, old man," Slater says. "Get some ice on those old bones. Because tonight we're going to get our dancing shoes on." Slater shuffles like an out-of-rhythm white man.

"Dancing shoes?" Funk says.

"Yeah. I want you to channel your inner Travolta."

"Which one?" Funk says. "There are multiple incarnations."

"Anything pre-hairpiece."

"*Urban Cowboy?*"

Slater points. "No line dancing. I can assure you of that."

"Bob Shapiro?"

"Fuck Bob Shapiro. I'm talking Danny Zuko, Tony Manero. Dudes with game."

The elevator door slides open and they step inside.

Funk punches the eighth-floor button and the elevator door closes. "About tonight," he says. "Angie's band is playing at the Whisky. I got us on the guest list. So if you're not dead set on Tony Manero, we could just chill out and listen to some really good music."

Slater's face drains white, and he says in a voice higher than Funk expected, "What? Mrs. Robinson? No way, bro. I've got a big night planned. That is not going to happen."

"It's just down the street," Funk says.

The elevator slows, moans, and grinds to a halt on the eighth floor. The door opens and Funk hobbles out, Slater on his swollen heels.

"Look," Slater says in a measured voice. "I've moved a lot of things around to make this a great birthday for you. I've even invested some of my own money. Just roll with me on this. It's going to be great. *Trust me.*"

Funk stops in the middle of the hallway and stares into the jaundiced eyes of Slater. They jiggle like fried eggs in a pan. *Trust me.* How many times has he heard that in Hollywood? In a town that prides itself on being able to cry on cue, it's hard to separate the crocodile tears from the real thing. Genuine emotion is rare here. So all you can do is follow your gut, and hope to God it steers you right.

Funk feels pressured to comply. "Okay," he says. "I'll catch her band another time." He playfully snaps his towel on Slater's leg. "But only because you made plans."

Slater laughs. "That's my little buddy. Tell you what. Get cleaned up. Order lunch in, and I'll meet you in the lobby at two. I've got a killer man-date lined up for the afternoon."

"That sounds dangerously close to *Jersey Shore*."

"That's right, hoss. GTL. Gym, tan, laundry. Or in our case, massage, steam, and haircuts." Slater winks. "Gotta clean up for the ladies."

Funk thinks for a moment. "A trip to the spa does sound good."

"It sure does," Slater says. "Especially when the production is picking up the tab."

Funk's ears prick. "They have a spa here at the hotel?"

"No, no. It's somewhere off Sunset. They've got a Lincoln Town Car picking us up, whisking us away to the ultimate man-cave experience. Cocktails. Big-screen TVs. Mani-pedis. Haircuts. The works. Sound good?"

Funk nods, makes a yes grunt. He's presumably in. But it is still open to interpretation.

"So that's a yes?" Slater says.

"What part of my head nod did you not decipher?"

Funk knows that in today's hectic world his leisure time is a luxury, an embarrassment of riches. Given this, it is something that he will never take for granted.

Ever.

Otium cum dignitate.

Leisure with dignity.

A slanted smile falls from Slater's poker face. "Great," he says. "I'll see you in the lobby at two. Don't be late." As he thunders down the hallway, his large, buffoonish body breaks into a full gallop.

Four minutes later an exuberant Slater bursts through the control room door, surprising the crew. On the main monitor, Funk is seen entering his hotel suite.

Slater rushes to Dungworth's director's chair and begins rocking the wood frame like an excited child. "Did you see that, superstar? Funk serving up leather to Lopez on the B-ball court. Score me, baby. *Score me.*"

At ease, Dungworth flicks a speck of dirt off Slater's gold jersey. "He got the men's vote," Dungworth says. "I'll give him that. But the women were unimpressed." He casually points to the bar graph scoreboard on the curved computer monitor. Although the green bar has moved up slightly, it is still well behind red. "Now get your dirty paws off my chair."

Slater pumps a fist and slaps Marty on the back. "It's a start. Am I right, Big Marty?"

Marty, turning knobs on the console, agrees. "Funk's blowing up low-key."

Dungworth shakes his head and shouts to no one in particular, "Which one of you clown tossers has got the helmet cam!"

There is mumbling among the crew members, production jargon buzzes. Loggers, audio specialists, camera operators, fixers, and editors talk among themselves.

There is plenty of blame to go around.

Out of the unnecessary chaos, a young black man in a Minecraft T-shirt scrambles over, arms outstretched, and offers Dungworth a red construction helmet. There is a GoPro Fusion mounted on top of the hard hat—a 360-degree action camera with simple one-button control.

Dungworth rips the helmet from the production assistant's grasp and shuffles over to Slater. "Are you ready for some movement, Agent Orange?"

Slater shrugs. "Do I have a choice?"

As Dungworth places the hard hat on Slater's head, he smacks it down with the palm of his hand, producing a sharp, loud cracking noise.

"Ouch," Slater says. "I just lost an inch in height. What am I, a wine bottle?"

Dungworth grins. "Just making sure we have the right fit."

Slater's mind fills with medieval images and torture racks. What's next? *Sword swallowing?*

Slater's face is gray now, the color of a waterlogged book. It suggests that things have gone horribly wrong, or pear-shaped, as the Brits like to say.

Dungworth is clearly enjoying the moment. He adjusts the leather strap under Slater's chin and cinches it tight, like he would a donkey's harness. Slater groans and clamps his jaws, breathing heavy through his nose.

"You seem shaky," Dungworth says.

"Do I?" Slater says, his face white around the gills. "Whatever gave you that impression?"

"So you're doing okay?"

"Craptastic."

Dungworth pauses. "You are a strange sight to behold, Mr. Slater. And looking at you reminds me of some gain-of-function experiment gone wrong, some sleepy-eyed bridge troll that has just climbed his way out of the deepest, darkest recesses of the metaverse. But you are here right now to deliver your finest hour of television. Your last...brave...heroic hour. I salute you."

Slater despises millennials. Hates everything about them. Everything from their crude Harry Potter tattoos to their ill-advised gender-reveal parties. *Hey, can anybody recommend a decent decompression capsule? Something to take the edge off?* Pathetic. The only thing these entitled punks want from society is a long life and money.

Lots of money.

As far as he is concerned, they are the most cruel and hard-hearted individuals to ever walk the planet Earth. It's not hard to look into their eyes and see the end of civilization.

This is the same generation of amateur propagandists that will rescue a wounded fly from the windshield of a speeding automobile but have no qualms about running over another human being in the crosswalk. The last thing the dying person sees as the luxury SUV flees the scene is a "Kindness Matters" bumper sticker.

Come to think of it, Slater has never met one cool millennial in his entire life. Not one. *Not ever.* There's something basically wrong with that.

Slater says, "Just tell me what's going on, please."

"It's called young bulls harassing old bulls, Mr. Slater."

"I know that. What the hell is this contraption on my head?"

"A very expensive camera. All mic'd up. And I must say, the red helmet matches your hair color well."

Slater rubs the back of his neck and says with injured dignity, "I disagree. It's more of a strawberry blond."

"Whatever. Use the helmet cam only if Funk strays. If he wanders, goes off property, follow him and livestream every-thing. It's your last chance to capture the magic."

Slater reaches up with a trembling right hand and loosens the chinstrap. "Do I look like a stuntman?"

"You wish, bacon neck. More like a walking flop sweat of ineptitude. Like I said, use the helmet cam only for emergen-cies. Now, is Funk ready for the spa?"

Slater unconsciously wipes his nose on his jersey. "Yeah. We'll be there at two. Haircuts at four."

"Good," Dungworth says. "Because we're going to shave his head on camera."

Slater yanks off the construction helmet, his eyes wide and frenetic. "What!"

"You heard me. If you want the money, your friend goes zero guard. Buzzed to the skull."

Dread sweeps over Slater. "The naked blade?"

Dungworth nods with gloating eyes.

"But—but he'll never go for that," Slater says. "I mean, he's talked about it...but no!"

Dungworth goes chest to chest, gets up in Slater's beet-red face. "He shaves his head...*or you go home*. Understand?"

Slater slumps, his weak spine curved. "But how can I convince him to do that?"

Dungworth walks toward the door, turns. "It's tough out there for a pimp, Mr. Slater. I'm sure you'll think of something."

29

THAT AFTERNOON, Funk and Slater sit naked in the steam room drinking lemon drop martinis, their torsos glistening with sweat. Slater plucks at his gray chest hair and says, "I'm thinking about having all this lasered. My back, too."

Funk offers his thoughts, his face void of emotion. "It's going to take several sessions to tame that undomesticated pelt. We're talking Marlin Perkins, *Wild Kingdom* country."

Slater nods, muffling a rebuttal.

They sit in silence for a moment, the aroma of eucalyptus filling their noses.

Funk leans back and takes a deep breath. He is totally relaxed, his body melting into the room. He looks up at the maple ceiling and blinks away the pearls of sweat, still thinking about his deep-tissue massage with Jorge. It had been pure bliss. A total back reconstruction. From traps to shoulders.

Afterward, he was so loose, he found himself facedown on the massage table, unable to move a muscle. When he could finally form a complete sentence, what leaked out of his mouth surprised him: "Don't tase me, bro." He smiles at the thought of it, looking forward to the soothing, dual-head rainfall shower.

Eventually Slater breaks the silence and says, "Speaking of hair. You remember what you said last week…about shaving your head?"

Funk drains his martini. "I was just talking out loud. I've decided to let nature take its course. Go the Euro route."

Slater is aghast. "The power donut?"

"Yeah," Funk says. "It appears that shaving one's head has gone the way of the soul patch. Very uncool."

"Maybe, but you're the one who said his hairline was retreating faster than the Germans at Haguenau."

"It was a joke."

Slater wags his head in dismay. "The power donut is a very difficult look to pull off. There are only three men in modern history that have been able to rock it. Sean Connery, also known as James Bond. Prince William, soon to be king. And Ed Harris. The man with the chiseled face." He pauses. "You, well, let's face it. You're Long Shot Larry."

Funk puts a hand to his heart. "Thank you for your vote of confidence."

"Be that as it may, don't you feel cheated?"

"Why would I feel cheated?"

"Your hair. Most rock gods have kept their locks. It's in the genes. Just like bums."

"What are you getting at?"

"What I'm saying is…nature shortchanged you. So fuck nature. Be bold. Shave it off. Today would be a great day to do it. The haircuts are free."

Funk lowers his head and studies the tops of his bare feet. "I'm not ready for that."

"The hottie I ran into at the salon begs to differ."

"What hottie?"

Slater picks the lint from his belly button. "The chick that saw you out on the basketball court this morning. Know what she said?"

"What?"

"She said, 'Your friend would be way cuter if he shaved his head.'"

Funk, surprised: "Really? Is she crazy?"

"I'm serious, bro. And I know you've been thinking about it. And you even said a transplant was out. So let's face it, there's nowhere else to go with that fly rink. Unless you fully commit to the bald ponytail look. Which is, of course, boldly going where few men dare." Slater pauses. "What do you say? I think it will give you cosmic game."

Funk rubs his temples, his wet brown hair pasted to his scalp. "What time's our appointment?"

"Four."

Funk thinking, nodding. "All right," he finally says. "I'll do it. But under one condition."

"What's that?"

"I'll take the buzz cut, but *only* if you agree to get a flattop." Funk extends his hand. "Deal?"

Slater stiffens. At its essence, he wears the petrified look of a caged bird with an open door to the outside world. *Should I stay or should I go?* The decision between hair and money is a difficult one in Hollywood. It's rare to have one without the other. In this moment of tense indecision, Slater does not shake Funk's hand. Instead, he stands in all his naked glory and pumps up the volume. "A flattop? *Are you insane?!* I am not equipped for that psychological hurdle. And you know it. I won't do it, Larry. I won't!"

30

AT FOUR P.M. SHARP, in an upscale men's grooming lounge in West Hollywood, an electric hair clipper buzzes as Slater's ginormous head is trimmed down to something more manageable. Wrapped in a white cape, he sits silent in the salon chair, watching his dyed orange locks float helplessly to the floor. Maria, a hip young hairstylist, attends to his aging mane. Short and thick, her pink jaw-length bob frames her round Hispanic face. She says, "You doing all right, Mr. Slater?"

"I'd feel a lot better if everybody stopped calling me Mr. Slater."

She laughs. "I'm almost done."

Funk stands at the window, arms at his sides, anxiously awaiting his turn at the guillotine. It is hard to watch, so he swings his eyes and stares out at the city in motion. Shifting from foot to foot, he licks his dry lips as the colors of Los Angeles flash by: wildfire reds, Dodger blues, coastal grays, and desert browns. These are the true tones of L.A., he thinks.

"Hey!" Slater calls out, jarring Funk from his thoughts. "How bad is it? Do I look too corporate?"

Funk turns from the long rectangular window, his lean form

washed out in the lazy afternoon sunlight. He stares at Slater's new hairdo and chuckles. "No, man. It's actually not that bad. You kind of remind me of Coach Carter. My old high school football coach. A work-hard, play-hard kind of thing."

"Great comfort," Slater says.

Maria circles Slater, admiring her pruning skills. "I think it makes you look younger. Are you ready to see?"

Slater hyperventilates and closes his eyes. "Don't hurt me, baby. Just take it slow and easy."

Maria plants her feet and slowly spins the barber chair around. He sits motionless, his eyes tightly shut.

"It's okay," Maria says. "The ride's over. You can look now."

Slater's eyes flicker open as he stares into the mirror. His long orange animal hair is gone, and all that remains is a tight gray flattop.

And the roots of old age.

Crazy-eyed, he says, "Younger! I look like fucking Johnny Unitas!"

Funk laughs. He's thinking more Gus Grissom than Johnny U. But Slater is on point: he has just joined a long list of brush-heads. From H. R. Haldeman to Kid 'n Play.

Hard angles and hardballers.

Don't screw the pooch.

"Yeah, laugh it up, snow globe," Slater says. "Your follicular reckoning is near."

Funk's face drops. His moment of truth has arrived.

Maria trains her big brown eyes on him and holds up the clippers. "Your turn."

In the control room, Dungworth and the crew watch Funk slide into the salon chair.

Dungworth paces between the workstations and speaks a series of commands into his headset. "Stand by for tape. Ready A." He points a finger. "Marty, cue the music."

"On it," Marty says.

"Roll camera," Dungworth says. "Speed, nice and quiet in the salon, people. Annnd...*action*."

On the big screen, Funk sits in a semiconscious state—dead-eyed, like a Marine Corps recruit in an Oceanside barbershop.

"Give me a tight shot on his face," Dungworth says.

The camera closes in on Funk, his vacant mug a stock image of scared straight.

"Great shot," Dungworth says into a walkie-talkie. "Hold nine. Gimme the music. Music!"

Over Funk's blanched image, the theme song from *M*A*S*H*—"Suicide Is Painless"—kicks in over the sound system.

"Killer choice," a PA says.

Dungworth grins, proud of his selection. "Yeah. We're spoofing that famous suicide scene from the movie."

Marty looks at Funk on the monitor, and does a double take. Some past recollection has just resurfaced in his nascent brain-pan. He points and says, "I swear I know that dude."

"Yeah, you go way back," Dungworth says. "You met him yesterday."

"No," Marty says. "Before that. I don't know where, though."

On-screen, Maria, the hairstylist, ceremoniously wraps Funk in a black barber cape as the control room looks on.

There is no talking, only the haunting music.

As a somber line of salon workers approaches Funk, one by one they say their last goodbyes and pay their respects as they would to a dying man on his deathbed.

First to greet Funk is a young woman with long lavender

hair and black eyeshadow. She approaches the chair slowly, as if walking barefoot over a bed of hot stones. She stares down at her combat boots and holds out her hand, palm up. The young woman wants something, and Funk knows what it is. He hesitates, and she gives him that "hand it over" look. Funk sighs. He fumbles under the black cape and produces a fine-toothed pocket comb with a tortoiseshell finish—his favorite.

Although the comb has seen little work in the last few years, he reluctantly slaps it into her open palm. She kisses him tenderly on the forehead and departs with her head down.

A thin blond man wearing a French sailor's shirt and high-waisted trousers is next in line. He stops at the chair and stares at Funk with paralyzed eyes, long-suffering eyes. Funk, not knowing what else to do, flashes a witless grin. The understanding blond man nods, and runs a thoughtful, shaky hand through Funk's thin brown hair.

Following him is a glum middle-aged black woman in a classic white shirt and flared jeans. She hands Funk two wallet-sized photos. One of Sir Patrick Stewart, and the other of Matt Damon in *Elysium*. Funk glances at the photos with stretched pupils, then back up at the woman. She nods consolingly, beaming him an afterlife smile.

Finally, a flattopped and sober Slater. He steps up to the salon chair, pounds his chest as if victory is imminent, and gives Funk a defiant fist raise and a "stay strong" look.

In the control room, Dungworth speaks into a walkie-talkie. "Cut the music. Tight on the clipper."

On the big screen, the image of a buzzing hair clipper roars to life.

Dungworth says, "Give me the beating heart and a wide shot on Funk."

Without delay, the sound of a beating heart thumps over

Funk's distressed image as he takes a deep breath and gapes at the hair clippers like they are the Jaws of Life.

THUMP...THUMP...THUMP...

"Do it!" Dungworth says.

Close-up on the hair clipper as it zips voraciously around Funk's head. Slater grimaces. The blond man chews his nails. And within moments, Funk is bald.

Fifty shades of bald.

The control room falls silent.

Time stops.

All stare as a speechless Funk processes his new alien look in the mirror.

My Favorite Martian?

Gaye Miller, the caramel-haired challenge producer, stands with a clipboard cradled against her chest. She wears a gray pinstriped suit and likes what she sees. "Wow, he looks so, *smoothly kewl.* Much younger."

"A lot younger," Marty says. "A tad ghostly, but nothing a spray-on tan won't cure."

Dungworth runs a hand through his coarse black hair. "Younger? Really? I was thinking more along the lines of the Pillowcase Rapist."

Marty glances up at the scoreboard. The green bar graph is now halfway to red. "Think all the negative vibes you want," he says, "but the tribe has spoken."

"What?" Dungworth says.

Marty points at the score on the curved monitor. Dungworth turns, sees Funk gaining on Lopez. Full of anger, he rips off his headset and heaves it. "Freakin' cue ball. No way he wins this. No way!"

———

In the salon, Funk sits in silence, blinking at his glazed reflection in the mirror. At this very moment, he is at the center of baldness—the far reaches of the hairless universe. The skullett is gone now, and there is nothing left to frame his face. It's as if he has just landed on some alternative planet. Some hellscape for the bald and the furious.

He turns his head, and his moody blue eyes seem to float in the air.

A chill breaks over him, shivers.

Maria the stylist says, "How do you like it?"

A blasé shrug from Funk.

"I think it looks great," she says. "You have the perfect-shaped head. No lumps, ridges, or valleys."

Funk, as still as a veined marble statue: "Never in a million years could I have ever imagined someone saying that to me."

An elderly Asian woman with cropped silver hair looks up from her manicure station and declares, "You're lucky. In my culture, a high forehead is a sign of wealth." She smiles and gives him the thumbs-up. "You're going to be rich."

The blond man in the high-waisted trousers now stares adoringly at Funk.

Slater is elated and dances a soft jig like a drunk Irishman. "It's tight, bro," he says. "You look like a mixed martial artist. Lean and mean. Bald with game."

Funk turns his head, still studying his reflection in the mirror. "You really think it looks good?"

"Dude," Slater says. "It oozes defiance. You're ready for the octagon."

"He doesn't look mean," says Maria. "Just edgy. Like Billy Corgan of Smashing Pumpkins."

"I think it's a compliment," Slater says. "Hell, I think we actually have a shot at winning this game."

Funk removes the black cape and stands up. "What game?"

OOPS.

Slater backpedals. "The, ah...game of life, buddy. The second half...yeah."

"You're an idiot, Slater."

Funk takes a dizzying breath. His entire body aches from the labor on the basketball court. He slowly turns to the stylist and says, "Does one normally tip for this?"

She laughs. "Not today. It's on the production."

Funk rubs his bald head, slightly removed. "Cool, okay...thanks."

Funk and Slater walk toward the exit, but the voice of Maria stops them.

"Hey, Larry," she calls.

Funk turns. "Yeah?"

"I always keep it real," she says. "Whether you believe it or not, it's a good look for you. It's back to rock star status."

She smiles, and Slater nudges Funk.

"You see?" Slater says. "What did I tell you? Chicks dig the dome. I mean, there's a lot of ways you can go with this newfound masculinity. Daughtry, Vin Diesel—"

"Don't say Bruce Willis," Funk says. "Because he had hair in *Moonlighting*, receding in *Die Hard*. He already had a boatload of money before he shaved."

"Jason Statham?"

"He doesn't count," Funk says. "He's British."

"Fine. Pick whoever makes you feel good. Now, c'mon. We gotta get back to the hotel. We're late for wardrobe."

Funk checks his watch and scratches his inner arm. "Wardrobe?"

31

BACK AT THE HOTEL, Funk and Slater stroll down the dimly lit tenth-floor hallway.

Funk says, "I told you I brought my own clothes."

Slater stops and stares at Funk's dated ensemble.

"How many times do I have to say it out loud?" He writes cursive in the air with his index finger. "Khakis plus square-toed shoes equal *no game*. You're a bald man now, a shiny bullet that requires a bold new look."

"Oh, that's high praise."

Slater pauses, studying Funk. "Is that your dad's Oleg Cassini shirt?"

Funk dips his head and stares down at his short-sleeved leisure shirt. Teal blue with chest pockets and epaulets. The finest '70s nylon. "Yeah," he mutters. "Sears catalog."

"C'mon, man. The only thing missing is the pocket protector. What's next, a ventilated shirt?"

There was a reason they bullied Slater in high school, Funk thinks. He just has that haughty face and discordant voice that bullies love to hit.

"I'll tell you this right now," Funk says emphatically. "I am not a fan of wardrobe. They always try to make you into something you're not. Next thing you know, I'm walking out of there with a crocheted beanie on my head."

"Relax," Slater says. "There will be no crocheted beanies. Geez, what is it with you? All I'm asking is that you lose the AARP collection. Jump into something more contemporary. Like you used to wear onstage. I want you to find that guy again and channel him. You can do it. I know you can."

It's a cruel slice of irony, Funk thinks. The gregarious stonewashed guy to the competent introvert. He looks up at Slater's boot-camp haircut and says with a ray of hope, "I'll try to find him."

Slater nods. "All right. Let's get you out of those stretch pants. The ladies in wardrobe will hook you up."

Something fires in the back of Funk's noggin. Another red flag waves. "I'm open to contemporary and modern," he says, "but I thought the shoot was finished. There's no reason for wardrobe."

Slater spits out: "We are. I am. But I still get to enjoy the fruits of my labor for the rest of the weekend. The production company said I could keep a few things. Expensive things. And you're invited."

Funk steps back, shrinks within himself. "I'm just hanging out here, man. I don't want any fuss, or any expensive things."

Slater tenses. "We are going to war tonight, okay? These are not the same women that you and I grew up with. These young women today are jaded, hypercritical, and expect same-day shipping. You're going to have to deliver—*and fast.*"

Funk nods. "Squad goals."

"That's it, buddy. We gotta stick together, otherwise they'll eat us alive. Now let me hear your war cry."

Funk gives him a quizzical look, shrugs.

"Your war cry," Slater says, gesturing with his left hand. "That crazy rebel yell. Let's hear it."

"I'm not sure where this is leading," Funk says, "but I've temporarily shelved the death chant for more serene meadows."

"Damn the meadows! I'm talking *Full Metal Jacket*. The Visigoths sacking Rome. It's time to get pumped up, bro. Here, watch me." Slater plants his feet and snarls, then sticks his tongue out like a Maori warrior and yells, "AAAHHHHH, AAAHHHHH." He pauses, wipes the spittle off his lips. "There. Now you try it."

Funk looks around, unsettled. Slater's demented war cry has shaken him to the core. And, presumably, half the hotel guests. He says, "If you do that again with me in public, I will put you down like the old dog you are."

Slater sighs. "I'm just trying to get you fired up. You're not on Medicare yet." He pauses. "In all sincerity, though, you're getting into that clickbait ad territory of celebrities that you thought were dead who are actually still alive. Just sayin'."

Abruptly, behind them, they hear a hotel door bang open. Passionate laughter is heard. It is blunt and coarse and peppered with slurs of *bitch* and *motherfucker*. The end of a well-told tale.

Funk and Slater glance down the hall at the disturbance. It is Lopez and Backstreet, spilling out of the wardrobe room with hangers of clothes slung neatly over their shoulders. Garments wrapped in plastic.

Slater says in a hushed tone, "Low-flying black swans twelve o'clock."

Funk draws an agitated breath, suffering a mild turn of outrage fatigue.

———

Team Lopez stops laughing when they spot the freshly shorn competition. They share a look in the hallway and, once on the same page, approach Funk and Slater, face-to-face.

Top guns meet pop guns.

Lopez adjusts his dry cleaning and says, "Well, well, look who made it upriver. Jughead and Eightball. Nice haircuts, gentlemen."

Slater points at Lopez's black tank top and gold neck chain. "Better than that *Grand Theft Auto* thing you got working."

Funk elbows Slater, says softly, "Why do these people keep confronting us?"

Slater says out of the corner of his mouth, "Let me handle this."

Let me handle this.

How many times has Lopez heard a white boy spout that shit? He's not dumb, *ese*. He knows exactly what's happening here. Dungworth with the typecast, portraying him as the Latin Satin. Some big-dicked Frito Bandito with a gold-toothed smile. That's him all right, the Mexican lover with a spicy dong. The lusty gardener with a razor-thin mustache and a red rose clamped between his teeth. *Hola, señora. It is very hot today. Yes, it is, Señor Lopez. Very hot. Would you like to come inside for a cool drink of water? A salty taco, perhaps?*

Fuck that. You can slice your own Boar's Head meat. Mama ain't no maid, and Papa ain't no butcher.

Born and raised in Southern California, Lopez is a proud third-generation Mexican American. No deportation concerns here. His dad owns thirty fish taco trucks in the Valley, a big house in Woodland Hills.

So screw Dungworth and the network horse he rode in on. I got your typecast right here, right between these big *huevos*.

There was a time in his life when Lopez pursued acting on a full-time basis. Went out on auditions and harbored dreams of breakthrough roles. Roles that he hoped would eventually shatter the Latin stereotypes. But that never happened. All they ever wanted to cast him as was the angry, macho East L.A. homeboy gangbanger. Some cholo loser sitting on the stoop, smoking blunts and drinking Budweiser from a can.

Lopez doesn't even have an accent. He speaks perfect English, watches British dramas, and wears a vintage cardigan on occasion. Along with that, he is well read and can talk on a variety of subjects ranging from deleveraging to fiscal constraints to social instability. The accent only comes out for roles. He is, as Rumsfeld liked to say, one of those known unknowns.

But unlike Slater, he never had a chance in the entertainment business.

He knows that now.

He still goes out on auditions, though, but only for the money. And lately, these reality shows have been paying extremely well. Something he can't say about his personal training business. Albeit that's what got him today's job. His history of seducing and shagging his rich white clients. The class of rich white trash who wears Ugg boots in August, chugs wine and Xanax, and steps out on her husband in between sushi lunch specials and soccer practice.

You want to check my emails, bro?

Lopez is not sure which stock "Latin Lover" character he should play today. He has narrowed it down to two: the suave Fernando Lamas or the more macho Antonio Banderas. It's a hard choice, and he wants to give his best performance.

So he stands here proudly, dramatically, plowing ahead in this stupid game of who gets the girl. He is not worried about the competition. This Funk fellow's newly shaved head reminds him of an active mall shooter—some crazed White House fence jumper. Shit only stupid white boys do. With that said, he harbors no ill will toward Slater or his egghead friend. There's no need for animosity.

They are all here for the same reason:

The money.

The cheddar.

The broccoli.

Call it what you will, dawg, it all spends the same.

Slater says, handling the situation, "We were just talking about you, Phil."

Lopez smiles and says, "Yeah? What about?"

"We were just wondering how you liked your synthetic breakfast this morning. You know...the roundball beatdown?"

Backstreet chimes in. "Pop off, cake tits, because tonight Phil makes Funk his bitch."

Funk cocks his bald head.

Slater shakes his hands, feigning extreme fear. "Oooh. So scared, errand boy."

Backstreet takes a step forward. "I ain't your boy, whiskey face."

Lopez puts a hand on Backstreet's Chicago Bulls jersey, curbs his aggression. He glowers at Slater. "We'll know in a few hours," he says. "Then we'll see who's got game, beta boy."

Lopez holds the menacing look, his dramatic dark eyes challenging Slater to a Mexican standoff. But he finds it hard not to giggle. Staring at Slater's *Back to the Future* flattop, and his oblivious buddy's bald head, is enough to make any actor break character and howl with laughter.

He realizes now that he's going to have to carry the scene.

Again.

So he turns up the macho.

Lopez cranes his neck, the gold cross on his throat catching light. He stares up at the ceiling and cases the area, his intense eyes flicking from side to side. *Where's the camera?* he thinks.

Where is it? Got to give the gringo audience what it wants, expects.

That dirty evil bandit stare.

The well-worn Mexican trope.

Cue the mariachi music, Dungworth. I'm ready for my close-up.

32

FUNK IS uneasy about the latest encounter with Lopez and Backstreet. Who are these two men? And why do they bring such an unsavory flavor to the room? Did Slater lose a bet? It wouldn't be the first time. And what was Lopez doing out in the hall, looking up at the security camera on the ceiling and smiling at it like he was clutching an AK at a block party shoot-out?

Weird, he can hear his mother say in her New Jersey accent.

"After you," Slater says, gesturing with a hairy right arm.

Funk is the first to enter the wardrobe room. The tenth-floor suite buzzes with activity, its opaque whiteness bathed in squishy afternoon sunlight. Several people scurry about the minimalist space, pushing rolling chrome garment racks and frantically fingering designer clothes. In a tufted upholstered armchair, a slender man with dark brown hair examines himself in a handheld mirror, picking his frosted bangs into place.

On the shoe-strewn bamboo floor, Funk spots a pair of gladiator sandals and wonders who might be the lucky recipient of those beauties. *The Great Pumpkin, perhaps?*

Both men stop in the center of the chaos and soak it all in. It is warm and stuffy inside, but the top of Funk's head is freezing.

It is just something that he is going to have to get used to, he thinks. *Welcome to the hat brigade.* He turns his head and glances at his reflection in a walnut floor mirror, rubbing his shaved skull. It is as rough and abrasive as sandpaper.

Are you an assassin?

After a moment, he trudges to the far window. He is reserved, quiet. His melancholy a shield of gratitude. In approximately seven hours, at the stroke of midnight, if he is lucky, he will turn fifty years old. He drops his head and inspects the top of his rough hands, the brown sunspots as big as dimes. They are the reminders of an outdoor life well lived—a life lived without sunscreen, without regret, and without protective helmets. He tells himself that he is still beautiful on the inside, and this induces a private chuckle.

He stares out at the hazy downtown skyline, watching a plane fly over the Wilshire Grand Center. The smog is back, he notices, and a gauzy cloudbank sits heavy over the city. With his hands in his pockets, he ponders eastern values in the western light and thinks about the things and people that have left L.A. The Japanese gardener, rock and roll—his hair. *I'd like to thank all the beautiful bald people for their love and support.*

Evolution and growth in Los Angeles does not come easy, he knows. It will take time.

Slater walks over to the window and nudges Funk. "Hey, bud," he says softly. "Don't leave me now."

"What?" Funk says.

"You're spacing, dude. Your mouth is open. It's not a good look."

Funk nods. "I was just thinking about that muscle-head, Lopez. Maybe if you'd stop egging him on, he'd chill. I mean, we're not on the court anymore."

"Screw him," Slater says. "You're the roundball shaman now."

Slater gets momentarily sidetracked when he sees a young obese guy stuffing his face over at the craft services table. "Look at that fat kid over there," he says. "Shoveling chocolate chip cookies in his mouth. He's a world-class eater, that one. Joey Jaws. I bet he has diabetes."

"You've got diabetes."

"Yeah," Slater says. "But it took me fifty years to get here. I earned it. These brats want everything now."

A tall, mature woman in black yoga pants and a gray T-shirt approaches. Thin and barefoot, she has shoulder-length brown hair streaked with gold. Her walk is graceful and strong, yet unhurried.

"Hi, I'm Carrie, your wardrobe stylist," she says. "You must be Larry and Ronnie."

She extends her gold-bangled hand, and Slater shakes it with a dead-fish grip. "Nice to meet you, Carrie."

Funk bows slightly. "Carrie."

It relieves Funk to finally meet someone who appears to be over the age of thirty. A confident woman with a sense of who she is and not what others expect her to be. He is not keen on being emasculated on a daily basis, but he does like strong women. Those secure in thought and mind, clear of purpose, and no *Sex and the City* searching. Maybe that's why he's tired of seeing the bored and skyward looks shot from the faces of babes.

Carrie says, "So, how can I help you guys?"

Slater flips through a rack of men's shirts. "We're looking for something for my friend here. Something other than his usual shuffleboard casual."

She laughs. "Well, you're in luck. We have all the latest designers."

"I see," Slater says. "Very cool threads. Love the ripped jeans."

Cool threads? Funk thinks. He remembers the time when you actually had to wear your jeans to gain "the look."

Funk, always one to thwart a wardrobe malfunction, steps forward with a list of his demands. "No back-to-school stuff," he says. "I don't want to look like an L.A. parent. What's more, there will be no wing collars, deep V-necks, or flight jackets. Save it for the Dierks Bentley concert. Holey jeans with embroidered back pockets are also a no-no, along with puffer vests. I'm not up for a People's Choice Award. And please, nothing tight. I don't want to look like the guy who presses ten plates at Gold's Gym." He pauses, holding a forefinger to his lips. "If I think of anything else, I'll let you know."

Slater's jaw flexes. He swallows hard and says, "That doesn't leave you with much, buddy."

Carrie nods, serious. "I got it. I know what he wants. Something age-appropriate. Modern, yet classic."

"But not too classic," Slater says.

Carrie picks through the racks. "I see him in a pair of fitted designer khakis and classic white sneakers. Stan Smith or Adidas Originals. Nothing fussy."

Fussy has never been Funk's middle name.

Funk says, "The pants are palatable. And the shirt?"

Carrie studies Funk's snow-white pate. It shines and blinds, like Rudolph's red nose in a storm. Her expression screams *Makeup!* But she says, "I'd probably stick with something neutral to match the lighter skin tone. Maybe an olive tee, a crewneck. We'll just have to see what works."

Funk nods. "I like the direction. But no graphics, stripes, studs, or tattoo themes. And if I see a gothic cross, *I'm walking.*"

"I got you," she says.

Slater's cell phone dings to announce a text. He digs into the front pocket of his size forty True Religion jeans and checks the screen. It is a message from Dungworth. The text reads: *It's a great time to be silver. Control room now.*

"Who is it?" Funk asks as Carrie holds up a black T-shirt against his chest.

"Niedermeyer," Slater says.

"Who?" Carrie says.

Slater looks crushed. His pop cultural reference has sailed a bit outside.

"The producer," Slater says. "Mr. Wonderful. The only android I know who frowns in his sleep."

Carrie smiles. "Oh, him. He can be a real doomer."

Slater laughs, but it is fake. No brain endorphins released. Funk recognizes its sociopathic form and hits Flattop with the big question. "What does the producer want? The shoot's over."

Slater thinks a moment, shrugs his shoulders. "He probably just needs my Social Security number or something…to get paid. It's nothing." Slater checks his oversized Fossil watch. The sparkly watch he bought at TJ Maxx a few weeks ago. The young saleslady at the counter, a small-town girl with big-city dreams, said it made him look "dope."

"Whoa, Funk," he says, tapping his watch crystal, "it's almost six. We gotta get ready for tonight. Why don't you finish up with Carrie while I clean things up with the production crew? Then it's time for the birthday blowout." He turns. "And, Carrie, baby, can you do me a huge favor?"

"I'll try."

"Send me up twenty pairs of the hippest jeans you've got. Room 834. Size forty, maybe a few forty-twos. Just to be on the safe side."

She nods. "On the safe side."

"Yeah. And several cool Italian shirts. I'm a 3XL. And don't kid yourself. I, unlike my drab friend here, like a lot of color. I'm not partial to sequins, but won't rule it out. Shiny, vulgar, and garrulous works for me."

"I think I can manage that," Carrie says. "Any shoes?"

Slater points at the gladiator sandals on the floor. "Those will do."

"Really?" Funk says. "The mandals?"

"I'm not wearing a toga, dude. I'm wearing jeans."

Welcome to the culling, Funk thinks.

After making a dramatic pause, Slater continues. "Like that old dude with the beard said in *Gladiator*, you gotta win the crowd before you can win the girl."

"Freedom," Funk corrects.

"That's what I said," Slater yips, grabbing the leather sandals from the shoe pile. He thanks Carrie and walks distractedly toward the door, glancing at his cell phone. "I'll meet you at your room around eight. The Funkster is about to rock."

Funk spreads his hands. "What about dinner?"

Slater puts the phone to his ear. "I'm ordering room service right now. How does triple lobster sound?"

"Drawn butter?"

"Two vats."

Funks nods in agreement, his bald head glowing like some faint, distant planet.

33

IT TAKES Slater six minutes to run from the wardrobe room, catch the elevator ten floors down to the lobby, and sprint to the control room. He enters panting, tripping over the doorsill. Out of breath and gasping for air, he leans back against the oak armoire and grips the sides of the piece like he is holding back an unruly mob.

"What did I miss?" he says, chest heaving.

"You're late," Dungworth says, nibbling on a celery stick.

"I had to make a stop."

"A leakage episode is no excuse, Mr. Slater."

"That is not my problem!"

Marty, seated at the console, points his stubby index finger at the wall of screens and says, "There he is."

Slater and Dungworth glance at the monitors as they watch Funk enter his hotel room with an armful of clothes. He carries the wardrobe garments over the threshold like he would a new bride.

Dungworth speaks into a headset. "Camera five, tight on Lopez. I want to see those pearly whites sparkle."

On the big screen, next to the image of Funk tossing his

clothes on the bed, is Lopez showering. He is shampooing his thick, lustrous black hair, massaging his scalp and working up a lather.

Dungworth turns to Slater. "The women love this guy. He's perfect bachelor material."

But Dungworth's praise for the "Latin Satin" is unexpectedly cut short when Lopez screams from the shower. "Hey, Backstreet! I'm ready to eat some hot *panocha* for dinner. What do you think? Pink tacos sound good?"

Lopez laughs and flicks his long tongue out like a snake in the low grass.

With her forefinger, Gaye, the caramel-haired challenge producer, mimes a gag as she looks at Marty. Marty nods in agreement.

Dungworth, assessing the damage, says, "Cut that remark."

Slater looks alarmed. "I thought the show was live?"

Dungworth shrugs. "Sometimes. The fact is, I edit for TV. There's a delay. Which is why we have additional focus groups for the night hunt." He smiles. "You and your boy Butt-Head are going to have to win this thing in the nightclub. Not on the basketball court."

Slater grits his teeth, nods. "It's like that?"

"Yeah," Dungworth says. "It's like that. Because tonight it's dancing and karaoke. And for some...*the tube steak boogie.*" A long, meditative pause. "Frankly, Mr. Slater, the best you could ever hope for tonight would be angry starfish sex. Good luck to you."

Slater's mouth turns down in despair. "We've reached peak dystopia."

"We have," Dungworth says. "Embrace it."

Marty shouts from his workstation. "Hey, you gotta see this!"

Dungworth and Slater look up, staring at the main monitor.

They stand spellbound, watching the image of a human mouth opening and closing—gasping for air.

Slater is gobsmacked. "Oh no. No, you don't."

"What's happening?" Dungworth says.

Slater drops his head, humbled. "Facial exercises."

"What?"

"Funk believes he can tighten his facial skin naturally. It's an organic face-lift, if you will." Slater shrugs. "He's not one to go under the knife."

Dungworth into a walkie-talkie: "Gimme a wide shot on the mouth."

The camera pulls back to reveal a shirtless Funk standing in front of the bathroom mirror, contorting and stretching his face and neck muscles like a man under a curse. He holds each facial pose for five counts, then repeats the process. The control room sits mesmerized, frozen, watching Funk stick his tongue out at his reflection and roll his eyes back into his head.

"He looks like a demon reptile from Madagascar," Dungworth says.

"Does it work?" Marty asks Slater.

"He swears by it."

"Coulda fooled me," Dungworth says. "How long does Happy Cheeks go on?"

"Three sets of eight each," Slater says. "Followed by smile crunches, jaw presses, and face curls."

"Oh, he likes face curls, does he?" Dungworth turns. "Marty, let the focus groups see this. I'm sure the ladies will be thrilled."

Slater throws up his arms. "Oh, come on! You cut Lopez and his ugly remarks."

Dungworth removes his black Buddy Holly glasses and casually wipes the lenses with the tail of his blue Oxford shirt. "I'll be honest with you, Mr. Slater. I find you extremely cringey and inauthentic. A dead meme walking. And watching you and your curved meat stick smashing the lifeblood out of that poor little streetwalker yesterday was beyond traumatizing. I'm not sure I'll ever get over it." He pauses. "Point-blank, and I take no pleasure in saying this, it was like watching someone trying to stuff a marshmallow into the tiny slot of a piggy bank."

Slater's face darkens. "Yikes."

"A big yikes, Mr. Slater. But, be that as it may, I want you and Mr. Funk in theater at eight. I suggest you get ready for the big night out. And if at all possible, dress to impress."

Slater pauses, glancing at the crew members at their workstations. After a long moment, he meets Dungworth's diagnostic gaze and says brashly, "At the stroke of midnight, you're going to see that green bar rise high above red. *I guarantee it.* And all of your sinister manipulation will be for naught."

Dungworth spins and walks bandy-legged down the galley. "Just get me that image release signed, you senile delinquent."

Slater points a stiff finger at Dungworth's back. "We're going to win this thing—you watch. Because tonight, Funk goes deep—*deep into the danger zone.*"

And without another word, Slater turns on his heels and rushes out the door.

Dungworth stops and rubs his chin, thinking out loud. "The danger zone? Huh. I like it." He looks to Marty. "*Top Gun.* Cue the music."

"'Danger Zone'?" Marty asks. "Are you sure? I mean, that's like a major fondue party. Serious cheese."

"Just do it, Marty."

The high-sounding, melodramatic music of Kenny Loggins plays over the control room's sound system. In a series of shots, accompanied by the iconic eighties song, Dungworth and the crew watch Funk and Lopez get ready for the big night out. Watch the action unfold on the main monitor.

These images fill the big screen:

• Funk's facial exercises, his mouth opening and closing like a dying fish on a dry lakebed.

• Lopez shadowboxing in his tight white underwear. *Is this the best a man can get?*

• The men and women's focus groups watching the activity in their hotel suites. Hands and fingers voting, punching buttons —the red bar graph rising high above green.

• Funk wiggling into a pair of slim khaki pants on the bed, grimacing as he struggles to button the fly.

• Lopez slipping on a cream-colored suit, and meticulously jelling his perfect jet-black hair into a classic slick-backed look. *Well, hello there, handsome.*

And finally—

• A wistful-looking Funk, rubbing his bald head in the mirror. *Who is this unmasked man?*

Dungworth, in his director's chair, shouts to the crew, "This is it, people! The big night out! Split screen! Split screen!"

On the monitor, Funk and Slater, Lopez and Backstreet stride toward each other in slow motion like gunfighters in a spaghetti western.

Warriors prepared for battle.

Ancient myths and tragic heroes.

"Big Tits and a Bottle of Wine" author versus handsome fan favorite.

In blocky red font, *GAME OR NO GAME?* is superimposed over their larger-than-life images.

Ready or not. (And Funk is definitely *not* ready.)

It's showtime.

34

EIGHT P.M.

Saturday night.

Do you know where your children are?

The warm, star-studded L.A. dark has put Funk into an introspective mood. Now just four hours shy of fifty, he walks the moonlit hotel grounds with Slater in tow. They are en route to the Skybar lounge—the Mondrian Hotel's glamorous ivy-covered rooftop bar. This small hut-shaped structure has been, and still is, one of the most celebrated nightspots in the city. It is exclusive, trendy, and well stocked with A-list celebrities. As one Google reviewer put it, "It's true Hollywood essence." If you don't know who you are, Funk thinks, this is the kind of place that will be happy to tell you.

Plowing ahead, they pass walls of concrete and glass, the illuminated pool, and plush white loungers on the terraced wood deck. The footpath is lined with exotic flowers, and candle lanterns hang from the boughs of trees, flickering like fireflies.

As he walks through the lush tropical landscape, Funk wonders if his best days are behind him. He is a rambling man, and rambling men are clearly out of fashion. Will he ever have a hit song that reaches the top of the iTunes chart? Probably not. Maybe at this stage of his life, the key to happiness is low expectations.

Any chart will do.

When he was young, before he knew about the harsh realities of stringing the long zither, he often thought about Angie at school, and how she once told him that she liked his boy scent. That masculine concoction of Suave shampoo, third-period PE, and one-dollar gasoline. (His lawn mowing business finally paying extra dividends.)

Now, he imagines the two of them together again onstage, playing to a sold-out crowd. He on lead, and she on his hip shredding the bass. The mere thought of it stirs his inmost desires.

What am I doing here? he thinks.

I have to see her tonight.

And so he will.

Funk has decided that he will have one beer with Slater, humor him, and then mosey up the street to the Whisky a Go Go and see Angie's band play. He will watch her jam, drenched in violet light, marveling at her long, supple fingers strangling the chords of an ivory-white Fender Telecaster.

Yeah, that's the ticket.

That's how a fifty-year-old man rolls.

Funk's glance falls to Slater's man sandals, his hairy ankles. "All hail Caesar," he says.

Slater stops on the pool deck, arms akimbo. "That's the difference between you and me," he says. "I take chances. You ought to try it sometime. Besides, these sandals are on trend. Versace runway next season."

"Yeah? What's the excuse for the aloha shirt?"

Slater, defensive. "No excuse. Just pure fire."

"And the tight pants?"

"Ready for the horizontal hula."

Funk stares at Slater's ill-conceived outfit and shakes his head. Along with the kooky gladiator mandals, Slater is ridiculously attired in a gaudy oversized *Magnum, P.I.* "jungle bird" shirt and a pair of skintight blue jeans. All compliments of wardrobe and their dark imaginings. At first glance, Slater's slim pencil pants and pipe-stem legs set off his fat abdomen, stretching his tropical plumed shirt to full duty. His gray flattop makes his head look smaller than it is, so it kind of floats on his shoulders, like a ping-pong ball on the ocean. His entire being gives Funk the impression of a Mardi Gras beetle walking upright on Fat Tuesday. A drunk beetle at that.

Slater says, "I'll have you know this shirt is an exact replica of the one Tom Selleck wore in the TV show."

"I understand, but you don't have the body of Tom Selleck. You look like the murder victim in a Hawaiian cozy."

"I was going for hot lava hipster. Lots of attention."

Funk looks him up and down. "Oh, you'll get lots of attention. Just not what you're hoping for."

"It's just a blooming shirt!"

"Maybe," Funk says, "but as you so eloquently stated earlier, these young people see things differently. Just sayin'."

The floral bird shirt is a classic, Funk knows, and the original hangs proudly in the Smithsonian's National Museum of American History. *But for how long?* According to what Funk recently read, only two kinds of men still rock the hibiscus print. Big fat party animals, and loony conspiracy theorists.

As is often the case, Slater fits the profile on both accounts.

"This is not a midlife crisis, Tommy Bahama," Slater says. "It's a *Gucci* shirt. Any hot chick will know that."

Funk pauses, sighs. "At least you didn't wear socks with the sandals. I'll give you that."

Slater takes a step forward and pats Funk on the back. "Don't overthink things. I'm wearing the shirt. But what about you? *How are you feeling?*"

Funk nods. "All things considered, not too shabby."

Thanks to Carrie the stylist, Funk feels and looks as good as any bald man of fifty could. Wearing a pair of slim khakis (but not package huggers), a classic pair of white Stan Smith Adidas tennis shoes, and a dark gray Foghat "Fool for the City" T-shirt, he is comfortable in his own skin. Everything breathes. He knows that he has broken his own cardinal rule regarding the shirt graphics. But he can live with it.

It's Foghat.

Yet there is still something about the evening that doesn't feel right. It weighs heavy and seems to sit on him.

Slater says, "We both look great, okay? Different strokes for different folks. Now, I want you to focus on having fun. Just for tonight, I want you to stop thinking up here." Slater points at Funk's head. "And start feeling down there." Now pointing at Funk's groin. "It's time to let your boner be your master."

"Who said that?"

"I dunno. I think it was Bruce Lee. Anyway, forget uptown. Tonight you're going *downtown.*"

Funk nods. He is hungry again. Thinking about the octopus salad.

"Don't brocrastinate on this," Slater says. "I don't need any half senders on this mission. It's all or nothing. You got it?"

Funk blinks, willing to let Slater think what he wants.

"Good," Slater says. "But first, a couple of things before we storm the beach. I want to pass along a piece of advice that a lesbian friend once gave me. She said that when you go down on a woman, you lick like a lollipop, then lap like a dog. You do that, and I see a lot of clam digging in your future."

"Oh, you do?"

"Yeah. Let the dick want what it wants."

"What's that?"

"Freshness."

"Jesus Christ, Slater."

Funk hasn't been out on the town in years, but here he is, returning to the heat of the night with a flatulent heathen in Italian clothes.

At last, they land at the red velvet rope, the entrance to the Skybar. The young and attractive spring break set begins to arrive as Funk slouches toward the back of the line. He watches the fashionable elite enter the venue: the women in heels and bright sundresses, and the men suited up with gold chains and expensive sneakers. There is a frantic, expectant energy in the air now, and one that is unique only to Hollywood. If one is highly attuned, Funk thinks, they can almost hear the dreams of stardom crackling.

As the rest of the youngsters jostle for a place in line, Funk stares at a slender person with short white hair wearing a black caftan. He is not sure if it is a man or a woman. It is androgynous, mysterious, akin to Pat on SNL. Fortunately, it doesn't bother him. He's all for bathroom choice.

But is it wrong to sneak a peek?

Slater elbows Funk. "Here they come."

"Who?" Funk says.

Slater points. Funk glances over his shoulder and sees Lopez and Backstreet exiting a poolside cabana, heading their way. In a slim-fitting vanilla-colored suit, Lopez looks confident, his dark hair swept back and still buffed for his age. Conversely, Backstreet appears to be another victim of the wardrobe department. He mirrors Al Capone's bagman in a black double-breasted pinstripe blazer, wide-leg gray pants, and a scuffed pair of black-and-white two-tone shoes.

Last Funk heard, Prohibition ended in 1933.

Lopez stops and eyes Slater. "I'm impressed, wingman. I didn't think you'd show."

"Oh, yeah, Phil?" Slater says. "Why's that?"

"Because I didn't think a couch captain of your age could get it out of the holster anymore."

Backstreet laughs.

Unfazed, Slater gives it back. "Dream on, weak stream."

Lopez nods, as if the entire weight of the macho world rests on his broad shoulders. "Dreams are for losers, pigeon chest." He points at Slater's unbuttoned Hawaiian shirt, his bouncy man breasts. "I see you're showing some cleavage tonight."

Oh yeah, he is.

"Just more to love," Slater says, volleying at the net.

Lopez flashes a kingly smile. "Let it go, bruh. There comes a time in every man's life when he has to settle for the bronze. Me, I'm a high-value man. You, you're on Tinder." He places a hand on his sidekick's shoulder. "Let's bounce, Backstreet. It's game time. I gotta get paid."

Funk secretly wishes that a falling palm frond would lance the coconut of Phil Lopez. Split it in half with one clean shot. He finds this juvenile exchange between Slater and these two men crass, the discourse of spoiled children. Having to deal with all this chronic narcissism has worn him out.

Soon, it will be time to bail.

Funk and Slater watch Lopez and Backstreet approach the large black doorman guarding the Skybar entrance. Backstreet shakes the large man's hand, street-style.

The doorman says, "What's up, my brother?"

Backstreet says, "Oh, you know, you know. It's all good. My boy here's ready to get his party on."

"I'm down with that," the doorman says. "Have a good one." He smiles and lifts the red velvet rope.

Funk watches Lopez and Backstreet climb the wooden

steps to the ivy-covered venue. Backstreet enters the open-air pavilion, but Lopez pauses on the last step. Standing tall above the crowd, he smiles and waves to the Laurel Canyon beau monde with the same enthusiasm as a politician boarding a plane.

More like snakes on a plane, Funk thinks.

"C'mon," Slater says. "We're at the rope. This is it. It's time to bring the A game."

Funk pumps a fist and mumbles, "Same-day shipping."

They approach the beefy doorman.

"This is a private party, gentlemen," the doorman says. "If you're not on the list, I can't let you in."

Slater sneers and flashes his room key like it's a police badge.

"Sorry," the doorman says. "The flattop threw me."

"It throws me," Slater says.

The gentle-giant doorman unhooks the red velvet rope, and they walk up the steps into the bar.

The moment Funk sees the youthful crowd, he thinks of FIFO—the first in, first out method. It is an accounting inventory valuation tool that he uses for all of his social functions. It works like this: You show up early to a party that you don't want to be at, schmooze the host you don't want to see, then slip out the back door an hour later before anyone notices. It works wonders. At first it disappoints the aggrieved host that you left, but later they are just happy that you showed. *He is a man about town, you know. He had other engagements.*

There has always been a method to his madness.

Funk and Slater head for the bar, shouldering through a packed house. The dark and intimate lounge is filled with beautiful, leggy people less than half their age, drinking, boasting, and moving to disco music. All around them there is laughter and humor, but little humility.

One tall young man dressed in a charcoal suit and a straw fedora hat yells drunkenly over the music, "This place is too lit!"

Too lit? Funks thinks. More like a thirst trap. *Did you see the poseurs by the pool?*

"It looks like a Forever 21 party in here," Funk says.

Slater shrugs. "It's this or the sea bass crowd at the restaurant."

Funk sighs and says longingly, "I like sea bass."

"Focus," Slater says. "You're a vagitarian now." He grabs Funk's shoulders, spins him around, and they belly up to the bar. Funk sees a TV in the corner, showing a college basketball game. Michigan is playing Houston, and some guy behind him wants to know the score. Don't we all, Funk thinks.

Welcome to March Madness.

"I want you to stop feeling old," Slater says. "It's time to reprogram yourself. Unleash the animal spirits." Slater points at a frisky young couple necking on the plush banquette seating along the wall. "Like my man over there."

"The kraken?"

"That's it, buddy. Release it. So what do you say we turn back the clock and see if you can convince these young ladies that you are pro surfer Kelly Slater. I'll be your crazy uncle. You think you can pull that off?"

"Pull that off?" Funk says. "Let me see, when was the last time I got barreled at Pipeline?" He thinks a moment. "Oh, now I remember. *Never!*" He shakes his head. "Pull that off. Just get me a beer."

"Okay. Okay, tough guy. What do you want?"

Funk cracks his neck. "Kelly Slater will have Heineken, please."

"That's the spirit."

Slater waves at the black-haired bartender. The stoic young

man, rocking a samurai topknot, steps forward and raises his chin. As if this implies, "What can I get you?"

"Two Heinekens, please," Slater says, almost shouting.

The detached bartender half nods and pulls two sweaty green bottles from the fridge. He opens them with flair, flips the caps into the trash, and slides them over. Slater grabs the brews and gives one to Funk. Their drinks in hand, they lean back against the bar and marvel at the beautiful and the damned.

"Look at all this tender Virginia ham," Slater says in awe.

But Funk is looking beyond the "ham." He makes a sour face and stares at a long silver-haired woman in Capri pants and ballerina flats pulling back the white silk curtains from the tall rectangular windows like she is unveiling an artist's master-piece. When the curtains are fully drawn and the picture windows are open, the city lights of Los Angeles are revealed. In the darkness, the lights twinkle with promise and mystique.

L.A. in full, Funk thinks.

The right time of the night.

He shifts his eyes and steals a glance at a gorgeous cream-soda blonde, her wavy hair shining like fool's gold under the grainy light. He sips his beer casually, thoughtfully, like he always does, waiting for something to happen.

Patience has its own reward.

Slater says, "See anything you like?"

"I have," Funk says, beer bottle perched at his lips, "but she's not in here." Funk aims the bottle at Lopez. "Looks like your buddy has, though."

An anxious Slater turns his head and sees Lopez and Back-street entertaining a group of three young ladies in the far corner of the room. They are lounging on the plush yellow banquettes, and their small table holds three bottles of wine: one red and two whites. The young women clutch their glasses with both hands, wholly absorbed in the conversation as the handsome Lopez gesticulates wildly.

Slater whispers under his breath, "Shit, the guy's already got bottle service."

"What was that?" Funk says, watching Lopez reach for a bottle of German Riesling.

"Nothing," Slater says.

Glutted laughter rises from the table as Lopez refills everyone's glass. At that exact moment, just as Lopez sets the wine bottle down, he looks up and catches Slater's eye. In a toast, he raises his glass and winks.

It's clown time in modern Babylon.

Slater nudges Funk with a disturbed look on his face. "Hotties behind you," he says. "Six o'clock. Go talk to them." He nods in the direction of two young women. "Time is running out."

"Maybe for you," Funk says. "But I've got all the time in the world."

Which he doesn't. He just says it to annoy Slater. Any little thing will set him off these days.

Slater leans his elbows on the bar and begs, "For me, Larry? Would you do it for me?"

"Do it for you? For the same guy who got pepper-sprayed at the Oscars?"

"I thought I knew her! Come on, just go talk to them."

Funk ruminates over the song that Slater sang into the phone the other day: Neil Young's "Old Man." Perhaps a little brush-up with the opposite sex is just what he needs. So he obeys Slater's command like he would any director on set and throws a lazy smile at a chestnut-haired woman in a shapeless black dress. She sucks in her cheeks and quickly looks away.

"She's not interested," Funk says, turning around. "It must be the crystal ball on my shoulders."

"She's just shy. Go on. *Talk to her.*"

Funk slowly turns his bald head and smiles again at the chestnut-haired lady. "Hey, how's it goin'?"

The woman looks at her friends and rolls her black agate eyes. She says coldly, "Dude. I'm not here to date my dad. I'm a senior in college."

Funk smiles like a weary harem guard and spins around. He doesn't blame the young woman for the harsh delivery. He doesn't want to date her dad either.

Slater watches the girls grab their drinks off the bar and walk off, laughing. He draws a long breath and says with an incredulous tone, "*Hey, how's it going? Really? Is that what it's come down to?*"

Evidently, Funk thinks.

It used to work. But times change. It turns out that rock stars are mortal, just like the rest of us. In the end, he's nothing more than a commoner, another bald old fogey who likes sea bass.

And five-dollar footlongs.

Funk says, "Seriously, what do you want me to say to a woman thirty years my junior? *I'm thinking about shorting crypto. What do you think?* C'mon. Get real." Funk sips his beer. "Just let the night happen."

"No, no," Slater says edgily. "You are going to make something happen. You are going to mark your territory and attract a mate. *Don't think, just do.* With these young chicks, you gotta get nutty. Make them laugh."

Slater points out a duck-lipped woman in a tight cobalt-blue dress at the end of the bar. She has long platinum hair, dark eyebrows, and wears vampy red lipstick. She stares down at her glowing phone, swiping at it, her huge store-bought breasts blocking half the television screen.

"Look at cartoon-tits over there," Slater says. "She's got that thousand-cock stare. I bet she's got serious throat game. You can see she's down for it. Full Goblin mode."

"She's looking at her phone, Slater."

"That's what she wants you to think. The key is to entertain her. Wipe that fuzzy frown off her face. Here, watch me. Watch game in action."

Why bother? Funk thinks. She looks like a porn star. A pro that works the pole at the local gentlemen's club. She might be a wonderful human, but she is not a woman you would bring home to Mom. Even at this young age, her face is cheap and apathetic, a darkened portrait well beyond the romp. But to each his own, he reckons. His eyes follow Slater's movement as he pushes his way through the inebriated crowd and squares up on the artificially large-bosomed woman standing at the end of the bar.

Slater says with intensity, a little too much volume, "Hey, baby. You playing Pokémon?"

She doesn't look up from her phone.

"I don't play Pokémon," she says gloomily.

"You want to learn?"

She looks up and tries to speak, but her words catch in her throat. Her dull face now wears the expression of a silent scream. And after a long moment of waving a frantic hand in front of her frightened face, she finally calls out, "Maggie! Maggie! Safe space! Help!"

To Slater's amazement, another young woman in a plus-sized yellow dress muscles her way through the crowd like a linebacker after a fumble. She has big arms and legs and an aggressive oval face that is focused and taut. When Yellow Dress ultimately reaches her bodacious friend, she hugs her and asks what's wrong. The friend points hysterically at Slater's loud tropical shirt, grunting in horror.

Yellow Dress turns to Slater. "Oh my gawd! You're triggering her."

"What?" Slater says. "I just asked her if she was playing Pokémon."

He casually pops a Tic Tac and shrugs.

Yellow Dress gently strokes the platinum hair of her weepy friend and says to Slater, "It's your Hawaiian shirt. It reeks of white privilege and colonialism."

"It can't be the shirt," Slater says. "This is pure flora fuego."

"It's hideous, and culturally insensitive."

"Is there any room for nuance?"

"No! You are too old to be talking to her. You are a fat predator with a fuzz cut. Some pervy silverback out on patrol."

"I don't see—"

"You will see," says Yellow Dress, clutching her friend tightly. "You will see very soon. Because the movement is happening. It's real, and it's coming for bottom-slappers like you."

"What are you talking about?" Slater says.

"Just leave, creep. Leave our safe space."

"What?"

"Stranger danger! Stranger danger! Help!"

The big black doorman quickly arrives on scene. He says to Slater, "You're harassing people, sir." He grabs Slater's right arm, squeezes it like he is popping a teenage pimple, and "escorts" him across the open hut.

"We were having a consensual conversation," Slater says over his shoulder. "I swear to God, I didn't touch her sandbox."

The doorman deposits Slater at the other end of the bar, right next to Funk. "Don't be a jerk," the doorman says. He points with a stiff finger. "You're on notice."

Slater raises both hands, making the surrender gesture. The doorman gives him one last look and walks away.

Lopez and Backstreet are laughing at him from across the room. Both have slinky women in their arms, confident of the night's ROI.

Funk glances over at Slater with a flat, interchangeable look. Says out of the corner of his mouth, "So how'd the shirt work out?"

"*Fuck her.* That crick-necked bitch. She's a bunny boiler, that one."

"And you're convinced of that?"

Slater pounds his fist on the bar top. "Stop cock-blocking my amplification!"

35

IN THE DARKENED CONTROL ROOM, the crew watches a sweaty and heavy-handed Slater lecture Funk on the fine art of seducing young women in a bar. The fine art of eating overripe minge.

Appalled by the lecture, Marty swivels in his high-backed workstation chair and says, "That bird-shirt dude looks like the stockroom troll at Trader Joe's. Not only that, he suffers from a serious case of OCD. Obsessive creepy disorder."

Dungworth, now sitting on an orthopedic donut cushion in his director's chair, bares his teeth and says, "He's a dirt age savage, Marty."

"You can add smug to the list," Marty says.

Dungworth nods and speaks a series of commands into a headset. "I need those time code burn-ins, people...and give me another establishing shot. An OTF with Lopez." He pauses. "Roll 81...fade up. Fade up, dammit!"

Dungworth throws his headset down in disgust. "*Shit.* Somebody get that scoundrel Slater on the phone. It's time to send in the cavalry. Bring in the reinforcements. There must be somebody that can kick that lackadaisical Funk into gear." He looks at Marty moon-eyed, unmanned, like they are taking heavy fire in a foxhole. "*Marty*, send in one of the actors."

"Who?" Marty says.

"I dunno," Dungworth says, his voice hoarse and hangry. "But we need a hero. Someone raw and unfiltered. Someone cool."

Marty holds up a headshot. "What about Bobby James Bond?"

"The ass-pincher? No way. That backdoor cuddler almost got us sued on the last shoot. Forget Edward Forty Hands. What I need is somebody larger than life, somebody strong and sexual that makes it look easy."

Gaye, the challenge producer, stands up from her workstation and removes her gray pinstriped blazer, placing it on the back of her chair. "What about Donnie Williams?"

"Who?" Dungworth asks.

"They call him the Nighthawk. Donnie 'Nighthawk' Williams. He does a lot of those dating shows and was a runner-up on *Big Brother*. I've seen him perform. He's smooth with the women, but he's also very direct."

Dungworth shifts his rear end on the hemorrhoid cushion. "Smooth we need," he says. "Direct we *definitely* need."

Gaye nods. "Then he's our man?"

Dungworth grimaces, trying hard to get comfortable on the inflatable donut. "Yeah," he bleats. "Send him in."

36

FUNK and Slater chill at the bar.

The action swirls around them. As if one big word salad, the loud conversations are jumbled and tossed.

In their line of view, a pretentious young man in a gaucho hat chats with a starry-eyed girl about his California ambitions. He tells her that he specializes in chicken-wire topiary. Bird shapes, mostly. The occasional unicorn. Enthralled, she smiles and shows her crooked teeth, hanging on his every word.

Oh, the trappings of minor league success, Funk thinks.

Slater's cell phone rings. He fishes it from his pants pocket and checks the number. "Sweet mother of Jesus," he says. "It's the producer again. Captain Fantastic. I'll be back in a minute."

"For a show that's already wrapped," Funk says, "you seem to do a lot of work."

Slater wipes the sweat off his forehead. He is all damp fat. "Tell me about it," he says. "But I gotta eat."

Funk nods. He can't argue with that.

As Slater heads for the back door, Funk bobs his head to the sounds of yesteryear. The instrumental tune on the sound system is familiar. Herb Alpert and the Tijuana Brass performing

"Spanish Flea," the theme song from *The Dating Game*. It is the perfect choice of music, he believes. Even better than listening to some twit in a gaucho hat humming "Midnight at the Oasis."

Funk thinks back to when he was nineteen and his manager told him they wanted the band on the show. After a brief huddle, Purple Onion politely passed, but Funk always regretted not hearing the genial host Jim Lange introduce him as one of *The Dating Game*'s eligible bachelors: *"Bachelor number three is a free spirit and music is his bag. He's a rock and roll star who enjoys making whoopee in the back seat of a Ford Pinto and is famous for penning songs like 'Dune Buggy Horizontal' and the wildly popular 'She Shot My Wad in San Francisco.' Please welcome..."*

Smiling, Funk taps his foot to the trumpet-heavy song and imagines large thought bubbles hovering above the crowd. Most are filled with huge question marks.

His included.

A handsome black man in a steel-gray fedora has just sidled up next to Funk at the bar. The man is tall and slim, yet strong like an NFL quarterback. He wears a three-quarter-length brown rocker jacket over a white V-neck T-shirt and a peacock's feather in his hat.

The stone-faced man does not order a drink; he just stands with his back to the bar and stares out into the crowd.

Funk glances over, thinking the man is one strikingly cool character.

Soon after, a young bald guy with a five-o'clock shadow approaches. He points to the man with the gray fedora and says, *"Dude,* I know you. You're Nighthawk Williams."

Nighthawk tips his cap. "I am."

The bald guy nods and says enthusiastically, *"I knew it.* Nice to meet you, man. I'm Harold. I for sure thought you were going to win season twenty of *The Bachelorette*. You were my girlfriend's favorite."

Nighthawk smiles. "I appreciate you."

Funk watches the two men execute the homie handshake, and watches the young bald guy disappear into the crowd.

Nighthawk, still staring straight ahead like a spy in a Cold War film, finally says in a deep baritone, "Instead of drinking, you should be out chasing some of these beautiful ladies."

Funk looks over. "You talking to me?"

Nighthawk nods yes.

"I don't recall asking a stranger how to hunt," Funk says.

"Maybe so," Nighthawk says. "But drinkin' and thinkin' ain't gonna serve the love piston. It's time to represent."

Funk smiles. "I'm not here to represent. Some of us are just comfortable hanging out on the margins."

"That's white boy speak for no play."

His concentrated look makes Funk squirm.

"Perhaps," Funk says. "But that's not always such a bad thing."

"Shoot," Nighthawk says, laughing, "what we got here is a reluctant playboy."

True. Funk has never had to slip anyone the Cosby or chase anybody around the room in a bathrobe. He is way too lazy for that.

"I see now why you're losing," Nighthawk says.

Funk cocks his head. "Losing?"

"My man. It's time you channeled your inner Hugh Hefner. Love him or loathe him, he lived the life he wanted. Few people can say that. Liberator or exploiter? The debate will rage on, but he definitely had play."

"And you've got play?"

"Always," Nighthawk says. "I'm an exotic—a fantasy fuck.

Black poles for white holes. Eventually, all women want a taste of the mahogany bone. You feel me?"

Funk shrugs.

The lack of urgency forces Nighthawk to turn up the heat, get in Funk's grill. "What I'm saying is, you gotta be the *exotic*, brother. Because a bald man like you ain't got no game with these young white women. Not unless you're famous." He pauses. "Well, almost famous."

"Point, please."

Nighthawk leans in. "Brother, I'm going to give it to you real. These white women want hair. And lots of it. And that's something you ain't got. But now the sisters, and the Latinas, they don't give a mind about hair." He points. "There's your play."

Funk sips his beer without concern. You don't have to tell him he's not first choice. Life had long since robbed him of his pretty privilege. "You're probably right," he says. "Thanks for the tip."

"Ain't no thing," Nighthawk says.

Funk stands silently and clears his throat. After a long moment, he says, half-curious, "Any more tips? Last words of wisdom before we depart?"

Nighthawk grabs the lapels of his rocker jacket and says, "Look, bruh, I ain't your magical black man here to save the day. They ain't paying me enough to move your needle. But I'll leave you with this. Once you hit fifty, you gotta go Third World. *Peace out.*"

Mic drop.

Funk watches the suave man coolly dance his way into the revolving crowd, arms raised high above his head, his athletic body swaying to the rhythm of the music. He certainly is one cool dude, Funk thinks, but what was he trying to tell him?

Losing?

Move his needle?

They ain't paying me enough?

And how did the man know he is turning fifty? Slater better not be throwing him a surprise birthday party. Just when he was feeling comfortable with the night, he feels the obligations mount.

He understands what the black dude was trying to say about the ladies, though. He's like a pretty white woman on *Soul Train* who can't dance. And when you can't dance, you get zero camera time. *None.* Not even a chance to shine in the "Soul Train Line." At best, one could only hope to be part of the Scramble Board.

Funk shakes his head at the incongruity of it all. Has he just tired of L.A.? Or has L.A. tired of him? No matter, he thinks. It's time to make a move.

FIFO on out of here.

As if on cue, Slater returns in a flop sweat, his aloha shirt sticking to his big torso. "What the hell are you still doing at the bar?" he says. "You gotta mingle."

"I'm just chillin'," Funk says. "Like I always do. Besides, I've been around long enough to know who's interested and who's not."

"Apparently, it's more of a who's not. So no more chilling. We don't have time."

"Relax, Slater. Do a Jell-O shot."

"All I'm saying is you're a bald man now."

"Which means?"

"Which means you're no longer dessert. You're an acquired taste."

Funk, sarcastic: "Heavy seeds of encouragement."

"Hey, somebody's got to welcome you back."

"Welcome me back to what?"

"To the life you used to have."

"I don't want the life I used to have. Simple suits me fine now."

Funk has been told that if you don't stay in touch with your fans today, they will forget you. But did anybody ever stop and think that's what he wants? And since when did an artist ever need to appease his fans? Loyal fans will always stick by you. Because true fans, he knows, appreciate what you did for them yesterday. Not what you can do for them tomorrow.

The DJ suddenly screams over the sound system, "*Spring break! Spring break! Yo, yo, check it out! It's old-school all night long. And for those who like to dance, it's time to get your fever on! Time to get outside on the dance floor and party, people!*"

While the lithe crowd exits the rooftop bar, the Bee Gees song "More Than a Woman" blares out into the night as they make their way down the steps and out into the garden oasis. The late-winter evening is warm and still, the sky the color of dark denim. The mobile DJ has set up poolside on the teak deck, and the trees have become deep red from the stage lights.

Funk and Slater join the outdoor party. Standing near a cabana, they cool themselves next to a large pedestal fan, watching the smart set crowd the dance floor. Funk likes the Bee Gees tune, but he prefers the Tavares cover. That's another thing about getting old, he thinks. You don't get to DJ anymore.

Funk sniffs the air and checks the vibe. The seventy-nine-degree night smells of men's aftershave, skunky weed, and tainted love.

Just as it should.

Slater says, "You got your blue suede shoes ready?"

"I'm debating," Funk says, missing his father's orthopedic trainers. "My feet hurt."

Slater can't hear him over the din of music and leans in. "What's that?"

Funk shouts, "My feet hurt!"

It dawns on him now that his voice was too loud. *Way too loud.* He looks around, ready to do damage control. But none is needed. All eyes are pinned on Lopez and Backstreet, twirling their partners on the dance floor.

It's *Saturday Night Fever* and the Latinos rule.

Slater taps his watch face and says, "It's almost ten. You turn fifty at midnight. That means you've got two hours left with these young women. If you want to turn into an old man at midnight, that's up to you. But you will not get many chances like this again. It's all about access with this tight tail. Think smash and grab. *Smash and grab.*"

Funk lowers his head and studies the tops of his shoes. "Like, two ships passing in the night?"

"Yeah, buddy, because once you turn fifty you're going to have to lie about your age. At the very outside, you're a perpetual forty-five and holding. Stuck somewhere between Lieutenant Dan and the Priceline Negotiator." Slater pauses. "My advice is to keep the old photo on LinkedIn as long as possible."

"I'm not on LinkedIn."

"Then think of your age like a casting call. One day you're the leading man. Then the next thing you know the only part available is the crazy high school janitor. I know, it's happened to me."

"But you've always been the crazy high school janitor."

Slater nods. "My point exactly."

Funk shakes his head and peers out at the young women gyrating on the dance floor, their round asses as tight as jawbreakers. He's eaten this hard candy many times before, he thinks. *Many times.* But what he wants now is something soft inside, something more mature in the middle. He has only been with one older woman in his entire life. She was sixty-one. He was twenty-five.

The dark-headed beauty had picked him up at a restaurant on La Cienega, Alzado's if memory serves. Back at her place in Beverly Hills adjacent, in her fanciful wrought-iron bed, he had peeled off her black stockings with his teeth, licked the varicose veins on her leg, and worked his tongue up somewhere it had never been before. Like some ancient temple, the mystical experience had meaning and substance, something beefy to chew on. But later, after the rolling thunder in bed, she told him that she was the wife of a famous TV actor. This upset him greatly. It was never his intention to sleep with another man's wife. He never had to.

Poaching is not his style.

So, like a summer-school fling, it would end there—with a guilty bullet and a doleful goodbye. As for her, she would be out again the following night, her fake breasts as hard as day-old bread.

Now, in the spotlight, Lopez and his long-waisted lady friend are all alone on the dance floor. As the bass-heavy music blasts from the Peavey speakers, Lopez charms the creatures of the night with his disco moves. The young crowd claps and whistles as he slings his white linen blazer out into the pool, followed quickly by his T-shirt. Lopez is bare-chested now, his sweaty six-pack rippling in the moonlight like an oiled-up Tongan.

Funk is unimpressed. There is no way on earth he is turning fifty here. *No way.* It's time to improvise the melody and go off the page. He turns to Slater and says, "I gotta take a piss."

"What? And leave me here with the Menendez brothers?"

"I'll be right back."

"All right," Slater says. "But don't take too long. We've got karaoke coming up. That's your strong suit."

Funk looks off, lets it hang a moment. "Whatever you say, coach."

37

INSIDE THE CONTROL ROOM, Dungworth and the crew watch Funk exit the bathroom, look both ways, and walk toward the hotel lobby.

"What's he doing?" Dungworth says. "Is he leaving?"

"Either that," Marty says, "or looking for love in all the right places."

"I thought it was *wrong* places."

"Maybe for you," Marty says.

Dungworth is quaking in his Birkenstocks. Cold panic sets in. Tapping his knee with a No. 2 pencil, he swings his head and yells, "Where's my challenge producer? Gaye! Gaye!"

Gaye rises from her workstation and speed walks across the room. "Right here," she says, waving.

Dungworth, doubled over in his director's chair, winces from the pain in his gastrointestinal tract. He looks up at the score and sees the green bar graph is barely a quarter of red. It's not significant, but it is alarming. Gaye now stands at his side, waiting for direction.

"What's up?" she says.

"Get Slater on the line. Do it now."

She desperately dials her cell phone, pauses, and shakes her head. "Voice mail."

"*I knew it*," Dungworth says. "The old git is hard of hearing. Just like everything else in his despicable life, he probably cheated on the online hearing test. But that's what you get when you employ geezers. No wonder VH1 is a shell of its former self."

Gaye says, "You want me to try Mr. Slater again?"

"No," Dungworth says. "Get Backstreet on the horn. It's time that hobbit earned his pay."

38

SLATER, hopelessly seeking a wayback machine, ducks behind a palm tree and pops a Valium. Hastily, he washes it down with a Stella beer and pitches the empty bottle into the landscaped flowerbed. *Steady as she goes, big guy. You will not lose the house.*

All he needs now is a Funk miracle. More importantly, he needs that release signed—and pronto. Without that, even the loser's check will be lost.

You dig?

Honestly, how can you lead a Funk to water if he doesn't want to drink? It's crazy.

Slater wipes the sweatstache off his upper lip and slyly peeks around the trunk of a palm tree. The spring break party rages on. In his line of sight, a shirtless Lopez twerks to the sounds of Abba, while Backstreet plays a sloppy game of beer pong with a sunburned coed in a polka-dot bikini.

Jesus, he thinks. It's *Night of the Living Douche.* If his friends could see him now. From the Governor's Ball to the Backstreet.

Slater's insides are wobbling like a Jamaican bobsled. His

hands tremble as laser beam lights from the karaoke stage rake fingers of color across his squirrely face.

Then—

He feels something on his ankle.

A splash from the pool, perhaps?

With a raised eyebrow, Slater looks down and sees his weekend nemesis, the shaggy white-haired mutt with the vintage red bandanna. Its leg is lifted now, and it's pissing freely on his gladiator sandal like it's the most natural thing in the world. "Christ alive!" he says, sidestepping the warm urine stream. "Beat it, you sorry..."

"Hey! Hey! What is happening here?"

Oh great, Slater thinks. It's the mutt's millennial owner, that skinny kid with a black bowl haircut and Carmen Sandiego T-shirt pitching out of the warm, inky night.

"What are you doing to my dog?" the kid demands.

"I did nothing," Slater says, furiously shaking his wet leg. "Your domestic partner was urinating on me."

"That's because you probably deserved it." The skinny kid picks up his dog and says, "This is not cool, bro. Not cool."

"And your dog off-leash on hotel grounds is?"

"This is a service dog."

Slater scoffs. "Ha! And I'm sure you have the phony certification to prove it."

The kid nods. "I do."

"Yeah, right. Look, pal. That is not the demeanor of a service dog, and you know it. Service dogs do not free willy on humans."

"He's just a little nervous. He has a big meet coming up." The kid's thin, cryptic face flashes in and out of the white strobe lights.

"What meet?" Slater says. "The Canine Cologne Classic?"

The kid calmly strokes the dog's head while the dog growls

at Slater. "I'll have you know, sir, that this is a champion Frisbee dog. A gold medal winner. The pee shivers just happen to come with the package."

Slater says, "Oh, okay. So he doubles as a champion by day, and by night he's a lovely comfort animal with an overactive bladder."

The kid lifts his chin. "Yeah, that's about the gist of it."

Slater is incensed. "What a load of crap. That dog couldn't catch a Frisbee if I shoved it down its throat. Now you keep his mangy, avocado-eating ass away from me, or I'm calling security."

"Calling security?" the kid says. "Go ahead. You don't scare me. Because I know a bully when I see one."

"Good for you," Slater says. "You've earned another participation medal."

"You're a vile, dog-hating human."

"And you're an overly entitled punk. Your parents must be proud." He pauses, looking into space. "If you haven't killed them yet."

At least we have one thing in common, Slater thinks. We're both assholes.

Slater points at the kid's oversized T-shirt. "And what is it with you millennials and your obsession with the nineties? You want to know where Carmen Sandiego is? I'll tell you. Drunk under the Venice pier. Wearing a vintage Tommy Hilfiger flag shirt and getting finger-banged by Urkel from *Family Matters*." He sighs a deep shuddering sigh, his eyes not quite focused. "In all seriousness, tell me, was *Full House* really that good?"

The kid shrugs, his mouth opening and closing without sound.

"I figured," Slater says. "Now if you hurry, I'm sure the tattoo guy down the street would be happy to ink you up with Voldemort's malformed face on your left ass cheek. Or maybe a

Spanish Galleon across your sunken chest. He might even have an Xbox while you wait. Pretty cool, huh? So stop bothering people and run along, junior."

The kid clutches his dog tight and says, "You haven't seen the last of us. We outnumber you. We're eighty-three million strong. *We do what we want.*"

Slater shoos him away. "Yeah, yeah. Beat it, Potterhead."

Millennials.

Slater steps out from the thicket of palm trees and surveys the spring break soiree. After a moment of searching for Funk, he spots Backstreet in his gangster suit, frantically waving at him from across the dance floor. *What does that idiot want?*

Slater taps his chest and mouths the word ME?

Backstreet emphatically shakes his head YES!

Slater staggers through the blitzed crowd, his shifty green eyes as small as a hummingbird's.

When he finally reaches Backstreet, he shakes the Valium fog from his head and says thickly, "What do you want?"

Backstreet gives him that convict stare, points at his phone, and shouts over the music. "I got the producer on the line. It seems your boy's gone AWOL!"

Slater leans in, eyes wide shut. "AWOL?"

"Yeah, man. *AWOL.*"

"That can't be," Slater says. "He just went to the bathroom."

Backstreet laughs superior and hands Slater the phone. Lopez, oblivious to the mayhem surrounding him, twirls his fair-haired lady nearby.

Slater raises the phone to his mouth and almost eats it. "What's up?"

"Mr. Funk has left the building," Dungworth's voice says. "I repeat, Mr. Funk has left the building. Find him—*or forfeit.*"

Slater's jaw drops. "Left the building? That can't be. I—"

"Find him!"

"Okay, okay," Slater says, nodding. "Don't panic. I think I know where he is."

Slater is panicking. If he were wearing pearls, he would clutch them now. He turns quickly and underhand tosses the phone to Backstreet. Thinking hard, he looks up at the stars and grinds his teeth. The navy blue sky seems to go on forever, and yet it holds no answers. No promises of a fruitful resolution.

"Ain't no matter," Backstreet says. "Dungworth told me our lead was off the charts."

A loopy Slater looks at him cross-eyed. "What?"

"That's right. My boy will be nibbling crotch spiders by midnight. And you? You'll be left slapping the bag. It's over, bro."

He laughs as an emotionally out-of-control Slater stumbles across the dance floor.

Backstreet cups both hands around his mouth and yells over the wall of sound, "It's gonna take a miracle for your boy! Fifty Gs." He pumps his right arm. "*KA-CHING!*"

39

FUNK'S ON THE MOVE.

He walks silently in the darkness, hands in pockets, the bright headlights of traffic on Sunset Boulevard floating in the road. He carries no cell phone, and his digital footprint is invisible.

No friend requests, no drunken tweets, no late-night texts.

It's face-to-face conversation that he wants.

One-on-one combat.

His dark shadow walks patiently beside him, its svelte profile unrecognizable on the sidewalk. Out of habit, he stops momentarily to fix his hair in the window of a parked four-door sedan, and remembers what was there this afternoon is now on the cutting room floor. His smooth, pale reflection in the car window reminds him of that. *You're not bald, you're just taller than your hair.* The sad fact is his days of stealing the little shampoos at the hotel are over, but it isn't something that he dwells on. Although he will miss those tiny Vidal Sassoon travel bottles.

Before he is even finished thinking about it, the driver's-side window of the parked sedan suddenly slides down, startling

Funk. A white funnel cloud of marijuana smoke escapes from inside, rising and twisting up into the warm March night like a mini-tornado. When the smoke finally clears, the bearded face of a disheveled brown-haired man stares back at him. After a moment of rubbing his nose, the bearded man says, "People like to use my window as a mirror."

Is that you, Snowden?

The stranger's voice is thick and gummy, the result of too much weed. "Sorry," Funk says. "Just making sure I look presentable for the club. But it appears I'm as presentable as I'm going to get."

The bearded man is most likely homeless and living in his car, Funk thinks. The old sedan is filled to the roof with boxes, trash bags, canned food, rolls of toilet paper, and soiled blankets. Even though he is greasy and unkempt, his deep-set red eyes offer a glimmer of hope—a flicker of curiosity. Still, the man looks sixty but is probably closer to forty.

The street ages you like that.

The guy coughs and says, "No worries about the window, man. Where you headed?"

Funk points up the road. "The Whisky."

The guy nods and places both hands on the steering wheel. "I used to go there. In the seventies and eighties. When music still mattered. Now it's all about algos and keywords. Messenger bots and shit." He points at the brightly lit Apple watch billboard high in the sky. "We're just one ad away from corporate colonization. That's right, brother, the developers are at the gate. Just look around the Strip. Look at all the construction cranes. The vulture capitalists are here, and they have stolen the vibe."

"The vibe?"

"Yeah, man. The House of Blues is gone. Just disappeared into thin air. And even Burning Man has sold out. Can you believe it? Catering to those rich tech assholes in spirit animal fur."

Funk steps off the curb and leans his head in the window. "I hear you. But what I want to know is, what bands did you see back in the day?"

The guy flashes a stoner smile. "A lot of brilliant shows, man. The Germs. X. Guns N' Roses and Blondie, just to name a few."

"Sounds like a great time."

"It was," the man says. "But the best show I ever saw was Purple Onion. The 'Big Tits and a Bottle of Wine' tour."

Dial N for Nostalgia, Funk thinks.

"Enjoyed yourself, did you?"

The man lights a joint. He inhales deeply and squeaks, "It was killer." He sticks his rough, callused hand out and offers the spliff.

Funk politely declines. "No, thanks. I'm still adjusting to the time change."

"Me too," the man says, inhaling. "Every day. Say, who are you voting for?"

"Don't know yet. What about you?"

"Anything green," the man says. "Anything green."

Funk smiles and takes a few steps back.

"Hey, I'd offer you a ride," the man says, "but as you can see —it's kinda messy."

Funk turns on the sidewalk. "No problem. I like to walk."

"Cool. One last thing I gotta tell ya."

"Okay."

The man leans out the window, resting both arms on the door. "I know I may not be the engine of the future. But I can still be a booster rocket. You know, give someone that kick in the ass they need."

Funk looks puzzled.

The man laughs and says, "I guess some things are unexplainable. Like my love affair with maturations, saturations, machinations, and all things -ations." He pauses. "It's only less befuddling than my love of isms."

Funk's musical skills have made him catnip to a certain class of fans. Those of the deranged variety. His eyes slide away from the man's mustard-dripped shirt, and up to the moon above the palm trees. Dusty clouds distort its white face, making it appear powdery and lopsided, like crushed aspirin. "Well," Funk says in a thoughtful tone, "I'd better get going. Leave you to your isms."

Funk stuffs his hands in his pants pockets and heads west on Sunset.

The bearded man waves out the car door window and yells, "Enjoy the show, man! But remember, it's all about the music. All true artists are attracted by the light. Move toward the light! Move toward the light!"

40

FIFTEEN MINUTES LATER, Funk stands on the corner of Sunset and Clark, staring up at the Whisky a Go Go's world-famous marquee. It reads: THE MOTELS. And under that: SOUND LADY.

Like a wayward son returning to his childhood home, the former bank building seems much smaller than he remembers, no bigger than himself. But the strong odor of urine on the sidewalk quickly reminds him of where he is. The urban core.

A thin man in a backward baseball cap approaches and hands him a flyer for an upcoming show. It looks like some costume band is hosting a weenie roast. Funk, hardly a fan of the frankfurter, thanks the guy and files it under JOMO.

The joy of missing out.

Standing on the sidewalk, he shifts his attention to the long line of people waiting to get in. Bless those hearty souls for their commitment, he thinks, but he doesn't possess that gene. He watches for a moment as the burly security guards begin to pat people down for weapons and drugs. Something unheard of thirty years ago. Well, the weapons anyway.

As Funk approaches the entrance to the famous rock venue,

he hears the muffled music inside. He walks slowly but confidently to the front of the line and mouths the words "guest list" to the hefty bouncer guarding the door.

The bouncer shines a flashlight in Funk's face and says, "Name?"

"Funk. Larry Funk."

The bouncer checks his list, nods, and Funk traipses into the Whisky like a man on a submerged mission. If there is one thing he would like to impart to his adoring fans about this simple moment, it is this: always be on the guest list in L.A.

Never wait in line.

The line is for chumps, and a prop to be exploited for those with no game.

Don't be a dude with no game.

41

THE CONTROL ROOM has pinpointed Funk's position. A cameraman in a GMC van parked across the road from the Whisky has just captured him slipping into the rock club with a wan smile and a chin nod.

Hot and bothered by Funk's effortless maneuver, Dungworth taps the shoulder of an editor seated at the console and says, "Cut that."

Marty looks over, astounded. "Seriously? That was *sick game*. The Whisky is known for its tough security. He didn't even get his hand stamped. No ticket, no will call, no ID. He just cruised right up there like a boss. Not many people can make that happen."

"Make what happen?" Dungworth says. "Walking into a nightclub? Maybe we ought to try something harder, like seeing if he can walk and chew gum at the same time. Would that satisfy your fat aggression?"

Marty leans back in his chair. "You know what? You can fat-shame me all you want. It doesn't hurt me one bit, because I know I'm flabulous. But you, you're a hater."

"Dread to think someone has a different opinion than you do, Marty. But you're right. I am a hater."

As Dungworth straightens, he places his hands on his hips. His bloated stomach appears to have grown larger, and his face distorts in agony. The drugs have been of no help, he thinks, because he has the constitution of a horse. Something he blames on the medical bureaucrats and their ill-gotten gains.

Maybe it's time he started huffing shoe polish.

Marty says, "Hate all you want, but Funk's got old-school game, and you know it. That's what this show's all about. That's what the people want to see. And it's certainly not his problem, *or my problem*, that you can't go to the bathroom."

Dungworth shakes an angry fist at Funk's clean image on the monitor. "Damn you, bald man!"

ONCE INSIDE THE WHISKY, a sense of the familiar hits Funk. There is the obligatory thick smell of ripe humans, guest list drunks, and rock 'n' roll music. Like usual, some dude who looks like Benny Mardones is yelling for Dokken. A lot of Whisky, Funk thinks, and not much Go Go.

The iconic, intimate landmark still looks the same, though, dark and grungy and worn in all the right places. Much like his vintage Timex watch, the joint takes a licking and keeps on ticking.

Momentarily frozen near the entrance, he stares at the historic collection of photos hanging on the wall, photos of all the famous Southern California rock bands that have graced the stage. Everybody from the Byrds to Mötley Crüe, to the most famous house band of them all: the Doors.

Humbled to have played on the same stage as Jim Morrison, he slowly spins his head and eyeballs the scene. As expected, it is standing room only tonight, and the temperature simmers just below a sweatbox. New wave and gentrified post-punk is pretty much the crowd. Lots of Duran Duran and Joy Division T-shirts.

Inching closer toward the edge of the audience, he remembers Purple Onion's last show here in '89. Everything was heightened, amplified. Coke Bottle pounding out a primitive backbeat, Artie ripping the bass like he was plucking a chicken. He's not certain, but he thinks it was the same night he tossed his guitar pedal out into the crowd. The same night a strapping male voice shouted back, "Thanks for the good luck charm!" Funk savors the memory and often wonders if the owner of the guitar pedal still feels that way.

All at once he is slammed with emotion, his past and future colliding with the bright crash of cymbals onstage. Is that Angie's band? He can't tell; his depth perception is off. Despite this, he instinctively moves toward the pulsating light, to a familiar place where he can *feel* the music.

It's time to steal back the vibe.

He picks his way through the well-lubed crowd and rushes the stage. He recognizes the song now, recognizes the charismatic lead singer lit up under the violet lights. As he gets closer to the music, he can feel the room vibrating, the frenetic energy propelling him forward. He glances at the mosh pit. It is teeming with fist pumpers and crowd surfers and fangirls shaking their hair. Up on the high stage, Angie and her band are shredding an alternative metal cover of Blondie's "Call Me." She is clearly in command of her craft, Funk thinks, both hands gripping the microphone stand, her feathered brown hair blowing from the wind machine offstage.

Funk bobs his head to the driving new wave rock music and thinks the sound guy (or sound Nitz, as Coke Bottle liked to call him) nailed the mix. There are no earsplitting decibels, only the clean, pure sounds of Angie's voice.

When the volume drops and the song fades out, Angie bows and addresses the appreciative crowd. "Thank you! Thank you so much! We're Sound Lady. We're going to take a short break. So stick around. We'll be right back!"

Angie, wearing a dark floral dress with sheer sleeves and a silver moon pendant around her neck, is placing her guitar in a case when she hears a voice.

"I see you're still wowing the crowd."

Angie looks over her shoulder and smiles. Sees Funk standing there rubbing his bald head with a goofy eighth-grade grin on his face. "Wow. Look at you," she says.

He shrugs. "I went in a new direction. The only direction I had, really."

"I think it looks great. And I'm glad you made it."

There is a long awkward pause that follows, and Funk almost forgets what year it is. He searches for the right words but can only manage, "Killer set, and you were smoking hot up there."

Hot? Did he really just say that? Can he say that?

Pointing at the drum kit, he corrects himself. "I mean the band. The band was...kinda hot."

Angie laughs. "Thanks, Larry. But compliments aren't dead, you know." She hops off the stage and grabs him by the elbow. "Come on," she says. "Let me buy the birthday boy a drink."

He looks at her with an open heart, her earthy eyes shaping his future. "Lead the way."

43

AT THE HOTEL, Backstreet wants to scream. He stands with clenched teeth in front of the jury-rigged karaoke stage, watching a bare-chested and sweaty Lopez butcher a version of Christopher Cross's "Ride Like the Wind."

The performance is anything but pretty.

The high-pitched sound has so far chased birds from the trees and triggered a death howl from the scruffy white dog with a red bandanna.

How much more can man and beast take?

With a wireless microphone, Lopez unapologetically prowls the stage, high-kicking the air like Elvis and pumping his hips to the beat of the music. He certainly doesn't lack enthusiasm, Backstreet thinks, but you can chalk that up to the wine.

The young crowd seems to be enjoying the show, but Backstreet is reminded by the screechy voice of his friend that he needs to get the brakes fixed on his Mustang. Maybe a wash and a lube job while he's at it. He secretly hopes that Lopez will forget the chorus, bow out with a mic drop, but his prayers go unanswered. The shirtless wonder just lets it fly beyond his vocal range, his shrieky voice cracking in the dead of night.

Backstreet can't take it anymore. Soon it will be him howling at the moon. He plugs both ears with his index fingers and looks away, grimacing.

Please, cuz. No más!

44

SLATER IS DESPERATE.

The clock is ticking.

He scrambles into the hotel lobby wearing the red helmet cam and slides to a stop. His face is ghost white and wet, and he carries the haggard look of an overfed buzzard. At present, there is only one thought dipping into the secret sauce of his think box:

Gotta find Funk.

Gotta find Funk.

Gotta find Funk.

His morals are questionable, his work ethic is not.

Goofy and animated, fat arms outspread, he looks left, right, chews the air, and bolts from the lobby like a fan possessed.

It's Funk or bust.

45

NEAR THE STAGE, Funk and Angie sit in one of the Whisky's red leather VIP booths. The intimate space is dark and dingy, noisy and full, with a classic dive bar feel. Like a lot of longtime L.A. residents, Funk thinks, the old historic venue hides its age well.

He sips a light beer, and she cradles a ceramic mug of herbal tea and honey. It is to protect her voice, he knows, something to coat her throat. In his heyday, he chugged an entire bottle of honey before a show, but that's because he was screaming through most of the set.

"So is your friend coming?" Angie asks.

"No. He's busy with the spring break crowd."

"Yeah? What about you?"

"I'm just along for the ride, but..."

"But what?"

He pauses and stares at the Jack Daniels poster on the wall. "Have you ever outgrown someone? I mean, I'd always heard the expression, but I couldn't relate until now."

"Your friend?" Angie says.

Funk nods. "Yeah. Well, you know, he's one of those friends

you meet on the job somewhere. One of those guys you introduce nobody to."

"Gap people," Angie says. "People that bridge the space between your old married friends...or until you find someone."

"I guess. Anyway, he directed a few of Purple Onion's music videos when we first started out. So I'm indulging him for one more go-around. Wasn't like I had anything better to do." When he looks into her eyes, he smiles. "Until now."

She meets his gaze and returns the smile, and Funk senses the moment has arrived. He is giddy with anticipation, full of warm flaky layers ready to be peeled and eaten. The urge to caress her cheek, get lost in her lips, is strong. But he hesitates. Once again, the times have crushed his desires.

Is the surprise kiss dead?

Funk does his best to be culturally aware, but in such fluid times, it is hard to keep up. First it's a selfie, then it's a mug shot. So, in his quest to become a better earthling, to be absolutely sure that the woman before him tonight with the moist red lips and cornflower-blue eyes is really into him, he asks, "Would it be forward of me if I made a night move?"

She slides over and leans in, their knees touching under the table. "Are you falling for an older woman?"

"Only if she lets me."

He slouches toward her radiant face and gently gives her a tender but quick kiss on the lips. Her mouth is warm from the hot tea, her breath a sweet shot of honey. He pulls away slowly and says in the afterglow, "Submitted for your approval."

Baby steps, he thinks. Baby steps.

She pulls at a strand of her hair and smiles affectionately, lost in the satisfying haze of the moment. Funk has always enjoyed the breeziness of her being. Unlike some today, she does not possess a coarse bone in her body.

"Hey," he says, holding her hand. "I really want you and

your daughter to celebrate my birthday with me tomorrow. I know we talked about it, but I just wanted to confirm. Sea bass, maybe? I mean, lunch. Say around one?"

Funk feels a flush of heat around his neck. His heart is pounding wildly, and a blue vein bulges on his temple. He hasn't officially asked anybody out on a date since the fall of the Berlin Wall. He reaches for a bottle of water and takes a bird sip.

Must hydrate.

"I'd like that," she whispers. "One is perfect."

He feels relieved, almost dizzy. "Great," he says softly.

Just then, a bandmate sticks his head in the room and says, "Do you have the new set list, Ang?"

Angie looks over her shoulder. "We're still working on it."

"Cool. We're on soon."

She nods. "Okay. I'll be there in a minute."

The bandmate waves a hand and disappears.

"Your band is tight," Funk says.

"Yeah. They're great. They were even cool when I told them we had a special guest star playing tonight."

"Sweet," Funk says, placing the cap back on the water bottle. "Who did you line up? Slash? Exene?"

Angie stares at Funk. And after holding his gaze for a long moment, he finally gets it. "Oh no. Not me. I mean, *my feet hurt.*"

"Yes, you," Angie says. "It's time you got back onstage."

He offers a lame smile. "So what are we talking about? A thanks for the memories tour?"

"That's up to you," she says.

"My rock days are over."

Angie pauses, points at a black-and-white photograph of three young men hanging above the booth. "Are they?"

Funk fingers a bar coaster and stares at the vintage picture of his band on the wall. The power trio poses outside under the Whisky's marquee, with PURPLE ONION at the top of the bill. All three men wear faded Levi's jeans and white T-shirts, wasted eighties smiles plastered on their long-haired faces. He remembers the night well. It was their first headliner, and they had blown off a sound check and split a half case of Mickey's Big Mouth out in the alley. Just to take the edge off.

"It's hard to find dedicated people these days, Larry," Angie says. "And I really need another guitar player. So I'm just throwing it out there."

"Like a wild pitch?"

"More like a changeup. You remember what I said last night? About hopping in *The Lazy Faze* and going on tour?"

"Yeah."

"Well, I want you to join me. It's going to be big."

"I'm not going to ask you how big, but how big?"

She gapes at him. "Like we're opening for Guns N' Roses next weekend at Coachella big."

Whoa, Funk thinks. If GN'R can get it together, so can he.

"I do like the sound of *The Lazy Faze*," he says. "I'm just not sure I'm ready for the road."

"*The road* is only two hours east. Do the Coachella show and go home after that."

Funk mulls over the possibilities, but he doesn't take long. He knows that exploration of the mind always comes at the expense of others. He nods and mumbles, "Two hours east."

Angie keeps at him. "Yes. Look, Larry. It's not about being a rock star. You play because you love it. Not because of the money. And watching you play piano last night was magic. Those kids were awestruck. Just like the old days, when every funk rock band wanted to be you. Whether you played guitar or piano, they all wanted to watch Lightning Larry. You have a gift. You inspire. Okay, so maybe the money hasn't come yet. Maybe you weren't ready, or just unlucky. I don't know. But you're super talented, Larry, and it doesn't matter how old you are, or what you look like. Artists create. It's what we do. But if you don't believe in yourself, or it's not in your soul anymore...then sell real estate or backyard grills. Or whatever. I don't care. All I'm asking is that you play one song tonight, any song you want, and if it doesn't feel right, walk away. I'll never ask again. But I will always be there for you." She smiles. "And I'm still in for the sea bass."

Funk softens his eyes and remains silent. He'd been a fool for losing her, he tells himself. A fool for losing his lust for life.

"I know it's none of my business," Angie says. "I just hope you don't let the past strangle your future. But I know that if you got out there and sang one of your hits, the crowd would really appreciate it. And I think it would make you feel really good. I know it would."

"And how do you know that?"

She cradles her tea and sighs. "I'm no expert. But I just read about a new study. And I believe it, because it makes me feel good. It's something I've known all along. It said music is not only good for the soul, but good for the body. It lowers pain and anxiety, and it makes you feel better."

"I get that," he says. "But even if I were to play, I'm not sure that 'Big Tits and a Bottle of Wine' is right for the times."

She rolls her eyes. "Okay. I agree it is a little misogynistic. But it was written nearly thirty years ago in jest. I think people would forgive you. I hope they would. Besides, it's fun."

The clawback could be brutal, Funk thinks.

He knows that if he doesn't sing his anthem, the red-pill-popping brigade will call him a coward, and if he does, the social justice warriors will have his head on a platter. Something to justify their liberal arts degrees. He could only imagine playing the song at a college gig right now. The young radicals would have him tarred and feathered for blasphemy. He wonders if the world should cancel an artist for channeling the times. He hopes not. He's read that book before.

Years ago, he was a campus hit. Now he would be heckled and booed offstage, dodging rotten tomatoes all the way to the stockade.

Ah, the luxuries of youth.

And so the decision is made. He will not sing it. Putting politics aside, the song isn't that great. It was a sophomore effort that caught a little heat—nothing more. The ghastly irony of it is, he doesn't drink wine anymore. Big tits he still likes, but who doesn't?

So there it is. The song will stay corked and locked inside history's guitar case for the foreseeable future.

Angie rises from the table and says, "I've got a gig to play. If you're ready to do this, now is the time."

He nods and sips his beer in the dim light, watching her walk slowly toward the door. He says, "I've been a fool for far too long."

Angie stops and turns, sees Funk tapping the front of his Foghat T-shirt. "Can your guitarist keep up?"

She smiles. "He played with Dick Dale."

Funk stands, leveling his filmy gray eyes on her. "If he's good enough for Dick Dale, he's good enough for me."

She nods. "So, it's 'Fool for the City'?"

He was thinking more like "I Just Want to Make Love to You."

But baby steps.

"I ain't no farm boy," he says. "So, yeah. 'Fool for the City' it is."

She slings a guitar over her shoulder and grins. "It's your stage, Larry. I'm just playing on it."

46

IN THE CONTROL ROOM, Dungworth and the crew recoil at the sight of Phil Lopez "singing" Christopher Cross's "Ride Like the Wind" on the karaoke stage. Lopez, proud of his off-key performance, flings the microphone out into the crowd, and bows enthusiastically.

Near the wall of screens, Dungworth stands with his arms crossed. "Those were four of the most cat-kicking, painfully excruciating moments of my life," he says. "Talk about screechy."

Marty lifts his head. "Maybe he shoulda sung 'Wildfire.'"

Dungworth shoots him a withering look.

Then—

Gaye shouts joyfully, "I've got Mr. Slater!"

With stiff legs, Dungworth hobbles over to her computer monitor and leans in.

Gaye says, "He's up the street—at the Whisky a Go Go. And he's livestreaming with the GoPro helmet cam."

Dungworth grabs his headset and rushes to his director's chair. "Make sure we've got audio. And check your comms," he says. "Marty, open up the focus groups."

As Slater wades through the Whisky's packed house like a

heat-seeking missile, the crew watches his shaky point of view on the big screen. They hear rapid, heavy breathing as Slater passes several inebriated faces and some scary dude in a leather motorcycle jacket with black eye sockets.

At this moment, all monitors in the control room go dark.

Dungworth freaks. "Did we lose him? We lost him. Marty. Marty! Rolling blackout!"

"Relax," Marty says. "They dimmed the lights."

"What?"

"Get out much?" Marty says. "The place is known for its concerts. That might have something to do with it."

Seconds later, a lone male voice booms over the Whisky's PA. *"Tonight, playing with Sound Lady, please welcome a very special guest back to the stage. An old-schooler from the L.A. grunge scene and the world-famous Starwood. Ladies and gentlemen, please give it up for the frontman of Purple Onion. Mr. 'Big Tits and a Bottle of Wine' himself...Larrrrryy Funk!"*

Offstage, Funk fumbles with his earpiece and moves toward the light. Cymbals crash, and a lone beam of purple shines down on him. He stands center stage now, rose-cheeked, wielding his guitar like a battle-axe. The jubilant crowd cheers as he coolly leans back on a cocked right leg and starts jamming to the riffy intro of Foghat's "Fool for the City."

Now, in the frenzied mosh pit, an exuberant Slater wearing the red helmet cam pogos up and down, pumping both fists. With his ears bearing the blow of the decibels, he yells over the roar of the crowd, "I don't know if you can hear me, Dung-breath! But this is it, man. This is classic Funk! Doing that voodoo that he do!"

Dungworth leans over the console and sighs.

As Funk takes the song to the high octave, bits and pieces of Marty's adolescence break apart and bubble up to the surface of his gray matter. The cry in Funk's voice has dislodged a long-lost memory. The memory of a drunk uncle and two turntables and a microphone.

Marty slaps his knee and says, "Purple Onion! *That's where I know that dude!*" He can barely contain his excitement, pointing emphatically at Funk on the monitor. "*He's the lead singer of the Onion, man!* He once sat in for Brian Wilson as a touring member of the Beach Boys. Took over the falsetto harmonies. He stole the show."

"And how would you know that?" Dungworth says. "You weren't even born yet."

"No, but my uncle was. He's got all the Purple Onion albums. *Screamers in the Night. Bitchslap. She Shot My Wad in San Francisco.* He even caught a guitar pedal at the show."

"Why would anybody want a guitar pedal?"

"My uncle said it was his good luck charm, the best souvenir he ever got. And like a miracle, he met his wife at the bar later that night. They're still together. True story." Marty, with undisguised glee, bobs his head to the choogling backbeat and energetically drums his fingers on the desk. "Look at him go. He's *wailing* on guitar!"

"I am looking at him," Dungworth says. "And he's staring at the lady bass player like she's a can of Spam. Poor guy, probably hasn't gotten any in a while. No wonder he's jumping around the stage like a maniac."

"Call it what you want," Marty says, rallying to Funk's defense. "But the crowd loves it." He points to the scoreboard. Dungworth looks up, his tiny head twisting on its long neck like a periscope on a sub. He sees that the red bar still trumps green, but green is rising.

And fast.

"Okay, that's enough of the lovefest," Dungworth says. He rises from his chair. "Gaye, go dark on the men's focus group."

Gaye nods.

Marty says, "What? You gotta be kidding me? This is 'Fool for the City.' One of the greatest boogie rock songs ever recorded. I mean, that's a full-on instrumental attack. The men need to hear this."

"I'm not kidding, Marty."

"But that'll kill Mr. Funk's chance. He needs the men's vote to win."

Dungworth looks Marty in the eyes. "Let me ask you a question, big boy. Which movie would you rather watch? 20,000 *Leagues Under the Sea*, or 20,000 *Follicles Under the Drain?*"

"I'm not following."

"Look," Dungworth says, "it's not my call. The network doesn't want a bald man to win. What can I say?"

"They told you that? That's bald discrimination."

A hard stare from Dungworth. "No, Marty. That's show business. We'll let the women decide."

———

Inside their hotel room, the men's focus group rocks out to Funk's live performance.

With heads banging, their bodies moving and arching, one long-haired surfer guy plays air guitar on his knees, strumming the imaginary strings with his eyes closed. Others pretend to play the drums, while another man lip-syncs into a balled fist.

Then—*poof!*

The picture on the TV turns to fuzz, and they all ad-lib their displeasure. A hollow-cheeked man in a Comic-Con T-shirt hurls his voting console at the screen and yells, "Dude, that is the multiplicity of wrong!"

———

Three doors down from the men's group, in another hotel suite, the women's focus group is bored with Funk's Whisky performance—all but one, an alternative redhead named Apple. While the other women doomscroll on their phones, she sits riveted to the screen as Funk ends the Foghat song to wild applause.

A tawny-haired woman in a brown suede miniskirt and black studded moto boots looks up from her phone and says, "Oh my God. Is it over yet? That was such a rip-off of *That '70s Show*."

Another woman with hair the color of the rainbow says, "He seems like a really sweet guy. And I know Phil can't sing, but he's a total smokeshow, and he has really great hair."

Apple shrugs. "I don't know. I thought Larry was kinda cute."

All the women stare at her and snort, "*EEEEWWW*."

DUNGWORTH FEELS THE HEAT.

The momentum shifting.

It's time to send this old bald guy back to the Barcalounger.

He paces the dusky control room, barking a series of commands into his headset. "You heard me. I want a delay on everything. *Everything.* Got it? Okay. Ready one on your wide shot. Annnd...go! Ready two, bring it in. Close-up on Lopez. I want beefcake. Shiny slabs of meat."

Marty says with a look of scorn, "Why don't you have him take his pants off? A few cock shots might be nice."

"Don't push me, Marty."

On the monitor, a bare-chested Lopez and Backstreet entertain two young ladies in their hotel suite. They all sit barefoot and cross-legged on the California King bed, drinking champagne and trading off-color jokes. "Kung Fu Fighting" plays softly on the nightstand radio.

Dungworth says, "It's eleven o'clock. And as you can see, my main man Phil is in the pole position. Funk's got one hour left. It's conjugate or checkmate."

Marty shakes his head. "Maybe if you'd given him a chance."

Dungworth laughs. But it is cut short by the loud, brash talking of Phil Lopez on the monitor. Lopez is visibly intoxicated, slurring his words. He picks up a pillow off the bed and flings it aggressively across the room. Sucking in a hard breath he says, "Where the fuck's the camera?"

Gaye says, "It looks like someone was overserved."

Dungworth nods. "What was he drinking?"

"Everything," Marty says. "The guy was chugging highball leftovers off the tables. It reminded me of that Smails kid in *Caddyshack.*"

Gaye, unimpressed: "He seems to enjoy the shirt-free lifestyle."

"If you've got it, flaunt it," Dungworth says.

Marty points at the big screen. "It would appear he's flaunting it now."

Lopez continues his erratic behavior on-screen. He rolls off the bed onto the floor, laughing. Fighting for balance, he rises unsteadily from all fours and staggers around the room. "Where's the camera?" he demands with a fair amount of anger. "Where is it!"

Backstreet points at a Boston fern. "Right there, dawg. In the plant."

Lopez lurches over to the fern and rips off the leaves. Once he finds the camera, he puts his face on the lens. "You want me to sing it, Dungworth? Is that what you want?"

"What is he talking about?" Dungworth says.

Marty shrugs.

"Typecast me, bitch," Lopez says. "Number one, Dungheap, I do not listen to salsa music. I like Morrissey in my Bose headphones—LOUD. And number two, I want extra wasabi with my

California rolls next time. Don't short me, bro. Don't you *fucking* short me."

Backstreet pleads, "It's all good, Phil. Come over here and party with us."

Lopez says, "Not until I sing the song."

"What song?"

"The song that fool Dungheap wants me to sing. The stupid Frito Bandito song. You know the one." Lopez starts singing. "*Ai yi yi yi…I am the Frito Bandito.*"

Dungworth looks perplexed. "And who is the Frito Bandito?" He looks around the control room. "Anybody?"

Everyone shrugs.

Nobody's heard of him.

"I think he was in a Harvey Keitel film," a scrawny male intern with a new beard finally says. "Or maybe it was an afterschool special. I'm not sure which."

Nobody has heard of Harvey Keitel either.

"Oh, for fuck's sake," Dungworth says. "Somebody get in there and feed Lopez some lines. Get him back on track."

But the drama continues.

Lopez shouts on the monitor, "I swear to God, I said it!"

"Said what?" Backstreet says, looking uneasy. "C'mon, Phil. We got ladies in here."

Lopez points at one of the women on the bed. "You think I'm going to fuck that fat *puta*? Not me. I don't do fat hos."

Dungworth into a headset: "Cut that."

On the monitor, Backstreet looks over at the young women sitting on the bed and makes an apologetic shrug. The bigger of the two women flashes a boozy spring break grin. It's all good.

"Look at her," Backstreet says. "She ain't fat, cuz. She's just big-boned. Now c'mon over. You ain't gotta put a ring on it. It's fifty large." He turkey-fingers his hands. "*Fifty large.* Remember?"

Lopez waves him off. "Forget it. Nobody buys me." He turns back to the camera and grumbles, "How about this, Dungworth? I'll be your personal flamenco dancer. Your Mexican on call. How much is that worth to you...you knock-kneed *pendejo*?" He teeters, wobbles back, and collapses on the bed, laughing.

Dungworth shakes his head at Lopez's schnockered image. "And they wonder why millennials don't drink."

48

ON THE TENTH FLOOR, Apple, the alternative red-haired woman who liked Funk's Whisky performance, shoulders her vintage JanSport backpack and sneaks out of the women's focus group's room. In a hurry, she closes the door behind her and dashes down the hallway of the hotel.

It's Funk or bust.

49

SEVERAL MOMENTS LATER, a harried Slater shoves Funk inside the Mondrian's hotel lobby.

In a state of confusion and disappointment, Funk smooths down his Foghat T-shirt and tries to regain his composure. "Ronnie, what are you doing? I didn't have time to say goodbye to Angie. You practically dragged me out of the Whisky."

"You'll see her tomorrow," Slater says breathlessly, the red helmet cam crooked on his head. "I told you, I've got big birthday plans for you. It can't wait. It simply cannot wait."

Right now, Apple, the alternative redhead, exits the lobby elevator and approaches Funk.

She stops and says deadpan, "I just saw you play at the Whisky. It was total awesomesauce. You ripped."

Funk smiles bashfully at the young punker girl. "Thanks. But that's old-school stuff. Who turned you on to the music?"

"My dad," she says, playing with her silver nose ring. "Along with KISS, Sabbath—and the Winter brothers."

Funk nods. "You like 'Frankenstein?'"

"Yeah," she says. "But my favorite's 'Still Alive and Well.'"

Funk laughs. "Really? That's my favorite too. What's your name?"

She fixes her honey-brown eyes on him. "Apple."

"Apple," Funk says, almost tasting it. "I like that. I'm Larry, and this is my friend Ronnie."

"Yeah, I know," she says.

Funk appears troubled by her reply and momentarily stares at the black-and-white "I miss the '80s" button pinned to her backpack.

Slater, realizing that serendipity has provided him one last chance, seizes the opportunity. He gestures hysterically at Apple while smiling back at Funk. "Uhhh, here she is, Larry. *Apple.* My gift to you, buddy. Happy birthday!"

"What?" Funk says.

"You heard me." Slater shifts his predatory gaze to Apple. "Apple, honey, it's Larry's birthday at midnight. I'm sure he'd love to show you his suite." He winks. "It's the biggest in the hotel."

Apple smiles. "Holy crap," she says. "They ain't got shit on you."

Funk: "No, I guess not."

Apple says, "I'm not one of those Chihuahua girls, if that's what you think. I like rock and roll. Hard and fast."

So did Funk, at that age. Now a glass of warm milk and Yanni will do.

Slater says to Funk, "Is she great or what?"

Funk looks at Slater with a disapproving face, then back at the young ingenue. "Apple," he says, "could you excuse us a moment?"

She nods. "Yeah, sure."

Funk grabs Slater's arm and escorts him across the lobby. "I told you, no hookers."

"She's not a hooker," Slater says. "I swear. I just met her at the Whisky. She saw you play, man. *She digs you.* She likes all your music. And everything you're into." Slater leans in and whispers, "So this is what you do. Get her back to your room. Load up your Spotify playlist. Just be sure to start off with some high-energy tracks. Maybe dance around the room to take the pressure off. Then, *only then*, do you hit her with the slow stuff. Maybe a power ballad. I'm thinking the Scorpions or Whitesnake." Slater steps back and opens his arms. "Squeeze and release. What more do you want?"

Funk scratches his chin. "I don't know."

"At least have a drink with her. She's a fan. What do you say? One drink." He pauses, his lower lip quivering. "For old-time hockey?"

Funk looks over at Apple. The dewy-eyed redhead is wearing an Army green camo jacket with rolled-up sleeves, her backpack hanging loosely off her shoulder. There is an impatient air about her, he thinks. Like she's just skipped class and is ready for a smoke in the boys' room.

Hard to resist.

"She is kinda cute," Funk says.

"Kinda cute? Larry, her skin looks like teen spirit."

Funk does not respond.

After a moment, the hesitation brings a mad cry from Slater. "You gotta eat that Apple, bro. *Like right now.* Time's a-wasting."

"All right, all right," Funk says, waving him off. "One drink." He pauses. "For old-time hockey."

Slater smiles. "I'll leave the light on for you."

50

SLATER DARTS inside the lobby elevator and punches the UP button. Surely, he thinks, Funk's Whisky performance has evened the score. How could it not? The man was on fire.

With both hands raised high over his head, he prays to the love gods above. *Please, please, please. I am so close. I know I haven't been the best of boys, but I need this.*

He reminds himself, after this whole fiasco is over, to send Dungworth a thank-you gift. A ricin-filled package might be nice.

The elevator doors slide open and Slater sprints down the hallway, frantically careening around corners. To a maid's surprise, he moves exceptionally well for a big man. With an arched back, he explodes with short, quick bursts, like a fat ferret in search of a chicken wing.

He dodges several hotel guests along the way, hurdles an abandoned suitcase, and rushes headlong into the control room. Doubled over and out of breath, he says with some degree of difficulty, "Score me."

Dungworth rises. "What's wrong, Mr. Slater? A little winded from the Faster Pussycat concert?"

Slater hacks something up from his chest. "That's not it."

"I understand. Too much cowbell?"

"Just give me the score!"

Dungworth stiffens at the controls. "Unfortunately, the egg man is all but cooked. So let his pallid pate be the sole reminder of all that has gone wrong in your perverted universe."

"Cooked?" Slater says, confounded. "What are you talking about? He just rocked the house."

"Sadly, the women's focus group didn't see it that way. But it was a moment. I'll give him that. I suggest you file it for future reference. Play it back when you're both old and feeble." He smiles. "Or just feeble."

Slater clenches a fist and shows it to Dungworth. "I am not old. And this game is not over." Slater inches closer. "Because I swear to you, Dungworth, if you screw me now, you're going to hear a bell ring. And I can assure you, it will not be your wings. It will be your thick skull taking a major thumping!"

Dungworth is not intimidated. He does not rise to this level of hostility. Slater has just thrown all that he's got at him, but the young buck strides forward with his big columnar legs, like Godzilla marching into a forgotten city. He squares up on Slater and says face-to-face, "You boomers always resort to violence first. That's your downfall."

Slater holds his tongue, watching Dungworth's hazel eyes fluttering rapidly through his thick black glasses. Mostly, they are clear and keen, but there is also something disturbing about them. The tiny glint of crazy. Besides, Slater thinks, the kid stands a full three inches taller than him.

Not sure how to respond, Slater turns his head, giving Dungworth his side profile. Dungworth pounces, circling Slater like a drill sergeant. "The game is over when I say it's over. Face it. *You lost.* Now wipe the foam off your mouth and put down the pom-poms. It's time to throw in the towel."

Slater whips his head. "Throw in the towel! Why would we do that? Funk's in his room right now with a hottie. Roll tape."

Dungworth pauses. He holds Slater's wretched gaze, and speaks into his headset. "Camera eight, anybody home?"

The wall of TV screens instantly switch to the picture of an empty hotel suite—Funk's suite. The California King is neatly made, and his blue wedge pillow sits at the foot of the bed. Nearby, Funk's Blackberry flip phone buzzes on the glass coffee table.

Dungworth turns and says with unsavory candor, "The unknown is now the known, Mr. Slater. Captain Picard is AWOL again." A beat. "Well, it's been great TV. And it's been a pleasure working with a man of such high honor and integrity."

"Thank you."

"I'm talking about Funk."

"Oh."

"I can't help the chronically self-absorbed, Mr. Slater. You're on your own there. So you're free to go now. Free to return to your sexbots, and your groping avatars, and whatever man-boosting formula you slam into your antiquated system in the back room." He pauses, affecting a look of disgruntlement. "The ten grand loser's check is still yours if you want it. Just get me Funk's signed release by noon tomorrow. And if there's anything I can do for you in the future, anything at all..."

"You could choke on a Tide POD."

Dungworth laughs. "People who feel aggrieved tend to be the most outspoken. Good luck to you, ol' boy." He pats Slater on the shoulder, pads across the room, and begins chatting with a production assistant.

Slater is devastated. He blows out a defeated breath and slumps against the armoire.

Marty, having overheard Slater's conversation, rises from his station, looks around furtively, and mutters to himself, "I gotta stretch my legs."

As Marty heads for the door, he discreetly gestures for Slater to follow him. Slater blinks twice, gets the message, and follows Marty out into the hall.

Slater is all ears as a serious Marty corners him. "You want to win this game, Mr. Slater?"

"What gave it away? The helmet cam, or the pee stain on my crotch?"

Marty exhales and props an arm against the wall. "Okay, look. Long story short. I'm not your biggest fan, but I do like Mr. Funk. You've got one shot left. Dungworth's rigged the game—edited everything. The focus groups have only seen Mr. Lopez at his best."

"And Funk?"

"Well, you know. Taking a shit. Blowing up his GERD pillow..."

"The reptile faces."

Marty nods. "All of it. The point is, he needs to sweep the last vote. Men and women. It's a slim chance, but it's still poss-ible."

Slater steels his nerves and gains confidence. With all things being equal, he knows that Funk is exactly the everyman protag-onist that America roots for during these violent and trying times. He has a certain *je ne sais quoi* about him, a dormant Barbary pirate swagger that still shines through a dull facade. It is undeniable that the man is a conduit, the glue that binds the old with the new. Perhaps Funk is no longer the face of a changing nation, Slater thinks, but his sneaky smile will do. Something to help ease the transition. *And what country doesn't need that?*

Slater says, "Listen, there has never been a moment too big for Funk. He can do it. Just give us the chance, Marty."

"It's a risk," Marty says. "*A big risk.*"

A psycho stare from Slater. "Marty, I'm fifty-five years old. Double nickels to you. I'm wearing men's jeggings and gladiator boots. Which means I am a walking billboard for ten mistakes older guys make trying to look young. Throw in the tacky aloha shirt, and I've gone full 'Funky Cold Medina.' So I ask you, compadre. What the fuck do I have to lose?"

"Okay, okay," Marty says. "You don't have to go all extra on me. Sheesh."

Marty leans in and whispers the plan.

Slater shakes his head, stunned. "You'd really put your job on the line like that?"

"There's still a few decent people left in Hollywood," Marty says. "I like to think I'm one of them. Besides, screw Dungworth. Telling me my job's gonna get outsourced to Bollywood. Forget him. I'm next level. I got skills."

Slater smiles and pats Marty on the back. "Let's do this. On my cue."

Slater and Marty enter the control room. Seeing the same burly workmen in blue coveralls who moved the armoire yesterday, Marty nods covertly to them as they fix a ceiling light. The smaller of the two men, the one with blond curls, acknowledges with a conspirator's wink. Marty sits down at the console. He steals a glance at Dungworth across the room, and back at Slater, who now protects the bathroom door.

Five seconds later, Slater chucks the helmet cam and shouts, "Help! There is a naked woman down in the bathroom! Naked woman down in the bathroom!"

Unmoved, Dungworth looks up from his monitor like an automaton. "It's just a hot flash, Mr. Slater. It'll pass."

"I'm serious, bro," Slater says. "She's passed out. And she might even be underage. That's a big liability."

Dungworth registers a look of concern and walks stiff-legged over to the bathroom. He gently raps on the door with a knuckle and says softly, "Hello. Anybody in there?" No answer. He twists the knob and opens the door an inch or two. He calls out in the dark. "Hello...hell-ooo."

"She's passed out," Slater says. "She can't hear you. You need to go get her. She could be hurt."

Dungworth looks at Slater, and takes a deep breath. "Okay. I'm going in."

"Now you're talking," Slater says. "Be the hero. One of the last of the jukebox heroes."

Dungworth gives him a "you idiot" look, opens the bathroom door, and walks in. A moment later he says, "I don't see jack—"

Slater slams the door shut, and just as quickly, the two brawny workmen slide the mammoth armoire in front of the bathroom door.

It's a primitive move, but effective.

Dungworth is trapped.

He vigorously slams the bathroom door up against the solid wood armoire several times before realizing his predicament.

"Marty! Marty!" he yells. "Open this door!"

Marty and Slater smile at each other.

"That's it, Marty!" Dungworth shouts. "You're finished. You hear me? Finished. You can't fuck with me. *I am unfuckwithable!* You're nothing but knob-cheese, a drama goldfish at the bottom of the entertainment ocean. You too, old man. You're both finished!"

Marty turns to Slater. "Colonic hydrotherapy is rarely pleasant. Let alone rectal rehydration. That's what awaits him."

"I did not know that."

"Yeah. He's been constipated for days. That's why he's been so cranky."

Slater nods. "Load management."

Dungworth's muffled voice comes again from the bathroom, only louder. "You'll pay for this clown coup! And the next time I see you two gut lords, you'll be serving cocktails in a tunic. Playing nursemaid to a bunch of drunk gamblers at an Indian casino. *Welcome to Morongo!*"

Slater has no time to process the pandemonium because Gaye's animated voice overshadows the producer's tirade. She says boldly from her workstation, "Mr. Funk's in his room. And he's with a woman from the focus group!"

Slater lights up. "That's my boy."

Marty hurries to the director's chair. He grabs Dungworth's donut cushion and zings it across the room.

He's in charge now.

"Camera one," he says into his headset. "When you lose light, pan left and up. Yeah, that's right, a two-shot."

On the main monitor, Funk sits on the opposite side of the sleek white couch from Apple. They talk politely, their posture like that of two high school kids feeling each other out at the prom. He drinks a Miller Lite from a can. She awkwardly swirls a glass of red wine.

Slater says to Funk's on-screen image, "Scoot over, buddy. This ain't *The Love Boat.*"

Marty says, "Gaye, show the women's group the Lopez conversation. The one where he fat-shames the girl on the bed. Bobby's got the time code."

Gaye smiles. "Now you're talking."

THE WOMEN in the focus group are appalled by what they see on the television screen. They watch the monitor with bated breath as Phil Lopez goes ballistic on a young woman in his hotel room. Stunned, they all cover their mouths in mute horror when they hear him calling her a "fat *puta*" and a "*ho.*"

———

Marty at the controls.

"Show the men Funk's entire jam. And double up on that filthy guitar solo. It's time to even the score."

———

The men's focus group sits glued to their chairs, watching an ear-splitting replay of Funk's sizzling guitar solo at the Whisky. Their heads rock in unison to the driving music as Funk's bald dome glistens with sweat under the multicolored stage lights.

A handsome raven-haired man with a cleft chin rises from

his chair and says with gunslinger bravado, "I'll tell you what. Mad props to the old dude. He's still got it!"

———

In the control room, Marty shifts his weight in the director's chair and says to the crew, "This is it, people. Funk on the couch. Last vote. It's his to win or lose. *Game or No Game?*"

52

INSIDE FUNK'S HOTEL ROOM, he and Apple sit quietly on the plush sofa, sipping wine. The distance between them has not changed. As stated earlier, Funk no longer drinks wine, doesn't like the acidity, but he reverts back to his old tactics. Tactics used to close the deal.

"Are you trying to get me drunk?" Apple says playfully. "Because your wineboarding strategy won't work with me."

A woozy smile from Funk.

She continues talking, going on about a scene in the movie *Training Day*. "Remember? And Denzel says, 'I'm surgical with—'"

She trails off when she sees him drifting, spacing in his own thoughts.

"Am I that boring?" Apple asks.

Funk looks at her with vacant eyes. She is blurry and out of focus, a gray blob before him. He soon realizes where he is and navigates out of it.

"How old are you?" he says.

He hates that question, rarely asks it. *But damn, she looks so young.* It occurs to him that she may be too young to consume alcohol. Should he ask for ID?

"Twenty-one," she says.

Funk sighs in relief. "Wonderful age."

He leans back on the couch and flashes on the night he turned twenty-one. Driving his demo tape over to the KXLU radio station in his graphite black Volkswagen Jetta, Coke Bottle and his skinny girlfriend Lily riding shotgun. True to form, Coke Bottle's grimy index finger was up someplace it shouldn't have been. Funk was fortunate that he had just picked up the car from the mechanic, and the disposable plastic covers were still on the seats.

The DJ at KXLU loved the tape, played the entire album on air. In some respects, it was the happiest moment of Funk's life. The experience of hearing yourself on the radio for the first time was transcendent, a huge milestone requiring celebration. Later that night, the three of them sat high on the bluffs of Westchester, looking out over the lights of L.A., drinking Swedish vodka from a stainless-steel canteen.

It was otherworldly magical, the best birthday ever.

Funk remembers the first song he played for the DJ on his Sony boom box. "Screamers in the Night." God, he hasn't thought about that song in years. It was song one on the album and was supposed to be the band's first single released. It was a cover of Sinatra's "Strangers in the Night" but with alternate lyrics and heavy drums. It went something like this:

Screamers in the night
A backdoor pounding
Screamers in the night
She loves to call my name...

Sinatra had sent a note: *Not bad, kid. Good to hear you're getting some.* He's not sure that it was Sinatra. It probably wasn't, but it was the thought that counts.

While Funk has never been a fan of groupies, he allows himself a moment to imagine Apple hiding backstage at the Roxy and smashing a sloppy wet kiss on his flushed cheeks after the show. He can feel that she genuinely loves music and has a deep understanding of it. Her ass isn't half-bad either.

"What are you thinking?" she says.

Women can always see when you're thinking.

Funk sips his wine. "Nothing, really."

"*C'mon.*"

His eyes take on the bewitched expression of a man transported. Speaking softly, he says it as though it were a sacred place. "*Coachella.*"

"Oh, are you playing there?"

A drowsy nod from Funk. "Maybe."

"That's cool," Apple says, taking off her camo jacket. "I want to go."

Funk drifts again and hums a few bars of Foghat's "I Just Want to Make Love to You."

"Is that song stuck in your head?" Apple says. "Because sometimes a song gets stuck in my head, and I can't get it out."

"Those pesky earworms," Funk says. "But with me it's more like a sign...a harbinger of good things to come."

"What do you mean?"

"All my life," he says, "soundtracks have either showed me the way or reconfirmed where I was supposed to be. Or who I was supposed to be with."

She shakes her hands in jest. "Oooh. The signpost up ahead."

"Exactly. Like in high school, Frampton's 'Baby I Love Your Way' accompanied my first love." He pauses, looks up. "Jill

Solomon. I mean, every time I saw that girl, that song was playing somewhere. At a party. The school library...the Bean."

"The Bean?"

"My first car," Funk says proudly. "A 1976 powder-blue Ford Pinto—the blow-up model."

He chuckles at the recollection but soon realizes Apple wants more.

She slides her zaftig body close and says, "Maybe it's time we made some music of our own."

Funk's stomach knots. "Maybe."

Apple leans back on the sofa and lifts her undershirt, revealing two large milky-white breasts. "Do you have a song for these?"

Oh, the irony, Funk thinks.

"No," he lies.

"Then let's make one up." She pulls the coppery red hair off her face and leans in. "Go on," she says. "*Taste me.*"

Funk wrestles with a bout of nausea, puts a clumsy hand to her shoulder, and leans toward her open mouth. Her waiting lips are a supple pink in the shape of Cupid's bow, and he finds her plain but pretty, if not a little raw around the edges. There are smoke and chlorine scents in her hair, the smell of onions and Tommy's burgers on her breath. All the trimmings of spring break. He likes his women the way he takes his mud pie—gooey and sweet—and she checks all the boxes. And it has to be said that if he doesn't take a bite of this delicious Apple now, he will surely be banned from the Dirty Old Man's Hall of Fame.

But he stops.

The full truth of the moment slams him. He is going backward. Choosing access over feelings, flesh over love. He has a hot date with someone he cares about tomorrow, and he is not about to screw that up.

"Is something wrong?" Apple says.

"I'm not supposed to be here," he says. "I've already lived this moment. This life. Not only that, I have feelings for someone else."

"Don't worry," she says. "I'll turn the light off. The cameras can't see us then."

Funk looks at her with gigantic eyes. "Cameras? What cameras?"

"*I just wanted you to win,*" Apple says.

"Win what?"

She delivers it haltingly. "You know. *The game.*"

"I don't know what you're talking about."

"Oh snaps," she says. "You're a contestant on *Game or No Game?*, silly. I thought you knew that." She pulls down her shirt. "Or was it the other guy?"

"What other guy?"

"The macho man."

"Phil Lopez?"

She shakes her head yes.

Funk grits his teeth and pumps his fist. "*Slater!*"

Funk is furious. Beyond himself. He bolts up off the couch and stalks the room like a white tiger in heat. "Where is the camera?" he demands. "*Tell me.* Where is it!"

53

"HE LOOKS PISSED," Marty says.

Inside the control room, Slater and the crew watch an angry Funk ransack his hotel suite.

Watch him knock over a lamp.

Manhandle a ficus tree.

Punt a trash can.

"Your flair for the obvious is disconcerting," Slater says. "Either way, Marty, I'm sunk. Do you have a cry room?"

Gaye checks the score and announces, "Green bar is well over halfway to red...*and rising!*"

"He got most of the men's vote," Marty says. "But he'll need to sweep the women to win this thing."

An apprehensive look crosses Gaye's face as she glances at the bank of screens. "Uh-oh," she says, "he found the hidden camera inside the nose of the Buddha sculpture."

Marty rises from his director's chair, holds up a hand. The control room falls silent.

They all stare at the main monitor, watching Funk prepare to speak.

On-screen, Funk is incensed, his reaction anything but

cautious. He confronts the camera in the laughing Buddha sculpture and waves a flippant hand. "So that's it?" he says, his voice rocked with emotion. "I'm the Secret Square? The freakin' joker in the deck? *I can't believe this*, Slater. You sold me out, man." He steps back, points a stiff finger. "I am not your show pony! And there is a reason we are not friends. I'm through with you, buddy. *That's it.*"

Funk thoughtfully rubs his bald head and paces the hardwood floor. "All right, chill. I'm not going to get angry. I'm a big boy. Been sold out before. I should have known who I was running with. Should've been clear as day. All the people coming up to me with button-pushing questions—the free stuff. But did I listen to my gut? *No.* I just plowed ahead into the darkness like a rube in a fun house." He pauses. "But you know what? It's not about games or game. It's about growing up. About hiking your pants a little higher. Lord knows somebody in this town's got to do it. It might as well be me. So go ahead, throw me some shade, accuse me of sporting dad jeans. Hell, toss in a military cap and a pair of Crocs and I'll fly that freaky flag. And do you know why? Because I'm *dad as fuck!*"

The inhuman wail that leaves his body surprises Funk. He momentarily halts his rant and laps around the suite, the thought of cameras heavy on his mind. He takes a quick peek in the bathroom, then looks under the bed. Satisfied that they have exterminated all the bogeymen, he exhales and resumes his thoughts.

Is this a teachable moment?

A dad-as-fuck opportunity?

He thinks it is. It's the perfect time to air his dirty laundry, to let the universe in on the optimization of his future existence.

He calmly steps up to the camera and says in a low voice, "I'm sure Slater has told you all about me. Briefed you on my ignoble past. So the question is, which I'm sure you're all dying to know, where do I go from here? Where does a former rock star get his kicks?" Funk shrugs. "Shoot, I don't know, you tell me. If Justin Timberlake is dad pop, then what am I? Grandpa metal?"

He sighs and looks out the window, his full face as pale as the moon. "As you can see, or have seen," he says, "I have been going through some changes. Facing the strange as Bowie put it. And it happened fast. Take magazines. One minute I was laughing out loud at *Cracked*; then the next thing you know I was reading about transitory soft patches in *Kiplinger's*. And liking it!"

Funk pauses and blots the sweat off his face with the sleeve of his T-shirt. "And I can almost hear you young people laughing at me now, but I'm telling you, it happens to all of us. Candidly, the minute you see an actor your age playing somebody's grandfather or grandmother on-screen, then it's going to hit you like a ton of bricks. Or the moment you see your favorite TV show on the cover of a magazine: *Glee turns 50!* And that's when you sit down at the kitchen table and shakily pour that second cup of stale coffee and say to yourself: *Shit, I'm getting OLD.* But you know what? You deal with it. You put on your big boy pants and move on."

He glances at Apple sitting on the couch. "And I know what you're saying about her, about me. That the only reason I'm not hooking up with her tonight is because I forgot my Viagra single packs, or that my overcooked noodle is too soft. You think that, right? Point being, look at her, she's gorgeous. I should post this on Instagram. If I had an Instagram. And I can safely say now, that if I'd met her at any other time in my life..." He growls playfully. "Well...you get the picture."

Funk looks over at Apple. "Apple, who's got shit on me?"

Apple pumps a fist. "*Nobody.*"

"That's right," Funk says, staring back into the camera.

"*Nobody.* Because the truth is, I reconnected with a great lady tonight. And as E.M. Forster once said, 'Only connect.' That's what I did, *we did.* And if any of you saw me perform at the Whisky earlier, then you know it was the beautiful bass player, Angie. The crazy thing is, I don't know if I can even say 'beautiful' anymore. With corporations and societies outlawing handshakes, high fives, and smiles, what's a good guy to do? Get rid of his 'Free Hugs' T-shirt? I don't know, I'm rambling, but Angie made me feel something that I haven't felt in a very long time. And let me tell you something, people, it's hard to get your head, your heart, and your crotch to agree on anything. It's a miracle if it happens. So, in a perfect world, I'd end this show with *An Officer and a Gentleman* moment. A big finish where I storm her house, lift her up into my arms, and drive off into the sunset. But that will not happen. Not tonight, anyway. She's got a thirteen-year-old daughter asleep at home. So I'll do the grown-up thing and call her tomorrow. Take her and her daughter out to lunch. Maybe eat some sea bass. Who knows? After that, we'll see where it takes us."

Funk feels the blood abandon his face, his pulse slowing. A sure sign that it is time to wrap things up. "Look, minions," he says, "all I want to do now is see Apple out, grab some ice, and have a nightcap with my thoughts. Maybe a scotch—listen to some Miles Davis. That's what single fifty-year-old men do on their birthday. So please, turn off all the cameras. You don't need to see me anymore. And if the front desk can hear me, I will not be accepting any calls or visitors for the rest of my stay. The 'Do Not Disturb' sign is clearly out." He shrugs. "I guess that's about it. I hope you enjoyed the show. It's the end of the game...*the end of the playboy.*"

Slater reels back from the monitor and gravely quotes the late, great basketball announcer Chick Hearn. "The game is in the refrigerator. The door's closed, the lights are out, the eggs are cooling, the butter's getting hard, and the Jell-O's jiggling."

Marty looks completely baffled. "*What?*"

"Forget it," Slater says dejectedly. "It's another old reference." Like a frail octogenarian, Slater groans as he lowers himself onto a chair. "Just shoot me," he says. "I'm done."

Before Slater can snatch defeat from the jaws of victory, Marty shouts, "Green bar skyrocketing!"

Slater lurches up and hustles back to the computer monitor. "How can that be? I thought we were cooked."

Gaye looks over from her workstation and smiles. "Women are suckers for a good love story, Mr. Slater."

While holding his breath, Slater stares at the scoreboard, watching the green bar graph even up with red.

It stops and flickers, teases, and sputters.

"C'mon, you bastard," Slater says. "One time for Papa."

"One vote left," Marty says. "Camera six, zoom in on her finger."

The picture on the main monitor switches to a young woman's index finger with red nail polish, pushing a small green button in slow motion.

The wall clock strikes midnight.

The second-hand shadow sweeps across Slater's worried face.

The green bar inches up...up...up...and explodes well over red.

On-screen, Funk stares in awe as the word *WINNER!* flashes across his weary face in mint green letters. Glowing digital dollar signs flutter over his unwitting image like confetti at a parade.

With a knockout smile, Marty leans back in the director's chair and claps his hands. "Ball game."

The crew cheers and high-fives as if Apollo 11 has just

landed on the moon. Slater kisses Funk's image on the screen. "Yes! Yes! You flawed, beautiful bald man."

But wait, there's more.

Funk steps back up to the camera...again.

"He's not finished," Gaye says.

The control room falls silent.

On-screen, Funk stands with both hands in his back pockets. "Oh, one more thing before I retire. I'm not signing that release. Not for three grand, or whatever paltry amount was offered. Do you hear me? No release. I'm smart enough to know that without that, this show never airs. That's another thing about getting old—you seem to get smarter. And it takes a lot more for you to sell out. Sure, I'll talk, I'm not stupid, but the numbers have to be right. Otherwise, forget it. So with that..."

Funk steps back and spreads his arms. "Say goodnight to the bald guy."

Slater drops his head over the console. An intern comforts him and rubs his shoulder. On the monitor, Funk kisses Apple on the forehead and escorts her out the door. Marty and Gaye share a smile. Could there be something there? Maybe in another novel.

"Hold nine," Marty says, directing. "Right up on the sneakers. Cue the music!"

In the hotel hallway, Funk's white sneakers strut along to the iconic Bee Gees song "Stayin' Alive."

"I want A camera wide," Marty says. "Give it to me."

On-screen, stoic in expression, Funk's entire body lopes confidently to the beat of the music, his right arm swinging by his side.

Then—

Out of the blue, his pursed lips curl into a sneaky smile.

From Funk, with love.

He is in a flow state now.

Bald with game.

Rounding the corner, Funk and Apple are greeted by the applause of the focus groups as they now line the hallway, clapping and cheering. Funk strides past the women. Some wipe tears from their eyes; others smile approvingly.

The men wait at the end of the hall, and as he passes in slow motion, one by one, soft fist-bumps all around.

"Freeze frame!" Marty shouts into his headset.

The image of Funk coolly finger-pointing at no one in particular freezes on all screens in the control room.

In bold black letters, a single word zips across his triumphant image:

GAME.

SUNDAY

54

IT IS SUNDAY.

Funk's birthday.

The first official day of spring.

He walks through the hotel lobby, his overnight bag slung over his shoulder, the morning light hazy and unfiltered. The cleaning crew is busy mopping the marble floor, and the smell of disinfectant is heavy in the air.

It is 11:30 a.m.

Time for checkout.

After a good night's sleep, he is at ease with himself, his body finally adjusting to the time change. He looks forward to meeting Angie and her daughter for lunch and prays he can contain his excitement long enough to string a few coherent sentences together without sounding like a thirsty mess.

His excitation level is off the charts.

As he approaches the reception desk, he thinks about repainting the Bird Cage, his mind exploding with creative colors ranging from Pigeon Poop Gray to Greek Villa White. After that, maybe a big farm sink in the kitchen. *But is modern farm-*

house dead? These are the domestic DIY actions one thinks about when love has suddenly entered the picture.

He reaches the front desk, almost blushing. "Hi. Room 807."

"Checking out?"

"Yes."

The young woman working the desk is fair-skinned and brunette, and much to his surprise, extremely pleasant. (The Tripadvisor staff reviews had been mixed.)

"Great," the lady says. "Do you have your room key?"

Funk hands her the keycard, and she scans the computer.

"How was your stay?" she asks, eyes still locked on the screen. "Good?"

"I was not displeased," Funk says. "The hypoallergenic bedding was decent."

"Very well. I see you're all set, then."

Funk is hesitant, skeptical. "You sure? Because my friend has a way of duping me sometimes. Like not paying the bill."

She laughs. "Yes, I'm sure. You're all set. Oh, I almost forgot. These are for you." She hands him a stack of pink memos. "Messages," she says. "And some business cards. It seems you were quite popular last night."

Funk's Whisky performance has gone viral, and people are coming out of the woodwork.

He grabs the messages and riffles through the stack. Coke Bottle wanting to know if they're getting the band back together. Capitol Records, MTV, several Slater urgents, and a few soiled lipstick napkins with phone numbers.

All chicks digging the bald man.

Funk places the business cards in the back pocket of his faded jeans and hands the checkout woman the rest.

"You can trash these," he says, smiling.

"Right. Happy birthday, Mr. Funk."

Funk nods and heads for the exit. He cruises out of the hotel's signature thirty-foot-tall mahogany doors, his face aglow, and stops at the valet parking station. He hands the valet his ticket, whistling the day's latest earworm: Queen's "Crazy Little Thing Called Love." It's kind of cool how the right song at the right moment can do that, he thinks. Take up residence in your mind and stick around a while. On the flip side, he pities the fool who's got "Big Tits and a Bottle of Wine" on a loop in their headspace. The involuntary imagery is a cognitive itch you don't want to scratch.

Still suffering from stuck song syndrome, he looks up at the sky and squints. It is a cool and cloudy morning, with an onshore breeze and a hint of rain in the air. Spring break one weekend, he muses, Coachella the next. He is starting to feel like a real party animal.

But does he have that much clean laundry?

An instant later, he sees Lopez and Backstreet climbing into a classic Ford Mustang. A 1968, maybe a '69, with a flawless candy-apple-red paint job. Lopez, dressed in black Armani and supple white deerskin moccasins, appears hungover. He holds a blue ice bag on top of his head and moans loudly as he plops down in the passenger seat. Funk is unable to decipher the cursive in which he speaks.

Backstreet closes the door behind Lopez, spots Funk at the valet, and says, "You got lucky, bro. Everybody knows the fix was in."

A watery smile from Funk. "It always is. Not a judgment, just an observation."

Backstreet frowns and hops into the driver's seat. "Don't get it twisted, homie."

"It's nothing personal, gentlemen," Funk says. "It's just business." He waves goodbye as Backstreet guns it out of the hotel driveway, the Mustang's tires smoking and squealing down Sunset.

Lovely couple, Funk thinks. Great party chatter.

The valet, a young towheaded man with a mullet cut, approaches and informs Funk that he is so sorry that he couldn't retrieve his car, but it won't start.

"No problem," Funk says, holding out his hand. "I'll take care of it." He smiles. "I've got the magic touch."

Mullet Cut nods and drops the keys into Funk's open palm. Funk tips him a ten-spot and says, "You're still the man."

Funk doesn't walk far. His silver Porsche coupe is parked right up front. He climbs in and keys the ignition. And just as the valet said, it doesn't start. Deferred maintenance is a bitch, he thinks. He makes a mental note to fire that shade-tree mechanic he found on Craigslist and tries again.

Still nothing.

So much for the magic touch.

Normally at a moment like this, he would become agitated and edgy. Jump out of the car with clenched teeth and balled fists and kick the living daylights out of the freaking tires. But he doesn't do that today. Because Funk stands before you, a changed man. *Un hombre nuevo.* A man who will not show up to meet Angie in a playboy's car on his fiftieth birthday.

No, sir. Those days are over. Along with the lava lamp and the zebra-striped towels in the bathroom.

Thus, he makes another decision. He will sell the German toy. Maybe let the classic automobile appreciate for another year, and unload it to some plutocrat collector for a ridiculous sum of money.

Maybe Leno.

Lord knows.

He feels the blush of humiliation coming on, but it quickly

fades into vulnerability. And isn't that what he's been trying to achieve all this time?

His first step is to think like a millennial. What would they do in this situation? *Calmly request an Uber and hit the road.* So that's what he does. Although he has never taken Uber before, he figures out the app rather quickly and confirms his location. Like seasons in a year, he is riding out the generational cycles of history. The math alone tells him that his window is closing, but it is still far from shut.

Chair volleyball will have to wait.

Unmoored, he steps out of his Porsche like 99.9 percent of all Angelenos, as if the spotlight is upon him. He walks confidently toward the valet station and tells Mullet Cut he will have a tow truck pick up the car later that afternoon. Mullet Cut nods and says no problem. Funk slips him a "don't scratch the paint" twenty, just to be sure.

With his bag in hand, he walks quietly over to the curb and waits. The city sprawls out before him, a dry, incongruent land that feeds fires and floods. He sets his brown leather bag down on the sidewalk and stands up straight. Then, with no air of shame, he calmly hikes his relaxed fit jeans above his waist.

Love it or hate it, he is part of this cosmic ballet now.

This dark ring of fire.

No longer the recluse, he is ready to join the dance.

55

INSIDE THE HOTEL, the elevator doors slide open to the lobby.

Slater and Marty exit, walking and talking toward checkout. Marty appears relaxed, at ease with the moment, wearing beige cargo shorts, flip-flops, and a black crewneck T-shirt.

In contrast, a bleary-eyed Slater is anything but relaxed. Still sporting last night's clothes, he reeks of body odor, and his rumpled aloha shirt is stained dark from sweat. His spray-on jeans fit like sausage casings, and the gladiator sandals are on high alert. Anxious and fidgety, he looks like he's just escaped from a cruise ship brawl.

Looking to fight off some of that fat, Slater says with wild hand gestures, "Then everything's cool with Dungworth?"

"I wouldn't say cool," Marty says. "He had a severe bowel blockage. Evidently, he fell in the bathroom last night trying to pry the door open. Or trying to use the bathroom. I don't know which. They took him to the hospital. He's going to be okay, though. Word is a groin contusion. Possibly testicular torsion."

Slater smiles. "Life's a trip, huh?"

"I guess so. But Dungworth had a lot of drugs in his system.

Apparently, the guy was more medicated than the entire cast of *The Real Housewives of Orange County*."

"Huh. That explains a few things. So what about you? You still got a job?"

"Yeah. The network loved the show. They want me to direct."

"Hey, congrats, Marty."

A beat.

"Look, about that release agreement," Marty says, "I gotta have it if you guys want to get paid."

"I know," Slater says. "I thought maybe I could just scratch out his signature. You know, since we gave you such a great show."

"I can't do that, Mr. Slater."

Slater stops and places a heavy hand on Marty's shoulder. "C'mon, man. I tried all night. His calls were blocked and he wouldn't answer the door."

Marty shrugs. "I got to have it this morning."

Despondent, Slater looks out the window and spots Funk waiting outside on the sidewalk. Half-surprised, he fingers the release document from his breast pocket and says, "I'll get it to you, Marty. Just hang on."

Slater recklessly grabs a pen off the reception desk and races out of the lobby door, clutching the release paper like it's a relay baton. As he steps off the curb, the skinny millennial kid and his scruffy white dog greet him at the valet station. The anxiety-ridden dog stiffens at Slater's messy appearance, growling and snapping at his heels.

"Not now, you mangy hound," Slater says. He feigns a kick, and the dog owner yanks the leash and the dog out of harm's way.

Slater is not sure why dogs want to attack him. He has no explanation for it. Nervous energy, perhaps? The pit bull is understandable. But what has brought out the worst in beagles and labs? Not to mention lovable mutts with bandannas?

Since when has he become the distaste du jour?

"Hey," the skinny kid with the bowl cut says. "Dogs can sense bad people. And you, dude, are one terrible fellow."

"You know what?" Slater says. "I'd like your student debt to be forgiven. I really would. Then maybe you and your ilk would mellow out."

"Dude, you're the one who is so not mellow. I'll bet you own a Pet Rock. Got an ALF T-shirt in your closet."

Slater points. "Don't you bad-mouth ALF. And to think I was this close to sharing my Netflix password with you."

The kid blanches. "Why, I would *never...*"

Slater waves him off and trots up to Funk just as his Uber pulls into the driveway.

Funk's chariot has arrived.

A smoky-gray four-door Honda Accord.

"Larry! Larry!...*Wait.*"

Funk turns in the car park. "What do you want?"

Slater stops, huffing and puffing. "Look, I know I am not at the top of anybody's cloning list. But you got to help me, man. Sign the release. *Please.*" He holds the food-stained document out, the edges green from avocado.

"And I thought you just wanted to wish me a happy birthday."

"It's *ten thousand dollars,* Larry."

Funk, not surprised. "Oh, it's ten thousand now? Forget it."

Slater drops to his knees, hands clasped. "Please, Larry. I've got a mortgage. A soon-to-be ex-wife with expensive tastes. A gray divorce is the worst fleecing a man can take. I need this money. Seriously, has the boys' culture changed all that much? What's a red-blooded American male with a nice penis to do if he can't show it off?"

Funk looks down at the man groveling at his feet. "Feed it to the ducks. And stop sniveling."

"I can't help it. I yield to temptation."

Funk opens the car door. "You should have thought about that before you sold me out." He slings his overnight bag into the back seat of the Honda, crawls in, and closes the door.

Slater sticks his head in the open window, panicking. "Funk, listen to me. That's what married guys do. *We use single guys.* It's nothing personal."

"It's just business?"

"Yes."

"Not where I come from." Funk raises the window halfway up, wrenching Slater's neck.

"I beg of you, Larry. Save me! I'm this close, *this fucking close* to a Robert Kiyosaki seminar."

Funk holds Slater's whimpering gaze, then palms his face and stiff-arms him out of the cabin. He rolls up the window and gives the driver a quick hand chop.

It's go time.

The Uber driver nods, looks both ways, slowly pulls out of the Mondrian Hotel, and turns west onto Sunset Boulevard.

A distraught Slater chases the car down the street in his gladiator sandals, frantically waving the release document over his head. "Larry! Larry! Stop! I've got a preexisting condition!"

Panting furiously, and with its eyes locked on the release document, the scraggly mutt bolts from the skinny kid's grasp and fires out like a shot. Salivating, it smells its favorite food—why, avocado, of course.

Slater's face is twisted in comical concentration, and after two more awkward strides, he stumbles, loses his balance, and his big body crashes into the gutter. The release paper shoots out of his limp hand, floating and tumbling high in the wind.

Then—

Something extraordinary happens. That mangy mutt unexpectedly leaps up off the curb and, with great strength and agility, snatches the release paper midair. The acrobatic catch is an incredible display of athleticism, and one worthy of a gold medal.

They call me the sky hound.

After a moment of impressive hang time, the high-flying pooch returns to earth, landing squarely on all fours. With the release document firmly in its mouth, the dog cocks its scruffy white head at Slater.

Slater sits up in the gutter and pleads. "No. Don't you do it."

But the avocado-loving pup seems to savor every inch of the paper. It chews it slowly, methodically, like a goat chewing its cud.

Following this, with its bushy tail wagging and a "here goes" look on its face, the dog swallows the wrinkled document whole.

GULP!

Slater watches the lump pass down the mutt's furry gullet, and slumps in the gutter, resigned. Whores always get their due, he thinks.

Always have.

If you were a dog whisperer, then you might have heard the dog say at that exact moment, *"That dog couldn't catch a Frisbee if I shoved it down its throat. Dream on, Flattop. More avocado? Yes, please."*

FUNK'S FIRST UBER.

He sits slumped in the back seat, twitching his nose and tapping his foot. His driver has just passed gas, and the stale air inside the car holds the foul scent of dirty gym socks and propane.

Welcome to the sharing economy, he thinks.

"Is this where I'm supposed to sit?" Funk asks.

"You can sit wherever you want."

"Good answer," Funk says.

If they are willing to compromise, so is he.

"You want to hear some music?" the driver asks.

"That would be nice."

"Anything in particular?"

Funk looks out the window. "Your choice."

Funk has tried to keep up with the new music. *Who is Paramore again?*

The driver twists the dial on the radio and Fleetwood Mac's "Yesterday's Gone" cranks through the sound system.

Not bad, he reckons. Although Robert Palmer's "Bad Case of Loving You (Doctor, Doctor)" might have been a better choice. But he's not in charge anymore. It's all about letting go. That's what he will eventually tell Marty, many weeks later, when the production company brings him back to watch the show, hoping they can strike a deal. They will not. It's not so much the fact that he despises seeing himself on the toilet; it is Marty's choice of music. More notably, the end credits. While he will understand the substance behind "Stayin' Alive," he will opine that the theme song to *Welcome Back, Kotter* might have been a better choice. Something slow to ease him in. Chin nods all around. Upon leaving the meeting, he will thank them profusely for not playing him out with the theme song to *Rocky*.

That's just amateur hour.

He is mindful that this literary farce he's been starring in borders on the absurd—full of screwball and slapstick. But since when is making people laugh a crime? Unlike the movies, his life is not a three-act structure. He is free to roam about the cabin, free to stoke the artistic wildfires that burn brightly within. In other words, how far off from the climax and denouement has he really ventured?

Way off, bro. Way off.

But Funk has learned from his many creations that all art is subjective. Where one sees a closed door, another sees an opening to the universe. You can't please everybody. All you can do is stir your own animal juices.

When the Honda passes the Whisky a Go Go, Funk's mind cracks wide, and light enters. This transformation was never about a midlife crisis, he tells himself. Not about adventure travel, a keto diet, or a thirty-two-inch waist. It was about a journey—the journey of an artist in transition. (Without the pink lenses.) Just like the city, one of his greatest strengths has always been the ability to adapt.

As an artist, all he ever wanted to do was move people through words and music, and give the fans their money's worth. He is fully cognizant of the evidence that there will most likely never be a Larry Funk Bobblehead Day. And he's cool with that. A small tribute quartet will suffice; maybe play him out with a New Orleans Jazz Band funeral.

Above stated, he knows that old artists never die; they just rewrite their obituaries.

So he will go forward into this brave new world and create anew. And if it pleases him, purchase a gaucho hat and some fringy leather chaps for Coachella.

He'll keep you posted.

He sits in the Honda's back seat, looking out at the streets of West Hollywood. It too, it seems, is rebuilding. Construction cranes dot the Sunset Strip, and the sounds of prosperous car horns jockey for position. The midmorning fog begins to lift, and in the west he spots a sliver of orange on the horizon, a shuttering light.

In the distance, a new life calls, he thinks, a new soundtrack. Because he knows in his heart, beyond any doubt, that the world still needs dreamers like him.

A dreamer who has always been happy to oblige.

"Any special route you want me to take?" the driver asks.

Funk smiles and points through the windshield. "Yeah," he says. "Just keep moving toward the light."

Harlin Hailey
Author of East of Lincoln
The End
of the
Playboy
A NOVEL

I hope you enjoyed *The End of the Playboy* as much as I enjoyed writing it. Your reading is greatly appreciated. Like Funk, music has always showed me the way. These are just a few of the songs mentioned in the novel, though it is not a complete list. So, if you're in the mood for a little old school, grab the headphones, sit back and relax, and hit play. You might just discover, or rediscover, a gem or two.

"The Sound of Silence" by Simon and Garfunkel
"Fool for the City" by Foghat
"Miss You" by The Rolling Stones
"Old Man" by Neil Young
"Part-Time Lover" by Stevie Wonder
"One of These Nights" by Eagles
"In the Air Tonight" by Phil Collins
"Theme From Love Story" by Francis Lai
"Only the Lonely" by The Motels
"Call Me" by Blondie
"Stayin' Alive" by The Bee Gees
"More Than a Woman" by The Bee Gees/Tavares

"Ride Like the Wind" by Christopher Cross
"Kung Fu Fighting" by Carl Douglas
"Baby, I Love Your Way" by Peter Frampton

ACKNOWLEDGMENTS

As always, it takes a village to raise a book. I'd like to thank my awesome team of editors and proofreaders, Kira Rubenthaler, Donna Rich, and Eliza Dee, for taking my manuscript to the next level. Your work is never short of outstanding. Thank you.

To Edward Bettison for his killer cover design that truly is a work of art and for convincing me that a black and hot pink guitar cover was the only choice for my story. You're the man.

Thank you, also, to the Mondrian Los Angeles hotel. Any views or oversights by the characters are fictional, and certainly not my own. My stays and time there have always been wonderfully exquisite. Thank you for giving me the chance to dream and live among the stars.

It's worth noting that any liberties I took with the technical aspects of producing a reality show, or any errors I made, are my own. That's the beauty of fiction.

Last but not least, a big shout out to all my good friends who provided me honest feedback along the way. In no particular order, thanks to Rob and Sheri, Nick and Regan, Thomas and Natalie, Big Dave, and the Instacart grocery delivery girl who loved the cover art and wanted to know more about the story. The avocados were perfect, by the way.

Thanks to all of you, I am truly grateful.

ABOUT THE AUTHOR

HARLIN HAILEY was born in New Orleans and educated at the University of Southern California. He is the author of *The End of the Playboy, The Downsizing of Hudson Foster,* and the award-winning literary crime novel *East of Lincoln*, which won the 2020 Eric Hoffer Book Awards for best fiction. Having escaped Los Angeles, he now lives on the edge of the desert in a quiet California town. Fond of T-shirts and sweatpants, he writes among the lizards, howling coyotes, rambunctious hummingbirds, and the occasional chihuahua in a comfortable winter sweater. He welcomes all comments, rants, media inquiries, typo sightings, and emails from rabid fans who want the skinny on his upcoming new releases. Or those who just want to check in to say hi.

Contact him at harlinhailey.com or harlinhailey@gmail.com.

If you enjoyed the book, please consider leaving a review or rating on your favorite book-buying site. It is the fuel that keeps all authors running. Thank you for your support!